SWEET PUNK

LEILA JAMES

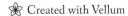 Created with Vellum

CREDITS

Editing & Proofreading by Krista Dapkey:
www.kdproofreading.com

Cover Design by Diana TC:
www.triumphbookcovers.com

ONE

KELLAN

This girl is leading me on a merry fucking chase. I run faster, trying to keep up with her, my heart pumping hard and my legs a blur. But damn, she's fast. And how the hell she's running in a pair of flip-flops like that, I'll never know. That fire alarm went off, and she hadn't even stopped to put different shoes on, which I can't really fault her for because I hadn't put on a shirt on my way out either. Maybe she didn't intend to run across campus when she fled Duke Hall, but here we are, doing just that. She makes a sharp left and darts across the quad, heading toward the academic buildings. What the fuck is she doing?

Star St. James is a mystery to me. Ever since she moved into the suite across the hall two months ago, I haven't known what to make of her funky blue-framed glasses or the pink stripe in her glossy dark hair. Or the fact that she holes up in her room more often than not with her computer. Or the way she sometimes sticks her foot in her mouth with how blunt she is.

As I run behind her, I smirk to myself. I guess I wonder about her because she's kinda like me with the same level of introversion and distaste for partying or even hanging out with people in general. She gets along well—at least I think she does—with her two suitemates, Lux and Raven. Thinking back, though, I'm unsure if I've ever seen her with anyone else, and I do occasionally spot her around campus—especially in the art building. She's taking some intro to art course, and her class ends at the same time my studio time is over. She's always alone.

I force myself to move faster, and the second Star senses me behind her, she whirls around, a mask of sheer terror on her face, and thrusts the small can of pepper spray that's attached to her lanyard and keys out in front of her, aiming it right at me.

"Don't fucking spray me again." I come to an abrupt halt about ten feet from her, throwing my hands up to shield my face. Memories of the intense burning sensation from our last unfortunate encounter are still fresh in my mind. That fucking aerosol caused my nose to run like a faucet and had irritated the hell out of my skin. My eyes had practically swelled shut. I don't want to go there again for anything. That shit hurt like a motherfucker. I shudder involuntarily, reliving the pain all over again.

We stare at each other for several moments, each of us taking the other in. Star's eyes wander over me from top to bottom, then back again, her breath hitching when her gaze returns to my face. Jesus, I have no idea what's in her head. Her hand shakes as she finally drops the canister, letting it dangle from her lanyard. Whatever she's thinking is on the tip of her tongue. Sure enough, a second later, she blurts, "Why the hell are you following me, Kellan?"

I rest my hands on my hips and work my jaw back and forth, assessing her. She's trembling all over, her face paler than I've ever noticed it being before. "Why are you acting so goddamn sketchy lately? That's why I came after you. You were safe in a crowd of people—it's just another pulled fire alarm, yet you ran off like the devil was chasing you."

Her eyes shift down and to the side, and she blinks rapidly before huffing, "I'm not acting sketchy. You're the one who keeps following me." She sucks in a breath, her eyes flicking to my chest and wandering over it, tattoo by tattoo, rose by inked-on rose. "Do you ever wear a shirt?" Her cheeks flush pink with her indignant question.

Staring right back at her, my brows draw together. She doesn't know me well enough for me to begin to answer that loaded question. I ignore it in favor of shooting my own back at her. "Seriously. Why'd you take off like that?" I can't deny it. I'm completely curious at this point, especially with the way her focus keeps darting around. And I have a habit of studying people, trying to figure out what exactly makes them tick—though most of the time, I observe and hypothesize. There's so much to be learned by paying attention to nonverbal cues. But with her? I want to know. And I want her to be the one to tell me.

"I don't like crowds." She pauses, fidgeting and refusing to meet my eyes. "Or very many people, period."

A harsh laugh trips out of me before I can stop it. "You're totally fucking lying." I surprise myself with how growly my voice sounds. I don't know what I'm reacting to that she's putting out there into the universe, but something's not quite tracking for me.

"Am not. I don't like crowds. Never have."

I narrow my eyes on her. She didn't answer the question. "That's not why you ran off."

She covers her face with her hands and speaks through them. "Just drop it, Kellan."

The plea in her voice stops me cold, the fear I sense in her words hits me square in the chest. I want to know what her deal is, but she's stubborn. "Fine. I'll walk with you wherever you're going."

She shakes her head, slowly backing away. "No. That's okay. I— Just let me go, okay?"

The fuck. I exhale sharply. I don't want this to be a battle of wills, but I also don't like the idea of her walking around campus by herself at this hour. Scraping my teeth over my bottom lip, I study her. I can tell I'm not getting any further with this tonight. "Fine." I look down at the ground between us for a few seconds before I meet her eyes again. "Would you text Lux or Raven and let them know where you're headed? If you can do that, I'll take off and leave you alone."

Finally giving in, she doesn't say a word but nods and pulls her phone out of her pocket. She thumbs it open and quickly taps out a text. I'm no dummy, though, I shoot a text to Hawk at the same time.

Me: Just checking—did Lux or Raven get a text from Star?

She glances up at me, her tone accusatory. "Um, what are you doing?"

"Isn't it obvious? Ensuring that someone is in contact with you." I grit my teeth, watching for Hawk's response.

"Is that seriously necessary? I'm not a child. And I'm not your responsibility." Her forehead pinches, leaving a crease right down the center.

I can totally tell she's not amused, but tough shit. "It is." I wouldn't feel right if no one else was paying attention, and I left her here alone. My jaw sets as I eye the way she's beginning to squirm uncomfortably and move from one foot to the other. Not only is our conversation wigging her out, but I bet she's cold out here, just like I am. A T-shirt, jeans, and flip-flops doesn't cut it against the late-October cold in Connecticut.

"Whatever,"—she tucks a chunk of her pink-streaked hair behind her ear and jerks her thumb over her shoulder—"I'm going." She begins to back away while I'm distracted by the incoming texts from Hawk. I glance down, quickly scanning his messages.

Hawk: Yes. Both Lux and Raven got one.
Hawk: WTF is going on?
Me: Your guess is as good as mine.

Before Star can get very far, I grit out, "Hey." She flinches, but stops in her tracks, her green eyes wide behind her glasses. "Tell me you're okay, and I'll back the fuck off."

I hate the look in her eyes. She turns and walks away

without answering me. *No.* She's most definitely *not* okay. Considering my limited but fucked-up experiences with women—well, one woman—I'm sure as hell not the person she needs to help her. But I also don't know how to turn a blind eye now that I know she's struggling with something.

TWO
STAR

Well, that was awkward. And downright humiliating. Kellan never did say why he followed me tonight, and I wonder if it has anything to do with what happened last week. But no matter the reason, he shouldn't have done it —being seen with me is the worst thing he could do.

While we stood outside the dorm, waiting for the fire department to give us the all clear, my senses had tingled with an internal alarm blaring louder than Duke Hall's. I didn't think it through, I simply knew I couldn't stand there another minute. Especially not with people I care about huddled around me. If there's even a slim chance that the shit show that is my former life has followed me here— I squeeze my eyes shut tight. I swear I'd caught a glimpse of a worn leather jacket on someone moving through the crowd.

Could I be overreacting? Absolutely. Do I feel like that's the case? *No.*

He turned eighteen in August. I should have prepared myself for this, but I don't know what I could have done differently. Being at Shadow River University helps. In the back of my head, though, I know without a doubt that if he wants to find me, he will. If this isn't all in my head, and he's actually followed me here, I don't know how I'll cope, how I'll lead any sort of normal life.

I walk quickly toward the Bean, glancing over my shoulder every few seconds the entire way there. I started coming here earlier this semester to hang out sometimes while Raven worked. This place is always filled with people, and to me, it feels safe. Not a minute goes by when I'm ever alone, not to mention this particular coffee shop has long hours. It's open super early so students and professors alike can grab their cup of joe before class, and it stays open later than late for those who choose to bring a laptop and study here. The best part is, no one bothers me when I come in, and all it costs me is a cup of coffee. And to me, coffee in exchange for peace of mind is a no-brainer. Because the dorm? I'm not entirely certain I'm safe there, and that thought chills me to the bone.

On autopilot, I enter the Bean, and the invigorating scent of coffee rolls over me like a great caffeinated wave. Even though it's Friday night, there are students dotted around the room with their laptops, hammering away at their keyboards. And *because* it's Friday night, there are also a lot of couples here, as well, grabbing coffee together. That's something I wish I could have. But I can't. There's no way I can let anyone get too close to me.

Hurrying up to the counter, I place an order for my usual—a mocha—mostly because I can't resist the hint of chocolate, but also because it's simple and no one ever messes it up. While I wait for my drink, I turn slightly, resting my hip against the counter as I scan each individual face, looking for any hint of black hair or darker-than-sin eyes, but not seeing anyone who matches that description.

"Here you go."

I startle at the sound of the deep voice behind me, my heart lodging painfully in my throat as I turn around. The barista nudges my mocha toward me with a curious smile. "You okay?"

I exhale an awkward breath that is part relief, part embarrassment. "Yeah, sorry. I was thinking about something else." I shoot him a grateful smile, collect my piping-hot coffee, and head for the row of stools over at the front window. Not many people sit over here, and I appreciate the fact that I can see every single person who enters the building before they ever set foot inside.

I live in a constant state of awareness, always on edge. It kinda sucks.

Heaving out a sigh, I sit down on the stool on the far right and blow carefully on my drink before taking a sip. A notification pinging on my phone grabs my attention, but there's no doubt in my mind that Lux and Raven are wondering what the hell is going on, especially once I texted them that I was coming here instead of heading back to the dorm. With Kellan. Because they have to know he came after me.

Why had he followed me? I chew on my lip as I think about the poor guy I literally pepper sprayed a week ago. I would have thought he'd want zero to do with me after that. But there he was, running halfway across campus. I'm impressed he'd kept up with me. As far as I know,

Kellan works out with Maddox and Hawk ... but that's no match for the miles I slog in the mornings before anyone is awake. I've got myself trained to be able to run far and fast if the need arises.

Would Kellan have come all the way to the Bean if I hadn't realized he was behind me? Then what would he have done? Watched me from outside? Come in and pretended like he was in the mood for a coffee, and it'd been nothing but sheer coincidence that the two of us wound up in exactly the same spot?

I take another sip of my coffee, then lick a bit of foam from my upper lip as I stare outside into the dark. Had Kellan told the guys I'd gotten him full in the face with that pepper spray? I swear it'd felt like someone was stalking me. And he *was* following me back to my dorm— the dorm where we both live. *Fuck. I'm such an idiot.* And apparently trigger-happy.

I let myself fall headlong into the memory of that day.

———

MY HEART RACES. *There's someone following me. Stalking me. I grip the tiny canister of pepper spray that hangs from my lanyard and turn with the cap flipped up and my finger on the depressor. I'm so startled to see a figure in a dark hoodie and jeans continuing to come at me that I shriek and fire away.*

Whoever he is drops hard to his knees, then falls forward, bracing his big body with his hands. He doesn't make a goddamn noise. Not a yell or a shout or a curse. After what feels like an eternity, he finally manages to grit out, "Star, what the hell?" That small question sends the hooded figure into a coughing fit.

My name. He knows my name. And holy shit. I recognize the voice. Realization dawns on me. "Oh my God. Kellan, is that you?"

He raises his head, blinking hard and gasping for breath.

Oh, shit. I pepper sprayed someone who ... well, I think I consider him a friend. Shit. I squat down next to him, gently tugging the hoodie off his head. "I'm sorry. I thought—"

He shakes his head and holds up a hand.

My teeth clamp down hard on my lower lip. My chest tightens. What should I do? Out of desperation, I scramble to pull my phone from my pocket. I quickly search for a remedy on Google and see that we need to flush his eyes and the surrounding skin with lots of cool water. I glance at the canister that I always carry around with me. Apparently, this shit is oil-based and not easy to get off. And sort of like poison ivy, we want to keep it from spreading around if we can help it. I can't believe I did this to him.

"Kellan, we need to get back to the dorm to rinse this off. Flush it out of your eyes. And whatever you do, don't touch or rub them. It'll only make it worse. So says Google." I huff out a breath and give him a tight smile that I'm unsure he can even see because, holy fucking shit, I've practically blinded him. "Do you think you can get up?"

He nods, still not speaking. I haven't a clue if he's not talking because he's in too much pain, if he's unable, or if he's simply pissed at me. I cringe. I hope it's not the latter. Not that I want him to be in so much pain that he physi-

cally can't speak. I grasp his bicep, helping him balance as he stands up.

Continuing to blink rapidly, he points in the direction of the dorms, which I take as a signal that he's ready to walk. I duck under his arm and slip mine around his back. His big hand clasps my shoulder and squeezes. I guide him to the dorm as quickly as possible, getting the odd look or ten from other students who pass by. I ignore them and forge forward.

When we reach Duke Hall, I heave out a breath, bringing him to the bottom of the stairs. "I think the smartest thing to do is to hit the gender-neutral bathroom on the main floor." We're almost there. He doesn't answer, so I assume he's in agreement. "Steps up. Ready?" I grip his waist firmly and peek up at him. He nods stoically. We climb the stairs without issue and stop momentarily at the door so that I can hold my ID up for the scanner. The light flashes green and the door lock makes a clicking sound, indicating that it's open. I grasp the handle with my free hand and tug it open. "Okay. And a step inside." I release him so he can step in before me, then am right back to guiding him. "We're stopping here." Once I've got us inside, I lock the door behind us.

We stop at the sink, and I blow out a breath, not completely sure where to start. Chewing on my lip, I tug on the hem of his hoodie. "This has pepper spray all over it. Let's get it off you." I shrug out from under his arm. "We'd better be careful how we do this."

Kellan grunts a bit then reaches back to grasp it at the nape and tug it off.

"Wait. Can you pull your arms out of the sleeves?

Then I can help you get your head through the neck without getting anything more on your face." He makes a little harrumphing noise but nods his understanding as he works to pull his arms in.

I slide my hands up to get under the material, inadvertently touching his chest—his very bare, very solid, very muscular chest—before I manage to get it gathered in my hands. He flinches hard, but whether it's because I touched him or he's hurting, I don't know. I begin to feel a slight burning sensation where I must have come into contact with some pepper spray, and it hits me how bad off he might be. "Shit, I'm so sorry." I grit my teeth as I work the collar wide and slip it over his head without touching his face. I set the offending hoodie on the counter next to us and hurriedly turn on the faucet, making sure it's running as cold as I can get it.

He exhales harshly before bending at the waist. The poor guy is still blinking like crazy. He cups his hands to catch the water and splashes it up into his face. Repeat. Over and over again.

I try to quell the sarcastic voice in my head that says I'm so sure he wants my advice—but I can't keep quiet. "Kellan, you've gotta try to keep your eyes open. What if you turn your head toward me, and I pour water over your eye? Maybe that'll help flush it out a little better."

For several beats, he hesitates, then murmurs thickly, "Yeah. Okay." Turning his head, he angles it as best he can over the sink. "We're making a huge fucking mess." His words end on a rough cough that immediately makes me feel like shit all over again.

"Don't worry about it. It's just water." I cup some water in my hands. *"Ready?"*

"Yeah."

I take a deep breath and carefully pour the cool liquid directly into his eye. "How was that?"

He nods, blinking rapidly. Water clings to his lashes. "Again."

We repeat the process several times for that eye, then switch sides and do the same for the other. At one point, he grasps my hip, holding on ... for balance? I don't care. He can do anything he wants right now.

"Okay. What do you think? Should I go again?"

Kellan shakes his head over the sink. His hair is drenched, and little droplets fling everywhere, some landing on me. It doesn't faze me. I want him to be okay. He rises to his full height and takes several breaths. His gaze is pinned somewhere over my head, his jaw rigid. He's holding his hands in front of his chest like he wants to touch his skin, but—oh man, I think he's afraid to.

The pepper spray must have seeped through his hoodie. Or maybe we got some on him when we removed it. Either way—

"I need to ..." He turns back to the sink and douses his chest with water, over and over. Now we really do have a mess. It's like a pipe burst in here.

And oh ... oh my. As I watch him, heat streaks through me. I've never had this reaction to him before. I'm totally used to seeing Kellan shirtless. It's like his natural state of being when he's "home" in his suite. It's not that I haven't looked. Because who wouldn't? But all this skin on display, glistening with water? Holy crap. It's something else entirely.

Kellan is magnificent. And I've never been in such close proximity before, so ... I look. At all the muscles, at the tattoos, at the entire delicious package. I'm nervous I'm going to start drooling or something as the poor guy continues to splash water over his very cut body. Droplets cascade over him, and my greedy eyes follow every single one as they trail downward until they disappear, absorbed by the waistband of his jeans.

"Can you grab me a few paper towels?" His deep voice hits me square in the chest, dragging me from my lust-induced stupor.

I pivot on my heel. "Yeah, sure." Only, the stupid dispenser is empty. My gaze flicks around the small room. Toilet paper is definitely not the answer here. I look down at my T-shirt, and without another thought, I peel it over my head.

Kellan's brows raise.

"Sorry, no paper towels. We can use my T-shirt." I hold it clutched in my hands between us. He stares at me, which is odd because up until now, he's been blinking fiercely. His gaze dips down to the teal-colored lacy bralette I'm wearing. Realization strikes as his eyes roam over my body that while the cups of this cute top have a bit of material backing them, the rest of it is fairly sheer, which is why I generally wear it under other things. For all intents and purposes, it's see-through. And Kellan ... is looking.

Hoping to diffuse some of the awkwardness, I step closer, reaching up to blot his face carefully, then his neck.

As I touch the shirt to his throat, I feel his rough swallow. He's staring down at me, fixated on my top ... or maybe what's under it. My heart jackhammers in my chest.

And then it's my turn to swallow. Why haven't I handed him the shirt? Why don't I let him dry himself? I don't want to think about the answer because maybe I'll stop what I'm doing. And I do not want to stop since my hands and this lucky shirt are gliding over his pecs. Through the fabric, my fingers brush over one of his nipples. I pause a fraction of a second, looking up at him with my lip clenched so tightly between my teeth that it hurts. Hurts. So. Good.

His ragged breath exits his mouth, and it feathers over my forehead. I blink a few times, hesitating before my hands drift lower. He doesn't stop me, but his jaw tenses and his cut abs jump at my touch. I slide the shirt over his stomach, soaking up the water.

That's when I glance down, noting the deep V lines leading into his pants. I want to inspect this part of his body with the utmost care. I can't resist running my shirt along one and then the other.

My breath hitches when I find myself fantasizing about touching him with my fingertips. And maybe my lips and tongue. Another wave of heat washes over me, making me a little dizzy.

He clears his throat, finally catching my hands between us with his. He softly murmurs, "I've gotta go."

Embarrassed, my cheeks flame pink, and I stutter. "O-oh. Right. Y-eah, me too." *I bunch my now damp shirt in my hands, my fingers reflexively squeezing it. I can't put this back on.*

He picks up his hoodie between two fingers. "I guess this goes straight to the washing machine."

"Yeah. You don't want to get that stuff all over everything. It transfers too easily." I wince. "I'm sorry. For all this. Do you want me to wash it for you?"

He gives a brief shake of his head before his gaze dips from my eyes to my lips and then down to my breasts. My nipples immediately peak. This is so, so not how I expected this to go.

I follow him to the door, which he unlocks and pulls open, letting me exit first.

"Whoa. Couldn't make it up to your room, huh?" This comes from some random dude sitting on the couch in the communal area in the foyer.

The other two guys sitting with him snicker, and one mumbles loud enough for us to hear, "Looks like she took him for a ride."

The third guy eyes me. "I don't blame him. I'd let her, too. Nice top, honey."

My cheeks flame red. I glance up to check Kellan's reaction, and to my surprise, his face is also flushed. Only ... maybe that's from the pepper spray.

"Shut the fuck up and mind your own business. Before I take care of it for you."

My brows raise. Whoa. Angry Kellan.

The first guy laughs. "I think that's the only time I've ever heard you speak, man."

"It'll be the last if you don't cut the shit," Kellan growls and throws his arm around my shoulders and walks up the stairs with me. Just like that. His bare skin against *mine. It's making my stomach feel like it's full of hummingbirds or something.*

At the landing, he pulls away. "Sorry. Those guys are dicks. They're in my fucking speech class. I kinda hate 'em."

I TRY to shake myself free from the memory of that day, but it's so difficult. It's one of the more exciting, normal things that's happened to me in a long time. I've been secretly reliving it over and over for the last week—well, the better parts of it, anyway. Though, it's hard to forget what an idiot I'd been and how he'd been in pain. Pain that I'd caused.

Taking a deeper swallow of my coffee now that it's cooled, I allow myself to remember how Kellan had waited until I'd unlocked the door to my suite before he did the same and entered his. I stood there for several minutes with my back to the door trying not to melt into a puddle on the floor. And ever since that day, I don't know if I'm imagining it, but it's felt like we're staying out of each other's way. Like neither of us is willing to admit the odd sense of intimacy that had developed between us in that little bathroom on the first floor of our dorm.

I have certainly spoken to no one about it. Haven't even hinted that anything happened. I wonder if Kellan relayed the entire story to Hawk and Maddox about what an idiot I was. But he's made zero mention of it within my earshot. Nor has anyone else asked me about it. I'd totally understand if he mentioned the pepper spraying. But dammit, no one has said a peep about it.

Is it too much to hope that at the very least he'd kept those odd stolen moments between us? I don't know what it meant, if anything. Propping my chin on my hand, I let myself daydream a little more.

Embarrassingly enough, I sit there for well over forty-five minutes, letting everything that happened replay in my head. Finally, I give myself a good shake. My coffee is long gone, and the girls are going to wonder where the hell I am. I tap out a quick message to our group chat.

Me: I'm on my way.
Raven: Oh, good. I was starting to worry.
Lux: And I was about to come after you.
Me: I'm fine. I'll explain in person.

But I won't. Not really. What am I supposed to say?

I still don't know the answer to that question by the time I let myself into the suite to find Lux and Raven waiting for me. They're sitting at the kitchen table with Oreos and milk.

"Hey," I offer, unsure where to take the conversation from here.

Raven smiles brightly. "Hey, yourself. Have you been at the coffee shop all this time?"

I nod. "Yeah, mostly."

"I'm going to jump right to it. What the hell?" Lux stops, her brows drawing together as her eyes drift over me.

Sighing, I pull out a chair and plop down into it, folding my arms across my chest. "Um. I should have mentioned this before, I guess. One of my biggest fears is fire. And not just any fire. Like the bonfire at Royal Revelry was cool. Controlled. Sort of." My eyes flick to theirs, first Lux, then Raven. I shrug. "It's more a fear of being trapped in a fire or something like that." Good enough. At least I'm not lying to them. But shit, I didn't say anything about fear of fires to Kellan at all. He'd caught me off guard. I should have just told him that instead of acting all weird. But the thing is, he *knows* there's more to it than that. Because he's the only one who knows how fucking terrified I am that someone would follow me. *Shit.*

Lux nods. "Ah. So whoever is pulling the fire alarm is triggering you."

"Yeah,"—I shrug—"I guess you could say that."

"But where's that fear come from? I mean, any of us would probably be terrified to be caught in a house fire or something. But this seems like it's more than that." Raven tilts her head to the side, studying me.

They can keep picking and poking at me, but I'm not someone they should ever figure out. And yeah, I feel like a total hypocrite. These girls have been so honest and forthcoming with their baggage and issues ... and here I am, hardly giving them any insight at all. I close my eyes and breathe out steadily, concentrating on the air passing between my lips. "It's better if you don't know." I worry the skin on the inside of my cheek.

Lux shakes her head and gestures with her finger back and forth between herself and Raven. She gazes steadily at me. "Our dirty laundry has been all over the suite. Eventually it'll be your turn. And I'm a tiny bit sad to find out you must not trust us. I thought we were pretty tight."

I shake my head, frowning. "I *do* trust you." My chest clenches. But I don't trust *him*. "And I need you to trust me—I promise I'll fill you in when I can, I just can't share this right now." I grit my teeth, and hope they understand the plea in my eyes. I can't let him see these girls mean the world to me. And I'm nervous that if I tell them what I'm dealing with, they'll freak the fuck out. For now, I can't let them all the way in. It'd be far too dangerous.

Raven and Lux simply won't allow me to keep them at a distance that will ensure their safety. And that scares the shit out of me.

THREE
STAR

Saturday evening arrives and with it, the themed Halloween party—Villains and Victims—that everyone has been talking about nonstop all week. Parties aren't my thing, but once again, Raven is insistent that we go check it out. There's a part of her that is still looking for acceptance, to fit in ... even though she has Maddox now and it's obvious he thinks the sun rises and sets in her eyes. And *he* doesn't give two shits whether he fits in anywhere.

But Raven still wants to go, so I'm trying not to be a party pooper. Never mind that the last two attempts we've made to attend parties have led to nothing but complete disaster.

"Quit fidgeting." Lux wrinkles her nose at me. "Actually, maybe we'd create a more realistic-looking jagged gash on your stomach if you keep that up." As our resident makeup expert, Lux has been making Raven and me look extra gross because we're playing the part of the victims at this party.

Raven shakes her head, inspecting herself in the mirror. "This is totally sexist. Why do we have to be the victims in skimpy clothing? Don't they think I could be a serial killer or ax murderer or whatever?"

I surprise myself by laughing. Maybe this is what I need to get out of the funk I've been in. "Raven, don't be offended, but you might be the least likely serial killer I've ever seen." She looks like a summer camp reject right out of the 1980 version of *Friday the 13th*, complete with Jason Voorhees-inflicted machete wounds.

Lux snorts a bit, winking at Raven. "And that's why they'd never catch her." She dabs at my fake gash with her finger. "There. I think you're gross enough now."

Lux and I have decided on characters from *Texas Chainsaw Massacre*, mostly because we had clothing that worked for it. Lux's costume was easy—jeans, a belt, a white tank top tied off to expose her stomach, and a cowgirl hat. I watch as she plunks it back on her head now that she's done goring us up. She's the protagonist in the film. That character doesn't even die, but she thinks being victimized in the film is plenty, even if she doesn't meet a horrific end. I personally don't think she wanted a ton of goop-like makeup all over her, though she did smear a bit of fake blood on her cheek, arms, and stomach.

"Thank you for that. I guess I'll enjoy being gross." I glance down, eyeing my outfit—a pink camisole top with a sweetheart neckline, a floral skirt that sits low on my hips, and Western boots. A huge nasty slice across my stomach means I'm supposed to be the girl who gets sawed in half in the movie. "Do I look okay?"

Raven, glances at me. "Are you kidding? You're perfect. This is going to be so much fun."

"What are the guys wearing, do you know?"

"I think Gage said he was going to be Leatherface so he can chase me around." Lux rolls her eyes.

"Maddox had the same idea Hawk did—he's going to be Jason so he can mess with me all night. He even got a fake machete."

"And Kellan?" I try not to sound too interested in the answer, but I kinda am.

"Gage said Kellan wasn't super into the whole blood and gore thing, but he has one of those *Scream* ghost face masks that he'll wear." Lux shrugs. "At least he's coming. From what Gage told me, horror stuff isn't his jam."

OUR GRUESOME GROUP walks to the Psi Chi house, which is located right next door to the Zeta Sigma Epsilon house. Lux gives a visible shudder as she glances at the other house. That place has no good memories for any of us, but especially Lux and Hawk. I wonder how those jackasses who drugged her are faring these days. It was quite a sight that morning when I encountered them tied to the trees near Royal Bridge. They got what they deserved, though, courtesy of these three guys. And even though our track record isn't great, I feel safe attending a party so long as they're with us.

The guys slip their masks on as we walk up the steps to the front door. I swallow. Kellan hasn't said a word to me tonight. He's always so damn quiet. Pensive. He hasn't so much as *looked* at me. He's either off in his own little world, coming along with us for the hell of it or because the guys asked him to. My brows pinch together. It's a tiny bit awkward that the other four members of our group are coupled up, leaving Kellan and me together. Or not. I truly don't know how this is going to work. Pushing my glasses up the bridge of my nose, let out a ragged sigh that I'm glad is hidden by the incessant thumping of the music as we enter the house. I'll probably end up standing at the edge of the party all night long. Alone.

Inside, I glance around, my eyes wide. This is pure mayhem, no other word for it. My gaze moves swiftly around the room, taking in the massive quantities of the most popular characters from horror movies. There are plenty more Jasons and Leatherheads and *Scream* ghosts ... but also lots of Michaels and Freddys and even a Chucky or two, which is actually hysterical. I nudge Lux and point to one of them, and both of us crack up.

Meanwhile, Raven is already across the room and in the kitchen—I swear, that girl does her own thing at parties—and is busily scoping out the alcohol situation. Hawk runs into Matty, who is wearing the *It* clown's mask on top of his head. That means Ryleigh must be around here somewhere, too. Those two go together like peanut butter and jelly. How we'll ever find her in this craziness, though, I have no clue. This place is an absolute madhouse.

The guys quickly become engrossed in their conversation, so the girls and I grab drinks and head out to the dance floor. We find ourselves a little bit of space near the far wall and amuse ourselves dancing to some classic Halloween-inspired tunes. Michael Jackson's "Thriller" is currently pumping through the house, and there's a group dead center in the room dancing like the zombies from the iconic video. It's entertaining to say the least.

I can do this. I can have fun at a party. This doesn't have to be a big deal. And for a while, we dance ... and I do have fun. As much fun as I can have while constantly scoping out the other partygoers, anyway.

Eventually, Hawk and Maddox find us, and we dance as a big group for a while until Hawk tucks Lux under his arm and takes off toward the back of the house with her. I have no idea where they're headed. I shrug and as I do, Maddox grabs Raven, and the two of them start to grind together in a way that is close to indecent. I suck in a breath, looking around, and that's when I spot Kellan coming directly toward me. He stays in character, which must be pretty easy for a guy who doesn't speak more than necessary. He doesn't say a word now either but crooks a finger at me. My heart thuds into the depths of my gut. I inhale sharply. I think he wants to dance with me.

I try to steady my breathing, but my lungs don't seem to understand that they're supposed to keep delivering oxygen to my brain so I can think. I glance from side to side, then give in, slowly walking toward him, and take his offered hand. He immediately whirls me around and begins to dance behind me. His hands rest possessively on my hips as he guides my body to move with his. I eventually get into it and relax against him, addicted to the sway of his body and the way his fingers dig into my bare skin. My pulse rockets, my heart beating so fast it feels like it might hop out of my chest and dance around among everyone on its own. And the alcohol—it probably helps that it's finally hitting me too. My head's a tiny bit foggy, but I feel good. *Star, just let go for once.*

Kellan's hands move from my hips up toward my rib cage, his fingers wandering, almost like he's counting each individual rib. He grazes the bottom of my bralette, fingers skimming underneath. My breath stutters, remembering that these are the hands of an artist. And how hot is it that he's touching me like this? Out here in the open where anyone can see him doing it, too. Granted, it's currently wall-to-wall bodies, so maybe what he's doing isn't so visible after all.

A second later, I gasp as he grinds closer to me. His hand lands on my lower stomach, holding me tightly to his body, and his hard cock practically nestles itself between my ass cheeks. My chest rises and falls so fast, I wonder if I'm going to hyperventilate. *Oh God.* A surge of lust rushes through me, making my pussy throb and dampening my panties.

He pulls me closer as he continues to rub his dick against my ass. My brain jolts. He cups the underside of my bare breast, teasing my skin with his fingers. The long, low groan that emanates from his chest heightens my awareness of him, and my own breath comes out in harsh pants. I can't believe this is happening. Desire streaks through me.

The revelation rocks me to my core. I want Kellan.

Across the room, I spot Ryleigh talking to someone. Not Matty. Matty was in that scary clown mask. This is another one of those *Scream* masks. I rest my head against Kellan's shoulder, hazarding a look up at him. "Everyone is wearing that mask tonight."

The guy Ryleigh's been chatting with lifts his mask to the top of his head to take a sip of his drink, and my heart slams around in my chest.

Kellan stands across the room from me. Kellan isn't behind me. I freeze in place. The arms that have been holding me so securely, let me go; the erection that's been pressed up against my backside for the better part of ten minutes disappears. I pivot on my heel ... but the guy who was just dancing with me is nowhere to be seen. Shock crashes through my brain, through my tingling, aroused body.

I blink, turning back around to focus on the pair across the room. Ryleigh points at me and holds up a hand to wave. When I don't respond, she tilts her head to the side, then says something to Kellan that I obviously can't hear over the din of the party. He looks this way. His soft green gaze connects with mine.

Oh, God. My face crumples, and my hand shakes as I touch my fingers to my lips. I squeeze my eyes shut, attempting to rein myself in, trying not to fall apart.

But I can't stop the fear from snaking through me. I spin around, shoving my way through the crowd. If I don't get some fresh air soon, I'm going to pass out or hyperventilate or something.

Outside, I grip the railing and hurry down the stairs

on unsteady feet, and when I hit the grassy lawn in front of Greek Row, I run as fast as I can in my goddamn boots toward Duke Hall.

Who the fuck had I been dancing with, and why did they think they could touch me like that?

FOUR
KELLAN

"Do you want me to go after her?" Ryleigh's quiet voice finally reaches me. I don't have the slightest idea what just transpired. One second, I'm discussing an art project with her that we'll be working on in the coming weeks for our art studio class, and the next, she's waving to someone. And by the time I'd looked in the same direction and found Star in the throng of dancers, she'd been standing so still, a look of tortured confusion on her face. Her eyes found mine across the crowded room. The bewildered expression, the disorientation ... she'd looked so goddamn lost, it tore at something inside of me. Her face had fallen, and I knew without a shadow of a doubt that something terrible had happened. But *what?*

I wait two heartbeats before I shake my head. "No. I will. Could you find Lux and Raven? Or even Hawk or Maddox so they can help locate the girls?"

Ryleigh is still nodding when I begin to move, plowing through the crowd of people dancing to "A Nightmare on My Street" before shoving the door open and stepping out into the dark. I can just make out Star in that sexy bra top and skirt quite a ways in the distance, headed for the dorm. Her legs are a blur, capped off by cowgirl boots.

I take off, not sure how this is happening again that I'm chasing after this girl. Except ... this time, I'd seen hurt in her eyes. Embarrassment, even. And I didn't like it. Not one damn bit. "Star!" My breath heaving, I shout her name several more times, until she comes to a stop. "Wait," I huff out.

"For what?" She turns to face me and shakes her head, her arms folding over her chest, like she's protecting herself.

From me? My brows draw together as I study her. She sways a little on her feet, and her eyes crash shut. I have the most intense desire to tug her into my arms and hold on tightly. And that's something I never do. Ever. I don't let anyone in. I definitely don't let them touch me. Yet ... I'd let her dry me off last week after the pepper spray incident. I've kept that piece of information tucked in the back of my head all week, not wanting to examine it for shit. I can't. "I wanted to make sure you're okay. What the hell happened back there?"

She takes a couple of deep breaths before she finally opens her eyes to look at me. "It's okay. I'm fine." But her body is racked with violent tremors, and I can see plain as day that she's struggling to take a breath.

Slowly, I close the distance between us, approaching as if she's a wounded animal. I finally stop when I'm within arm's reach of her. I could touch her right now. But I don't. Quietly, I murmur, "I'd like to help if I can."

Star begins to open her mouth to speak, but her lips wobble. "I—"

My jaw tenses, my chest tightens unbearably, and I wonder how I'm still breathing. Shit. My brain tumbles and spins, trying to work out why I'm so affected by the look in her eyes. "Did someone hurt you? Because if there's some douchebag back at that party who did something or said something that you didn't like, I'll track him down right now. Just tell me who it was."

Her gaze flicks around, first to the ground, then up toward the sky. Anywhere, really, but in my direction. I reach out and tug at the chunk of pink hair hanging near her cheek to get her attention. "That's the problem. I thought—" She jerks to a stop, her eyes finally meeting mine. A single tear trickles from the corner of one of them. "I-I don't know who it was. We were dancing. I was having a good time. It felt good. And then he began to touch me, and things got a little intense." She looks away from me. "Overwhelming. But—"

Her face crumples again, like it had inside the frat house right before she'd taken off. It makes my already-wrecked heart hurt to see her like this. And what she's telling me makes the blood bubble and boil in my veins. Some prick had his hands on her. Upset her.

I touch a few fingers under her chin, guiding her face back to mine. In the most soothing voice I can manage, I murmur, "Okay. But you don't know who it was?"

She squeezes her eyes shut again, and her cheeks turn a bright shade of red, like maraschino cherries. Another tear leaks out and falls down her cheek. When she opens her vibrant green eyes again, the frustration she's feeling is clear. Her voice low, she finally admits the truth, and in doing so, throws me for a massive loop. "He had a *Scream* mask on. I thought it was you, okay?" Her breath hitches, and I see humiliation in her eyes. "I thought I was dancing with *you.*" She laughs, but she practically chokes on it. "Funny, right?"

My mouth hangs open as I stare into her eyes, the implication of everything she's said rocking me to my damaged core. *No.* I— She can't—

Before I'm able to put my thoughts into words, Star turns and races for the dorm steps, slaps her ID card to the scanner, and heaves the door open. I haven't moved a fraction of an inch. I should go after her. I should talk to her. But my head is so twisted up. Is she saying what I think she was saying? Did she mean she thought it was me ... and she liked what I was doing to her? *Shit.* A girl like Star deserves someone who can give her what she needs. I don't think I'm ever going to be that person. She doesn't know that when she looks into my eyes, she's looking at a dark, devastated soul. One with irreparable damage. One that is so cracked and broken she shouldn't want any part of me.

FIVE

STAR

I'm going to have a heart attack. I race up the stairs to the second floor of the dorm as quickly as my feet will carry me and head down the hall toward our suite, my mind replaying on a loop. I thought I was dancing with Kellan. I thought it was him touching me, his erection pressing into my backside. Reliving it is the worst kind of torture. Because I wanted it to be real. And for those few minutes, I thought maybe things were finally going to happen for me. Even though I know it's a terrible idea to let anyone in, I wanted it. Him.

My chest hurts, and my head is so jammed up with all the questions clanging around in my head. If it wasn't Kellan, who the hell was I dancing with? I thought I was in a safe space, that he was taking care of me the way Hawk cares for Lux or Maddox treats Raven. And yeah, I thought it was a little odd that he'd touch me like that because he never has before, but I also thought that maybe the little interlude in the bathroom meant something to him, the way it had to me—that it had somehow brought us closer.

Stupid. I'm so stupid.

When I thought it was Kellan, I liked it. A lot. Everything from the way he'd swayed so effortlessly to the music with me in his arms to the sexy way he'd slid his hand under my bralette to touch my breast. But it wasn't Kellan. It was some guy getting his rocks off while groping me. Some jerk's dick rubbing up on me, some stranger breathing heavily behind me. I shudder. And that *Scream* ghost had disappeared fast the second he realized I was freaking out.

A horrible thought sinks into the back of my mind where I try to keep all things Milo. Could he have been so damn bold as to walk onto this campus and feel me up at a party? Is he *watching* me?

I get to our suite door and my hands are shaking so badly, it takes me three attempts to jam the key into the lock. Inside, I finally exhale, but then my breath hitches. My bedroom door. Standing open. What the hell?

Warning bells go off in my head. *No. No, no, no.* I swallow hard, taking a step forward to peek into the room.

My hands fly up in alarm, covering my mouth as I fall to my knees, ungracefully hitting the floor. A buzzing begins in my head and rings in my ears. My brain doesn't want to process this. I can't focus on anything but the wild disarray inside my room. Everything I own is upended. Tossed carelessly around. Broken. Shredded. Torn. *Ruined.*

In my mind, I cry out. But I can't make a sound, my

screams are caught in my throat. And then Kellan is there, squatting down next to me, his hand on my back. And I shriek, long and loud.

"Whoa, whoa, whoa." He holds his hands up as if he's been caught red-handed. His gaze follows mine to the disaster in front of us. Staring at it with wide eyes, he gets up and pokes his head into my room. For several seconds, he says nothing. But then a disturbed, "What the fuck," leaves his lips, and he blows out a hard breath. Stealing a look back at me, his brows pinch together. "Are you okay? Was someone here when you came in?" He's wearing this slack-jawed expression that betrays how thrown he is by what we've encountered.

"No. No one," I answer quietly. "The suite was locked, but my door was open."

"Did you go in?" His gaze swings from me back to the mess before us.

"Do I look like I went in?" My words would sound a lot stronger if my voice wasn't catching as I try to speak. I huff out a breath and sweep my fingers under my eyes, realizing there were tears forming.

He rubs his hand over his stubble-coated jaw. A stubble-coated jaw that'd been hidden under the *Scream* mask that was across the room from me earlier tonight. Not behind me. He wasn't dancing with me. Didn't touch me. My thoughts crash around my head, and I'm finding it harder and harder to concentrate. *Am I in shock?*

"We should report this. I'm going to text the resident advisor and see if they think we should contact campus security or go straight to the local police." Pulling out his phone, he begins to tap out a text.

I blink hard. "What? Wait." Scrambling to my feet, I grip his arm. "No. Please don't."

He frowns. "Why the hell would you not report someone smashing your entire room?" Glancing inside, he shakes his head. "It's bad."

Anytime I'd ever told my mom about something Milo had done, it'd only made things worse. She never believed me, and *he'd* find a way to punish me for it. Until that last time, anyway, when I submitted an anonymous tip. And now, all this time later, maybe my punishment is finally being swiftly delivered.

"What's going on?" Lux walks into the room, followed by Hawk, Raven, and Maddox.

Kellan's jaw is rigid—actually, his entire body is tense —as he grits out, "That's a fuckin' loaded question at this point."

Raven looks from me to where I'm still gripping Kellan's arm hard, then into my room. "Well, shit. What—?"

"Oh my God, if one more person asks me what happened, I'm going to go into full-on freak-out mode." I let go of Kellan's arm to press both hands to my cheeks, embarrassed by my outburst. "I'm sorry. I don't know. And I don't know what to do."

"Well, first, we're not staying here with your room ransacked like this. And I know it was primarily you that's been affected, but someone broke into *our* suite." Lux shrugs. "We need to report it. We need someone out here ASAP to change the locks on all the doors."

I want to argue. But I can't. She's right. This doesn't simply affect me. It's all three of us. But damn, I know it'll make things worse.

Maddox glances at Hawk. "It's not like they're hard to pick. I wonder if we can convince them to put something heavier duty on the suite door at least."

"Agreed." Hawk grimaces. "Sorry, I know it's nothing to brag about, but we can both get in here in under thirty seconds. The locks are shit."

I watch out of the corner of my eye as Kellan gets Lux's attention. I don't know if he's trying to be sly about it, but I can totally read the look in his eyes. He wants her to take me out of here.

And because she's a good friend, and it's not an awful idea, she obliges. "Let's go sit in the guys' suite." She holds out her hand to me. "Come on, let them handle this. They'll come get us if they want you to make a statement. We'll watch a movie or something. And maybe we can work on getting rid of all the bloody Halloween makeup while we're at it." Her eyes connect with Raven's. "Can you grab some of those makeup remover facial wipe thingies and meet us across the hall?"

Raven nods and scurries into her room, calling over her shoulder, "Yep, I'm on it."

I draw in an unsettled breath and let Lux guide me out of the room, but I hear the guys talking. In low tones, Kellan begins to relay how he found me on the floor outside my room, shaking. And I'm sure he's about to tell them about the stuff at the party, too, and why I left without everyone else in the first place. The question is does he realize it's probably all connected? Will anyone put it all together?

Lux ushers me to the couch, and I curl up on it, dragging a pillow to my chest before she goes over to the fridge and pulls out bottles of water for us. "I know this look. You're completely overwhelmed. Breathe, Star."

I nod, looking up as Raven comes into the room, her arms full of supplies. She has the package of wipes, fulfilling Lux's request, but also Oreos and some of the Halloween candy her parents had sent her in a care package—adorable that her parents are sweet like that—and packets of hot chocolate. She gives us a sheepish look. "I dunno, I went for anything chocolate."

I bite my lip, trying not to lose it. "That's sweet of you."

She gives me a tight smile and drops everything onto the coffee table before turning and planting herself on it as well. Digging into the Halloween candy, she hands me a Hershey bar. "Tell us what's going on."

I rip open the chocolate packaging and break a piece off. Chewing on it slowly, I close my eyes and shake my head before answering. "It started at the party."

"Yeah, Ryleigh found us. But we didn't know what the hell was happening and neither did she, really. She said she was talking to Kellan and they spotted you across the room, waved, but then you were scrambling through the crowd to get the hell out of there." Lux frowns. "Why didn't you come find us? You know we would have come back with you." She glances up, momentarily distracted by the commotion outside the suite door. I think the cops, or at the very least the campus police, are here.

I shove that out of my head for the time being, even though it makes me nervous that there will be someone poking into what's happened here tonight. I clear my throat. "There was this guy. We were dancing—"

Raven's white-blonde brows lift. "Oh yeah?" She studies me while Lux comes at me with the makeup remover wipe, moving the pillow out of the way so she can peel the nasty stuff off my stomach first.

"It wasn't who I thought it was. And it—" I exhale raggedly. "I was upset. And embarrassed. Let's leave it at that." I throw up my hands. *And then this happened.*

Lux gives a sharp laugh. "No. Let's not. At least tell us who you thought it was. It's time for some honesty, Star."

I blink rapidly, then lean forward to set the rest of my chocolate bar on the table. Pressing my lips together, I eye each of my friends in turn. As quietly as I can, I whisper, "I thought it was Kellan."

They exchange a look before Raven asks the obvious. "Why would you think that?"

And this is where everything gets all messy again. "Well, he had a *Scream* mask on for one."

"But there were lots of those. There must have been another reason you thought it was him ..." Lux picks up an Oreo and shoves it whole into her mouth, watching me as she chews.

"Has something happened? Between the two of you, I mean?" Raven glances over toward the door, but it remains shut, even though we can hear other people over there. "Maybe that's why he took off after you so damn quickly yesterday?"

My cheeks burn with embarrassment as I stare at my friends. "I sorta pepper sprayed him. Like a week ago. You know I've always been a little anxious about someone breaking in here, and then with the fire alarms, someone following me isn't any different—"

"Wait, what?" Lux's gaze immediately narrows in what I think might be fascination.

Oh my God, my cheeks are on fire.

Raven's pale-blue eyes have become comically large. "He was following you? And you hit him with your pepper spray." The second part isn't even a question. "Wow."

"Yes, he was following me. Technically. He was behind me on the way home one night and it was dark, and ... I freaked." I let out a disbelieving sigh. "I totally sprayed him good, too. But then I helped him flush his eyes, and it was okay. We were okay. I think."

Lux's forehead pinches. "I'm not following. How did we get from him following you and you pepper spraying him to you thinking he was dancing with you ... and liking it?"

Jesus, they're going to make me say it. "I kinda thought there was something there. That day I helped him. He looked at me. Like really looked at me. I thought we had one of those moments, you know?" I lift a hand to cover my mouth. "Oh God, I'm an idiot."

"No you're not. Would either of you have seen me ending up with Maddox? Why is it weird that you'd like Kellan? And vice versa?" Raven grabs an Oreo and twists it apart, not even waiting for us to comment before she continues. "So, when you thought you were dancing with him ...?" She scrapes the filling off her cookie with her teeth, her eyes never leaving mine.

"Whoever the asshole was, he touched me. You know, kinda possessive ... like he knew me. Like he wanted me."

"Oh, man. Some dude got handsy with you and because he was wearing the same mask Kellan was, you thought it was him. Now I get it." Lux groans. "What a mess. Forgive me for focusing on a potentially less important detail. But, did you like the way this guy was touching you because of what he was doing, or"—her head tilts—"because you thought it was Kellan?"

"I don't know the answer to that." I bite down on my lip as heat surges to my face again. I don't. But the intensity I'd felt was definitely because I thought it was Kellan. And now that I know it wasn't, and it could have been— fuck, probably was—Milo, it's throwing me into a tailspin. *Shit.*

"Wow." Lux presses her lips together. "Kellan's ... different. He's a good guy. But—"

Great. And now they'll be watching my every move and every interaction with him. It's entirely possible that she knows something that I don't. She's spent a lot of time in their suite with Hawk since the beginning of the semester.

I wouldn't feel right prying, though. It makes sense that I get to know him on my own terms. *Doesn't it?* And right now, the only knowledge I'm operating on is that when I thought I was dancing with him, things felt right for maybe the first time in my life. But what she's hinting at, I'm not entirely sure of. I don't know Kellan at all, and maybe that's an issue.

Raven's mind seems to bounce around as much as mine is. She shakes her head, a confused look passing over her face. "How'd you figure out it wasn't him? Like, did he say something, or ...?"

"Because he was across the damn room from me, talking to Ryleigh. He lifted his mask, and all hell broke loose in my head. I froze. It took me a few seconds to register what was happening, and by the time I turned around, my dance partner was gone."

"Oh, shit. So, how do we figure out who it was?" Raven pops the other half of her cookie in her mouth.

"I don't know. No idea. I don't think I want to know."

SIX

KELLAN

"Dude, pacing the suite isn't going to make them finish any faster." Hawk eyes me from where he's sitting with Lux on the couch. The campus police had wanted to ask Star some questions, and she'd asked Raven to stay with her.

And it's fucking weird, but I kinda wanted it to be me who she trusted enough; me who she needed. Not because I think any sort of *anything* would ever be possible with her because I'm so screwed up ... but— *Fuck.* I shouldn't even be letting my thoughts go in that direction. I'm so closed off, I'm barely able to maintain my few friendships. I think these guys only stick around because I don't let them all the way in. And maybe we get along because we're all kinda messed up in our own ways. But I haven't allowed them to see the true depths of my issues. Otherwise, they'd see me for what I am. Damaged beyond repair.

Maddox shakes his head, eyes pinned on me. "So

you're telling me that someone busts up Star's room the same night that some guy has his hands on her."

"And she thought it was you. Because he was wearing the same mask." A disturbed grimace slides over Hawk's face.

"Totally weird." Lux holds up a finger. "Don't forget how she's been completely spooked by these fire alarms." She narrows her eyes on me. "Oh, and why didn't you tell anyone she pepper sprayed you?"

Maddox's and Hawk's mouths drop open, and in unison, they blurt out, "What?"

Bracing my hands on my hips, I tip my head back, staring at the ceiling. "I didn't say anything because it wasn't important. I scared her." With a sigh, I meet their curious stares and grind my teeth together. "What's taking so long?"

"It's unlike you *not* to be the calm one." Maddox gets up and crosses the room to the kitchen, then rummages around in the cabinet until he finds a package of Twizzlers. He chucks them at my head, but I catch them right before they nail me in the face. "Have a fuckin' snack. Raven is with her. She said she'd text if anything unusual came up."

Just then, the suite door opens and both girls enter, grabbing our attention. Raven crosses the room to Maddox, slipping her arms around his middle and resting her head against his chest. In a very matter-of-fact way (that I presume is meant to help Star remain calm), she begins to fill everyone in on what campus police had asked, but I can't focus on what she's saying. My eyes are glued to Star. She hasn't come very far into the suite, and she looks decidedly twitchy, like she's going to take off running again at any given moment.

I want to say something to her, go to her, but I'm unsure where we stand after everything that's transpired in the last hour or so—hell, in the last week. Lifting one hand, I run it through my wavy hair, making it stand up in disarray and not giving two shits about it. She won't look at me, and I don't know what that means.

I could have been staring at her for minutes or hours, I have no idea. Hawk gets my attention by saying, "I think the girls should stay over here tonight. They aren't replacing locks until tomorrow." He meets my eyes, and I immediately know what he's getting at. Of course, Lux will stay with him, and Raven will stay with Maddox—as if this doesn't happen half the time anyway—but Star, she of the three of them, is in most need of a place to stay.

I nod my agreement. "Yeah. Star can have my room. I'll take the couch."

Flustered, Star waves her arms in front of her. "Oh, no. It's okay. I don't want to take your bed. I can camp out here." Her teeth clamp down on her lip before dragging over it. Her gaze darts around again, aimed anywhere except in my direction. She really does hate being the center of attention. *Yep.* I'm reading that correctly for sure. And more than that, I make her nervous ... which I can't fault her for. I'm exactly the kind of guy that she should stay away from. She needs someone stable. Someone lacking all the horrific baggage I carry.

But still, she's been through it tonight. And she should have somewhere to sleep where she feels completely safe. If I'm out here, and she's in my room, anyone would have to go through me first to get to her. I pause, realizing I'm making an assumption that someone might be coming for her. She hasn't said as much. But I feel it in my gut.

"Uh, nope. Not happening." I shake my head, lips pressed together.

Raven and Lux get up and walk past me, huddling with Star. Her head bobs at whatever they're saying, then they each peel off, heading for the other bedrooms.

"Breakfast in the morning? I can go grab stuff." Maddox calls over his shoulder as he stops at his doorway. Asshole is always thinking about food.

Hawk smiles as he heads for his room. "Yeah. Sounds good."

I don't answer, but it's understood that I'm in. Unless I specifically say no, I'm good with whatever they say. It's our usual way of communicating and they know it.

Both doors shut, and then it's just me and Star left alone. I inhale deeply. "I mean it, you can have my room."

Her eyes slide to my door. "I—"

"Please. I won't sleep tonight if I know you're out here alone." I pause, rifling my hand through my hair again. "It's not a big deal. Promise."

She wets her lips. "They said I can get in there tomorrow. See if anything can be salvaged. Start to clean things up."

I blow out a careful breath, stepping toward her. "Look, I'm sorry your room got jacked up. But don't worry about it if it takes you a little bit to get things squared away. You can have my room until it's all straightened out."

Her eyes meet mine. They shimmer brightly behind her glasses. "Thank you." She hesitates, her eyes flicking from me to my room. "Um. I should have asked Lux or Raven before they holed up with the guys—" She jerks to a stop, pressing a few fingers to her temple. "Do you have a spare toothbrush? And maybe, um. Uh—"

Oh. I interrupt, "Something to wear to bed. Don't worry. I've got you. Come on." I lead her toward my room, but then pause on the threshold, looking around to see what she's going to see. My room is not exactly what anyone would call clean. It's a chaotic mess of canvases, sketchbooks, boxes and bins of drawing pencils, markers, chalks, paints, and brushes. But the bed is made, so there's that.

At my swift intake of breath, she absentmindedly pats my arm as she continues to look around. "Don't worry. I don't care. My room is full of spare computer parts and all sorts of random stuff. Or ... it was, anyway." Her gaze drops to the floor before she releases a heavy sigh. "Thanks again for this."

Damn. I nod. "No problem. Hang on a sec." In the bathroom, I dig around in the drawers until I come up with a new toothbrush. Her eyes flick to mine as I reenter the room, holding the toothbrush up like it's some sort of award that I'm bestowing upon her. "Here you go."

"Thanks." Star takes it from me, the first genuine smile I've seen from her in days stretches her cheeks. "It's an artful mess in here, Kellan." She points out a giant bucket of markers on the corner of my desk. "And that's a *lot* of Sharpies."

I smirk the tiniest bit. "I can't help myself. I like all the different sizes and colors. I always have one with me."

"You never know when you'll need to sign a masterpiece, I guess, huh?" She winks and bestows a second smile on me. My chest tightens in response.

This girl. It's strange having her in my space. I've never had a girl in my room. Never wanted one in here. I blink, recognizing that I've been staring at her for way too long again. I can't help myself. Every time I look at her, I get a little lost in my head. "Sorry. Lemme get you a T-shirt or something." Stepping over a pile of painting supplies, I attempt to calm the racing of my heart. When I try to swallow, I find my throat's gone completely dry. *Shit, get it together, Kellan. It's just Star.* I glance over my shoulder at her to find her pushing her glasses up the bridge of her nose again. It's cute. And I like her glasses. The blue frames suit her. Trying to shake my nervousness, I tug open a drawer and rummage around until I find an old T-shirt she can wear to sleep in. "Um, do you want some joggers or something?" I pull out a pair for myself, glancing over my shoulder to check for her answer.

She smiles through gritted teeth. "Oh. Um. I'll just kick them off. I can't sleep in pants." A blush sweeps over her cheeks. "That's long enough that it'll be like a nightshirt. I'll be fine."

I swallow hard as I pivot to shut the drawer, my head full of images of Star lying in my bed, wearing my T-shirt and not much else. My cock twitches, and my eyes slam shut for a second before I turn around again, rapping my knuckles against the wood, as if what she said hasn't affected me in the slightest. "Well, they're in this drawer if you decide you want them for whatever reason. I don't have a problem with you borrowing whatever you need." With a jerk of my thumb over my shoulder, I murmur, "I'm going to brush my teeth, then I'll be out of your way."

She nods as she accepts the T-shirt from me. "Okay."

THERE'RE zero reasons why I should still be awake. It's been a long-ass night, and I'm exhausted. Yet, I haven't caught a single wink because I can't get my brain to shut off.

I'm totally lying to myself. It's my dick. I'm unable to shut my eyes without erection-inducing visions of Star in my bed floating through my mind. I've had a constant hard-on ever since I left her in my room. It's agonizing. Normally, I'd take care of business and not think further about it. But I can't fucking do that out here. Way too awkward. Especially since sex noises are coming from Maddox's room. I don't need to jack off to that soundtrack, no matter how hot it sounds.

My hands drift under the blanket, pressing on my dick over my joggers as I remind myself over and over again that I definitely should not stroke myself. I grit my teeth, pushing my head back into the pillow, and clench my eyes tightly shut. And then, like an idiot, I allow myself one stroke. Lust reaches out, smacking me in the face, and all the air whooshes from my lungs. *Jesus.*

The door to my room creaks open noisily, and my heart jumps into my throat. I jerk my hand away from my dick. There's never any sneaking in and out of my room because the hinge makes so much noise. Without a shadow of a doubt, Star's just opened that door, and here I am with an eight-person tent in my pants. I turn my head and slowly open my eyes.

"Kellan? Are you awake?" Star stands in my doorway with my shirt on. It barely fucking covers her. Her hair is tied back in a ponytail, and she's not wearing her glasses, which probably explains the squinting and asking if I'm awake, even though I think it's obvious I'm staring at her. *Shit.* And if I thought my cock was hard a second ago— ugh. I'm *so* fucked.

I clear my throat, but my voice still comes out gruff. "Yeah. You having trouble sleeping?" I wet my lips, my eyes roaming up and down her body, even though I already looked once. Apparently, I didn't get my fill. Or maybe it's my dick commanding me. I don't know. Those bare legs. The hint of the swell of her breasts under my shirt. The way she's chewing on her lip. Jesus. This is not helping what's happening in my pants.

"Yeah." Even in the dark, I can see her sigh more than hear it. It's like her entire body sags with disappointment that she's unable to rest.

I throw the blanket back, hoping that without her glasses on she can't see the current situation in my joggers. Resting my forearms on my thighs and letting my hands dangle between them, I eye her carefully. I haven't a clue what she's thinking. "Can I get you something to drink or eat? Or do you want to watch TV?"

She shakes her head. "I was wondering if you wanted to hang out in your bedroom. I thought maybe we could talk or—"

"Or?" *Or.* My brows inch up on my forehead as I tilt my head to the side and watch her fidget.

"Sleep. I'm exhausted, but every time I close my eyes, all the crap finds its way in."

Oh, man. She wants me to sleep in there with her. And for some insane reason, I can't fathom, I nod. My voice thick, I murmur, "Yeah. Okay. If you think it'll help." I draw in a breath as I stand, grabbing my pillow from the couch. I purposely hold it in front of me as she waits for me to join her.

After we're both inside the room, I shut the door behind us and lean against it for a second. It feels like we're crossing some sort of an invisible line by occupying the same room together overnight.

Star climbs into my bed, and I can't help but stare at her panty-covered ass cheeks as she moves to the far side. I wonder if she realizes they're showing or that I'm looking.

She curls up on her side, facing me. I can barely make out her eyes in the dark. She's waiting for me to get into that bed with her.

"Are you okay?" she whispers, then wets her lips in a way that has my cock swelling unbearably.

I blow out a hard breath and toss my pillow down on the nearside of the bed, then slip under the covers, pulling them up to my waist. I lie on my back for almost a full minute before I turn my head to answer her. "Yeah. I'm good." It's dark, but I know her eyes are scanning my face and down over my tattooed shoulders and chest. Fuck, this may be the worst idea ever. No way am I sleeping now. A little groan escapes me, unbidden, and I instantly regret it. I shift uncomfortably, no matter what I tell myself, I'm turned on. How could I not be with this girl lying beside me? I discreetly put my hand under the sheet in an attempt to push my dick down, somehow deliver the message that he's not getting any action tonight.

But the fucker knows there's a pretty female in his vicinity. My cock is as hard as a goddamn steel post. This might be the most brutal form of torture known to man.

Star shifts next to me and props herself up on her elbow. Her mouth curves down in a slight frown, and before I know what she's doing, she eases the sheet down off both of us. Her gaze lands on my hand, which is still covering my erection. "Oh." Her swallow is audible as it travels down her throat.

I must be in an alternate universe or something because she slowly reaches for my wrist and drags my hand away. My gaze is fixated on her as she stares at the raging boner I'm sporting. And before I can stop her, she grazes my aching length with her fingers. A strangled grunt erupts from my throat. "Star."

She lifts her eyes to meet mine at the same time she touches me firmly, wrapping her fingers around my dick through my joggers and boxer briefs. "I could maybe ...?" She tucks her lower lip between her teeth, her chest rising prominently inside my shirt as she draws in a deep inhale. She holds her breath for a few seconds before moving onto her knees beside me. "Do ... do you want me to?" Her eyes are big as she waits for me to say something.

In answer, my eyes remain locked on hers, but I hook my thumbs into the waistband of my joggers and lift my ass, shoving them down. My cock springs free, jutting straight into the air. I've been so hard for so fucking long, I don't think there's any way I'd deny myself this.

The second Star's hand wraps around my dick, my hips involuntarily thrust upward into her palm. I moan. I can't help myself. It's been so long since my cock has been in anyone's hand but my own. She slowly works me, her hand moving up and down my thick shaft at a steady pace. And the entire time, she watches me, and I swear to fuck, that's got to be what's making this so goddamn good. She stops for only a second to slide her thumb over the head of my cock where I'm leaking pre-cum like crazy. "Oh, fuck," I huff out as she uses it like lube, smearing it over me before stroking me again in earnest. My breath pants out harshly in the quiet room, and just when I think it can't get any better, she cups my balls with her other hand, gently squeezing and tugging.

"Do you like that?" she whispers.

But before I can answer, I erupt like a motherfucking geyser, cum spurting over her hand and landing on my stomach and chest. There'd been no warning. Just *boom*. My heart pounds so hard, I wouldn't be surprised if I'm about to die, but if I do, this is a good way to go.

When I finally have a tiny bit of oxygen circulating my brain, I blink a few times, then focus on her face. Her hand is still on my dick, but when she sees I'm watching her, she removes it.

"Um. Be right back." I hurry into the bathroom to clean up, but by the time I return, she's on her side again, only facing the other direction. I exhale heavily. *Fuck.* Tell me this wasn't a massive mistake. My brain is far too jumbled up to make heads or tails of anything after that orgasm. Gingerly, I crawl back into bed, trying not to disturb her. After a few seconds, though, it's obvious she's not asleep. In fact, she's moving around, squirming almost. "Star?"

She peeks over her shoulder at me, a slightly embarrassed look on her face, and that's when I realize what's going on. Her arousal scents the air. It's potent, traveling up my nose and invading my brain. *Fuuuck.*

Does she want me to reciprocate? Just like I haven't had any action in a while, I haven't touched a girl in what seems like forever either. Not since Tammy. And I don't want to think about how that relationship crashed and burned due to me being emotionally unavailable and unable to let her touch me the way she wanted to.

With Star's back to my front, I edge closer to her, then slowly run my fingertips down the length of her arm. When they reach her hand, mine covers hers. Together, we apply pressure to her clit, rubbing in slow circles. She whimpers, her hips thrusting a bit against our hands. "Will you touch me, Kellan?" The question comes out on a moan.

I nod near her head, and she must feel it because she slips her hand from under mine, leaving my fingers in direct contact with her panties. And fuck me, I knew they were probably damp, but they're soaked. I groan at the feel of her, my fingers working quickly. "Fuuuuck," I hiss out from between my teeth.

She languidly moves against my hand until she whispers, "Hold on a sec." Then she removes my hand and slips her panties down. My brain is close to imploding when she hooks her leg over mine, opening herself wide. I can't help myself, I want to feel her, want to touch her where she's throbbing for me. I slip my fingers between her legs once again. She's so wet and swollen, my eyes practically roll back in my head. "Is that okay?"

She moans low in answer and wastes no time, writhing against my fingers as I play with her clit. She's so beautiful, completely uninhibited. She knows what she wants. After a few moments, I allow my fingers to roam further, circling her opening and touching every inch of her pussy. Drawing her tightly against my body, I slide two fingers inside her and use my thumb to flick at her clit.

"Kel—" she gasps, unable to finish saying my name. Her strangled, throaty cries fill the room as I make her body tremble for me.

It's not a minute later that she's bucking against my hand and soaking my fingers when she comes. Her breathing is labored, and when she turns to look at me, she's dazed. "Sorry, I—"

"We helped each other," I rasp as I withdraw my fingers from between her legs. "It's fine. It meant nothing."

I feel the harsh exhale as her lungs eject the air she'd been holding. She stiffens against me. "Yeah ... *nothing.*"

I know this girl likes me. She revealed that much outside when she practically fell apart at the admission that she mistakenly thought she'd been dancing with me. But I can't let her like me. We can't be anything because I don't want to expose her to the depths of my devastation.

SEVEN

STAR

As I sneak out of Kellan's bedroom around five in the morning, humiliation rocks me. Because I'm not alone in their suite. Oh, *no.*

Maddox stands at the sink in the kitchen, drinking a glass of water. He looks sleepy as hell, his eyelids drooping until he spots me. He freezes in place. I do the same. We stare at each other, then after a few seconds, his gaze flicks behind me where the gentle sound of Kellan's snores are audible.

I cringe. Because yeah. Kellan was supposed to be sleeping out here. Not in the bedroom with me. And here I am, half-dressed in front of Maddox and tugging on the hem of Kellan's not-quite-big-enough-to-cover-my-panties T-shirt. It should be illegal to blush this hard so early. Fuck my life.

His brow quirks up, his eyes now wide open and alert. He's definitely awake, but his voice is still rough when he asks, "Something wrong?"

I wet my lips and shake my head. There's no way I'm

telling Maddox that his buddy rocked my world, then blew me off last night. And even though I don't say it, my face burns all the same at the fresh reminder. "No. I can't sleep. I thought maybe I'd go inspect my room. The cops said I was able to go in last night, but I couldn't handle it."

"Oh." His dark brow furrows. "I'm going to order breakfast soon from a pancake house not too far from here. Do you want me to get you anything? I'll order online and pick it up when they open at six."

As good as that sounds, I'm unsure if being around Kellan when he wakes up is something I want to subject myself to. I haven't slept. I'm embarrassed. And there's all this other bullshit to deal with today. I shake my head. "No, thank you." I jerk my thumb over my shoulder. "I'm going to get over there."

Maddox rubs his hand over the heavy stubble that's come in on his face overnight and steals another look at Kellan's partially open door that I hadn't gotten a chance to close behind me. "Are you sure you're okay?" A deep crease mars his forehead, a scowl darkening his features. If I thought I'd done anything to warrant it, I'd be fucking nervous right about now.

The swallow works painfully down the length of my throat before I find it in me to answer. "I asked him to come in there. If that's what you're wondering. He didn't force his way in or anything weird like that."

He draws in a deep, fortifying breath. "Look. I won't say much because I can't. But Kellan has some shit that he deals with. If he ... upset you, he probably didn't mean to. Or may not have realized he was doing it at the time."

"Are you making excuses for him?" My traitorous voice trembles as my heart jolts in my chest.

Maddox's jaw tenses. "No. Hell no. If he hurt you—" He hesitates, peering carefully at me while placing his hands on his hips, then shaking his head regretfully. "Fuck. I'm not good with this stuff." We're both quiet for the space of several seconds. "He's like a brother to me. But I'd still want to know if I needed to knock some sense into him. Are we clear?"

I nod, then point toward the suite door. "I really am going to go now." But midway out, I stop and turn around. "Maddox?"

He glances up from where he's setting his glass in the sink. "Yeah?"

"Thank you. Could you tell everyone I don't want to be disturbed?"

Scrubbing his hand over his hair, making it stand on end, he grits his teeth for a moment before subtly nodding. "You got it."

When I make it across the hall, I discover they haven't changed our lock yet, and in fact, the suite is completely unlocked, which pisses me off. I sigh, staring at the door. We were all off our game last night, that's for certain. I hope everything else is as we left it, and I'm not in for another round of unpleasant surprises.

Resting my hand on the doorknob, I finally give in, twisting it and allowing myself entry. Inside the suite, I flip the overhead light on, which we hardly use because it's so damn bright, but I want that obnoxious illumination now more than anything. I let my gaze travel the common area of our suite. Nothing else seems to have been disturbed. Raven's expensive coffee maker sits on the counter like it has since the day we moved in. A few plush blankets are neatly folded and stacked on one end of the couch. The TV mounted on the wall is also untouched. I cross to Raven's room first, check the door, and find it locked, then do the same with Lux's. Also locked.

Mine, however, stands open, my personal belongings strewn everywhere. I hadn't so much as set foot inside my room last night. I could see the destruction perfectly well from the doorway. I push the door wide and hit the light switch on the wall, then slowly make my way inside. I can't help it. I gasp. It's worse than I'd thought.

My laptop is open and facedown on the floor, the hinge smashed like someone stepped on it after tossing it carelessly to the ground. The computer parts that I'd mentioned to Kellan last night are mostly in pieces as well. The drawers of my dresser were pulled out completely and upended everywhere—articles of clothing, everything from leggings and jeans to socks, bras, and panties are scattered from one side of the room to the other. Inside the closet, my clothing is a mess on the floor.

I back out of the closet. What was the point of this? Unable to comprehend any of it, I turn and look at my bed. The duvet and sheets and pillows are a huge mess, ripped and torn.

And there on the nightstand lies a single matchbook. With a shaking hand, I pick it up. My thoughts scatter.

IT TAKES me a long time to process the fact that I'm now positive Milo has been in my room. I don't want to have to make the call, but I do. Pulling out my phone, I open my contacts and tap on my mother's number. We've never been super close, but she remarried several years ago, and our relationship hasn't been good since. Right now, I'd say it's mostly in the toilet. Ever since Raymond came into her life, she's been hard to deal with. I can hear her in my head. *Your stepfather has all the money we'll ever need. Don't be ungrateful, Star. Raymond can afford to send you to SRU like you've always wanted. I don't understand why you can't be appreciative of everything Raymond is doing for you.*

And all of that is great. Except Raymond and his fourteen-year-old son, Milo, had come to us as a pair. And for every kindness Raymond has ever extended to me, his son paid me back in awfulness and dirty deeds. Things started out okay. I even liked him at first. Soon though, it became apparent that there was something really, really wrong with him. Like he was sick in the head. Perverse. And most often, I was his target.

But no one wanted to listen to me. Because outwardly, to everyone else, he's the golden boy who can do no wrong.

It's a miracle I stopped that psycho. And it's unfortunate that he's now roaming about free. I listen as the phone rings several times before my mother's groggy voice answers. "Star? Why are you calling so early?"

Biting my lip, I close my eyes and gather my strength. "Um. I hate to ask this because I know every time I bring him up, shit hits the fan. But do you know where Milo is?"

EIGHT
KELLAN

What a fuckin' weekend. As if the fire alarm craziness and the Halloween party hadn't been enough, I'd let things go way too far with Star. When she asked if I wanted her to touch me—not in so many words because we'd both been nervous—I'm the one who got my dick out. And when we were done, and both satisfied, I brushed it aside like it meant less than nothing to me. Like we'd given each other a release and it was no big deal. Because I'd made a mistake. I shouldn't have touched her or let her touch me.

I can't let her think that I could ever have any sort of normal relationship with her. I'd known the second the words came out of my mouth that she wouldn't take it well. But what the fuck am I supposed to do? Fortunately, we hadn't crossed any of my boundaries, so I hadn't flipped out, but I'm sure she fuckin' hates me.

Jesus, and the looks the rest of our crew had given me yesterday morning. Maddox, true to his word, had gone out for food and coffee early, and he must have spoken to her because he shared that she'd had trouble sleeping and didn't want to be bothered by anyone.

Later in the day, I'd heard from Hawk and Lux that she'd been sorting through her things to see if anything was salvageable and had asked for some privacy. She's not even letting the girls help her.

And all that kinda makes me feel like shit because I hadn't handled things well. Why can't I be like other guys? Normal. Human. I should have held her close. Whispered comforting words in her ear. Told her she was beautiful and let her know how much I'd enjoyed the hell out of every second of what we'd done together. But no. I'm a grade A asshole. That's all there is to it.

I let out a pent-up sigh as I tuck the paintbrush I'm using behind my ear. Focus. I need to fucking focus. I only have so many art studio sessions before these paintings are due.

"That was quite a sigh." Ryleigh eyes me from her painting station about five feet away but doesn't say anything more. This girl will wait me out. She knows me too well. If it's something I need to say, it'll eventually come out. Not always verbally, though. Sometimes it's obvious in whatever project I work on that particular day, and we'll discuss it. Or sometimes she'll just nod, and understand what I'm pouring into my art.

Ryleigh has proved to be a good friend. We've been in art classes together since we started at Shadow River. She's a talented artist, and that's what'd caught my eye at first. I couldn't get enough of the images she created. And then we started talking more and more during our studio classes—well, as much as two quiet people talk, anyway. She gets me—and it's in a different way than Hawk and Maddox do, so that helps sometimes, though I don't know if she'd blindly go along with something I asked of her like they do. But she sure as hell will tell me the straight-up truth, and I appreciate the hell out of that. And now it might be nice to have a female opinion. Especially from someone who I know is completely and totally invested in their own relationship. She's been happily dating Matty Montclair, SRU's quarterback that Hawk hangs with all the time, for several years now. Honestly, she's like the sister I never knew I needed. Considering the shitty relationship I have with my younger brother, it's refreshing to know I have someone in my corner who feels like family.

With a shrug and a sigh, she looks back at her painting, tapping the end of the wide paintbrush she's been wielding against her lip. "What do you think? What does this say to you?"

Our current project is supposed to be a trio of paintings demonstrating a range of emotions. The trick is that the group of three works is also supposed to be cohesive in some way or another. Whether that's via color, brushstroke, or some other method, it's up to us how we think we can best express the feelings we're hoping to evoke in the viewer. It's an interesting project—especially since we don't have to tell anyone until the big art show at the end of the semester what it is we're expressing. There were no other instructions given, so we have free rein to tackle the assignment in any manner we choose, so long as the medium is paint.

I stop to look at what she's doing, and it's gorgeous as usual. Bold, vibrant colors applied to the canvas in lush, sweeping strokes. "Mm. Happiness. Or love, maybe."

Ryleigh gets a goofy look on her face. "Yeah. I'm so obvious."

I give her a little smirk. "What's obvious is that you're happy. That's not a bad thing. I like the way you're using that wide brush. I'll be interested to see the other two pieces once they're all complete."

She wrinkles her nose. "I think I probably need to go for something not so mushy on the next one, huh? Maybe something that's polar opposite." Very delicately, she sweeps the paintbrush she's just reloaded over an area of her canvas.

I laugh. "Well, maybe a little different, at least—but you could totally shake things up and go for something like envy or wrath."

"Ooh. Like one of the seven deadly sins? But then how would I keep Matty as my muse?" She jerks to a stop, her paintbrush held midair and her eyes going wide. "Oh. Oh. Oh. *Wait.* What about *lust?*" She wriggles her eyebrows at me and shoots me a wink. "Do you think Professor Zara would count that as an emotion?"

I wasn't expecting that one to pop out of her mouth with such glee. I cough to hide my surprise, bobbing my head. "That could be interesting." It's not the worst idea. Actually it's a great idea, conceptually. Love versus lust versus ...? Hmm.

The funny thing is, I don't know why the word lust popping out of Ryleigh's mouth had left me open-mouthed. Ryleigh looks sweet, but every once in a while, she'll spring something on me. Like the day not too long ago when she asked me if guys really like foreplay as much as Matty seems to or if they'd rather get to the main event. And then she'd gone on to say that he spends a long time going down on her and wondered if she should feel weird about that. *Holy fuck.* I assured her that if she's enjoying herself then it sounds like he knows what he's doing. So, yeah. Not sure why I'd been surprised at all by the word *lust* popping straight out of her mouth, or that she'd consider using it as the theme for one of her paintings. "What about hate for the third piece? Maybe put lust in the middle?" I shrug. "Just a thought."

"Oh. That's a good idea. I'll mull that over. But I'm liking it. There's a thin line between love and hate ... and I think lust resides right smack in the middle." She pauses for a few seconds to set her paintbrush down. "So, what's going on over there?" She nods at the painting I've been working on since last week.

I hadn't quite known what I was doing when I started it, but now that it's coming along, it's made itself obvious —at least in my head. The overriding emotion that I'm attempting to demonstrate is—

"Fear. You're totally doing fear." Ryleigh looks at me, excited. "Am I right?"

Oh, shit. Star's fear, to be exact. Not that Ryleigh knows whose fear I'm using as my inspiration, but I was trying to capture what I'd seen in Star's eyes—the wild frenzy of emotion she'd radiated. It's the feeling I got each time I experienced her panic for myself. The terror had flowed through her and shot right out of her eyes when she aimed that pepper spray at me. Absolute shock and fright had taken over her entire being at the Halloween party when she'd stared at me across the room. And last but definitely not least, the creeping, crawling anxiety upon the discovery of her ransacked room.

They say the eyes are the window to the soul. And if that's the truth, Star's soul is horrified by what she's experiencing, whatever it is. She's always on edge. Always ready to lash out to protect herself.

A voice whispers in my head, *But she trusted you enough to ask you to sleep in the same bed with her. And look what you fuckin' did.*

I press my lips together, scanning over my work again. "Yeah. It's definitely fear."

"But not yours." Ryleigh's brows raise. "Because I don't think you're scared of anything."

"It's hard to be afraid of much after having experienced certain things." When someone makes you feel so much less than. When they abuse you mentally and scar you physically. When that person is supposed to be one of the people who cares for you *the most*. My throat constricts with emotion.

"Sorry. I hit a nerve." Ryleigh blinks at me from behind her owlish glasses, which only serves to remind me of Star.

I hurt Star. I know I did. All I know is pushing people away. All I'm worth is nothing.

Ryleigh dips her brush into the paint on her tray,

making slow, intentional strokes onto her canvas. "Art is great therapy. But you know, actual therapists are helpful for this sort of thing, too. I mean, I know you pour your emotions into your work already, even without this assignment. And I know you don't like talking to people much. But maybe it would help. Or ... if not that, I'm happy to listen. I hope you already knew that. But you know, if you need someone. I'm here."

I nod and begin to work again as well. "Thanks, Ry." It's several more minutes before I say anything else. This isn't abnormal for us. Not when inspiration strikes for either of us. Not when we let it take over and get lost in what we're doing. We know better than to interrupt each other. Satisfied with what I've done, I pause, then wait for her to do the same. "I've never seen anyone. Therapy-wise, I mean." There are certain things I just don't talk about. Can't.

"Um, so don't answer if I'm being too pushy. But if this painting isn't about you, then ... who?"

The only way it's about me is that I saw this fear, right in her eyes. My breath hitches, and I set down my tray and brush, and pick up a cloth to wipe some paint off my hands. "Does it have to be someone in particular?"

She looks at my canvas again and raises a brow. "You're telling me that's not personal?"

"Okay. Maybe it is." My art *always* means something. Sometimes I don't even know what I'm doing until it's complete and I've had a chance to step back and examine it. But not this time. This time, I'm well aware of what I'm painting, as every stroke of my brush across the canvas burns inside me.

Ryleigh nods slowly, then points her paintbrush at me, a frown pulling at the corners of her lips. "It's totally a girl, isn't it." It's not a question. When Ryleigh is sure of something, she's usually right. She's obviously not wrong, but I'm unsure if I should admit it.

I glance at her out of the corner of my eye, quickly weigh my options, and decide there's no harm in sharing what's happening in vague terms. "This is ... just between you and me—" I hesitate. "I, uh, I don't actually know what it is yet. There's a girl. But I don't know what the hell I'm doing or feeling. And I think she's avoiding me now because I'm fucking dumb and clearly don't know how to handle things when anyone gets the slightest bit close to me. Because I'm not like other guys." My face burns with frustration and embarrassment.

Ryleigh sets her brush down. Her eyes roam over my anxious expression, taking it in. Figuring me out. Because she's good at that. Quietly, she says, "It's okay, Kellan. We don't always have to know how to navigate every little thing. And you aren't dumb. You're just—"

"Damaged. I'm fuckin' damaged. Call a spade a spade." Letting out an exasperated sound, I shake my head. "Can I be honest with you?"

"Always." I can tell from the concentration drifting over her features that she senses what I'm about to say is important, that she genuinely wants to help.

"I'm afraid I've messed it all up." What's stupid is that the second Star was in my bed, I'd started thinking of her as mine. I can't tell Ryleigh that. I can hardly admit it to myself. "Ry, I'm so fucked up, I don't even know where to begin, don't know how to be with someone." So, I'd let

Star think I used her to get off. I draw in a ragged breath. "I did what I always do. I pushed her away in the only way I've ever known. I said things I knew would hurt her."

NINE
KELLAN

I'm still in a shitty mood when I get to my speech class Tuesday. I'm one hundred percent sure that Star is avoiding me. And I'm not simply referring to her politely not speaking to me. I've literally not seen the girl for days. I stopped by their suite after my art studio class yesterday. I had it in my head that I should apologize or something. I don't know how to explain to her why I'd responded like I had or how to make sure she understands that it's not her. It's me. God, that sounds cliché. But it's the damn truth. She has her own issues, and I don't need to add my bullshit on top of whatever she's going through.

My chest is so tight, thinking about her, and I'm so goddamn embarrassed about it that I haven't said much to anyone, except that vague explanation I gave Ryleigh. It's hard to talk to Maddox or Hawk right now, and I don't know if I'm angry about that or what. They're in relationships with the girls who live with the person I hurt. Surely, there's talk among our friend group. But it's happening behind closed doors. And I'm the only one standing clueless on the other side.

"Mr. Murphy. Would you care to come up to the front of the room? It's your turn to give your speech." Professor Coggins eyes me, his bushy brows going up in question.

I blink, feeling every eye in the room on me. *Shit.* I must have zoned out. My speech class is definitely not my favorite, but it's one of the liberal studies requirements at SRU, so I figured I'd better get it the fuck over with sooner rather than later. And today we've got practice speeches. We'd all been given random topics to present, and Professor Coggins couldn't have selected a worse one for me if he'd tried.

I clear my throat, getting up from my seat. "Of c-course." I blink. *Fuck.* My concentration is screwed. Slowly, I walk to the front of the lecture hall, hoping I can calm the fuck down so I can deliver this speech and not make a complete fool of myself.

Setting my notes down on the podium, I face the sea of fifty faces, then look to our professor, and he nods that I may begin. This entire class is my worst fucking night-mare. Not only do I hate public speaking—speaking in general, really—but the assholes Star and I had run into at Duke Hall after the pepper spray incident are in this class. They're typical big-men-on-campus types, thinking they rule the damn school and can do no wrong. I call them The Assholes for a reason—and that's because ever since they picked up on this class as being a weakness of mine, they do nothing but taunt me. It reminds me so much of the way Jamie used to treat me when we were younger that it truly fucks with my head. It's bad.

And today will be no different, I can tell already. My ears buzz, and my palms begin to sweat as I stand at the front of the class, gathering the courage to begin. I take a few deep breaths to steady myself. Usually it works. "M-my topic t-today is childhood t-trauma." *Fuck.* I wince at how terrible I sound and how I can't seem to control it at all today.

"Dude. Seems like someone has experienced some trauma of his own." The Assholes cackle like maniacs even though Professor Coggins stands up and looks at them with a death glare. Their laughter reminds me of my brother every fucking time he did something better than me. Every time he won and I lost. Every time our father praised him and degraded me. These guys are a lot like him.

"WHY THE HELL *can't you be more like your brother, Kellan?" Our father glares, his eyes roaming over me with disdain as Jamie leaves the room. I hear that jerk brother of mine laughing all the way down the hall. He knows Dad's about to lay into me. He doesn't even care. He thinks it's funny.*

I look down at my feet. I'm still in my baseball uniform. My brother and I are on the same team, which I thought would be fun at first, but it's not. Not at all. The joke's on me, especially when Dad finally shows up to watch, and I strike out at every at bat, while my brother hits home runs.

"You're so fucking scrawny, kid. I have no clue where you came from. It must be your mother's genes. I can't believe my firstborn son is built like a goddamn pansy. Thank God for Jamie."

My brows draw together. Eight-year-old Jamie is Dad's favorite. Everyone thinks he's older than I am. He's bigger and stronger, though he's two years younger. I get picked on mercilessly at school because I haven't hit a good growth spurt yet. My grandma says it's coming, but I don't know about that. I think I might be doomed to be this size forever—the one everyone picks on and laughs at.

But no matter how bad it is at school, that's nothing compared to what it's like at home. Nothing. I'm scared I'm never going to get any bigger. Will never be able to defend myself. And if I can't, this will never stop. My lip wobbling, I whisper. "W-what was wrong with M-M-Mom? She was pretty. You m-married her."

"I'll tell you exactly what was wrong with her. Her entire goddamn family is full of weak, worthless people." He grits his teeth as he towers over me. "I swear to God, some days I don't think we share a single cell. How the fuck are you mine?"

My chest tightens, knowing full well what's coming next. "And Jesus Christ. What's the deal with the stutter? H-h-haven't y-y-you outgro-grown that yet?" he mocks me, then glares again, shooting an ugly smirk at me. He shakes his head, like he's disgusted by me.

I don't know why I ever think things will go differently. It's always the same. Always.

"Come here."

My heart skips a beat, then thumps hard as it resumes. I shake my head, my gaze flitting to the ashtray on his desk, terror shimmying down my spine. I feel sick to my stomach. "N-n-no. I-I don't want t-to." My breath stutters as much as my words do.

"Get your skinny little pathetic ass over here, right fucking now, Kellan." Dad's growling voice reaches inside me, squeezes my lungs, and makes it so hard to breathe. They don't even want to work anymore. It's like they've given up on me, too.

When I shake my head, my nerves getting the better of me, he pushes back from his desk, rising to his full six-feet-four inches. He towers over me, and before I can make my feet move from where they're rooted to the floor, his meaty hand lands on the back of my neck, gripping me so tightly, I cry out.

"Be a man, Kellan. This is the problem. You're a fucking baby, and you're always going to act like one unless I do my job and make you into a fucking man." He picks up the cigarette that's been sitting on the edge of the ashtray.

My entire body quakes in fear of what's coming. I try to be strong, I try to be quiet, like I know he wants me to be. I want to run, but he grips me so tightly, I can't get away.

And as I silently tremble, my father yanks the collar of my shirt to the side and puts out the cigarette on my shoulder, mashing the still-burning cigarette butt down good and hard into my skin.

I can't help it. I scream.

It's not the first time. And I know it won't be the last.

No matter how hard I try, my father hates me more and more with each passing day.

FUCK. That was so fucking embarrassing. From the look on Professor Coggins's face, that was a first. I'm sure he's had plenty of students nervous to give speeches before. Hell, who *isn't* a little anxious when they are required to get up in front of a crowd and spout off at the mouth for three full minutes? But fuck, within seconds of starting to speak, I'd given in to the stutter I've worked so hard to overcome.

I suck in a breath. Learning to master my body and my thoughts has taken me years of work. I'm upset I wasn't able to control myself better. There's nothing quite like feeling like you're ten years old again, ready to wet yourself at the prospect of being ridiculed. The fucking memories it'd dredged up as I stood there quaking hadn't fucking helped either.

Once the stutters had started, The Assholes had opened their mouths and broadcast their opinions, and I'd been reminded of each time Jamie made fun of me for the trouble I had speaking. Instead of coming to my defense, like I thought a brother should, he'd joined in with the other boys picking on me. And today, I let those ignorant, arrogant fuckers get to me just like my brother always used to.

If only they knew what I've gone through to overcome those issues. *Fuck.* Who the hell am I kidding?

They'd still be assholes because that's what assholes do. My dad's still an asshole. No matter how hard I try to be what he wants me to be, I'm never enough for him. My brother's an asshole, too. And I swear to fuck when Jamie gets here next year—because I know he'll end up coming to Shadow River—he'd better steer clear of me because thanks to the workouts with Maddox and Hawk, I will fucking knock him out if he says so much as a word to me. I shift my bag to a more comfortable position across my chest and pull my phone out of my pocket.

Me: Can anyone meet me at the gym?
Me: I know you guys are pissed or whatever.
Me: But I need to work out some frustration.
Maddox: Give me twenty minutes, and I'll meet you there.
Hawk: I can't get there right now.
Hawk: But beer later?
Me: Yeah. Anything.
Hawk: For the record, we aren't pissed.
Hawk: We're concerned. There's a difference.

True to his word, twenty minutes later, Maddox approaches me where I've been waiting for him on a bench outside the gym. I stand and we exchange a quick fist bump before he growls, "What's going on?"

"Can we just—? It's been a rough couple of days, culminating in a shit show of a speech presentation today." *Fuck.* I do want to talk. But I need to get my head straight first.

He exhales sharply through his nose, scanning my features for a moment. I don't know what he sees there, but whatever it is has him agreeing to my request. "Yeah, man. No worries. Let's go." He punches my bicep a little harder than necessary as we enter the building, heading directly for the locker room.

Inside, we don't exchange a word, we're all business as we quickly change into workout gear so we can fight. Because that's what this is and Maddox knows it. I need an outlet, and he's offered to be that for me today. He knows I'd do the same for him and have plenty of times before.

Out in the gym, we head for the area that's home to the punching bags and the large mats where we like to do our sparring. We make quick work of wrapping our hands for a bit of protection, put on our MMA gloves, and get to work. We circle each other, size the other up, and then the strikes begin. Maddox is a demon in a fight. He hits hard and fast, and has such good stamina, he rarely tires before I do. Usually, my job is to stay out of his way, and try to return the attack. Only today, I change my tactic, throwing the first punch, and catch him on the chin. Maddox's brows raise, but he gives his head a brief shake, and we carry on. It's an all-out battle, both of us throwing and landing vicious punches and jabs as well as harsh low kicks, until we're sweating buckets and heaving ragged breaths. My heart hammers in my chest. A flash of movement on my right causes me to glance away from Maddox.

The next thing I know, I'm on the floor, opening my eyes and blinking up at the overhead lights on the ceiling.

"Fuck. Sorry, Kellan." Maddox is stooped over me. "Between you and Hawk, I clearly need to ask for a full rundown of your current mental state and everything that's wrong in your world before I agree to fight you."

I wince, my head pounding. I groan, "You fuckin' rang my bell. Good job."

"What the hell happened?" Maddox grits his teeth, letting me have a few seconds to recover. He stands above me, making quick work of removing his gloves and unwrapping the tape from his hands.

I allow my eyes to shift back and forth, trying to recall how I ended up on the floor. Then it hits me, and I sit up slowly, looking around. "I thought I saw—" I jerk to a stop. Great. I'm fucking seeing things. I swear to God, I saw Star over by the treadmills. Just a flash of bright pink. Maybe it's dumb to think I saw that tiny lock of pink in her hair, but I guess whatever it'd been was enough to distract me.

Maddox runs his forearm over his brow, swiping sweat out of his eyes, then glances in the direction of my gaze. He shakes his head, huffing out a laugh. "Well, I'd say we're done for today." He holds his hand out to me. "Can you get up?"

I work my jaw back and forth, and when that checks out okay, I nod and grasp his hand and let him haul me to my feet.

In the locker room, we hit the showers before getting dressed again. We're quiet through the entire process. It isn't until Maddox is on the bench pulling on his shoes when I finally get up the nerve to tell him why he was able to knock me out. "I thought I saw Star," I mumble.

His eyes flick to mine. "Have you talked to her?" I shake my head, my gaze down, unable to meet his curious stare. "The fuck is going on, anyway? All the shit at the party and her room getting fucked, then all of a sudden the next goddamn morning, she's slinking out of your room, which wouldn't have been a big fucking deal, except I could see you in the bed."

"Did the two of you talk?"

"Look. She said she was fine. But she also hasn't wanted to talk to pretty much anyone since." He slaps his hands on his thighs. "Raven expressed concern that maybe something happened, and Star doesn't want to admit it."

What the fuck? "I didn't do anything she didn't want me to." My jaw clenches hard. Except treat her like it meant nothing to me. Because I had to.

"I have no fucking issues with you and Star. What I'm surprised about is the fact that you got into bed with her in the first place. You specifically told me and Hawk that your ex-girlfriend couldn't appreciate that you had certain boundaries that you didn't want crossed. You said you weren't interested in going through all that again with someone who didn't understand you, and that's why you weren't dating anyone. So, what I'm curious about is whether something has changed."

"Nothing has changed. Not really." I huff out a hard breath. "And I doubt anything ever will." Doesn't stop me from liking Star. Doesn't stop me from wishing things were different.

TEN

STAR

Milo is out there. Somewhere. Mom's words keep coming back to me. "They released him because he's eighteen. He's got an apartment in Freeport, and he's doing well. Let's not cause trouble." A disturbed laugh bursts from me. *He's* the trouble.

Someone was crazy enough to let my psycho step-brother out on the streets again. Boy, does he have them fooled. I know it was him who messed up my room. The matchbook left on my nightstand is his calling card.

It hadn't taken me long to figure out that there was no way I was keeping much of anything that'd been in my room when it'd been ransacked. The destruction was fairly thorough. Impressive, even. Fucking scary as hell. *Thanks, Milo.* And unfortunate for me since it left me to sleep on my torn-up bedding for a couple days, seeing as how there was no way I was going back to the guys' suite once my locks were changed.

In the interest of keeping things quiet, SRU had been quick to cut me a check to cover the loss of the contents of my room. They hadn't even questioned the list I'd sent them. With the money in hand, I'd spent most of Sunday evening ordering what I needed online. Quick delivery was promised, and sure enough, I got notice from the campus post office that a literal shit ton of packages had arrived for me.

In fact, there's so much they'd put everything in a van and brought it to the dorm instead of making me pick it all up, and for that, I'm grateful. But shit. They left it all in the foyer downstairs, and since there isn't an elevator in the building, it's going to take me forever to get it all upstairs. I'd love to ask for help, but I have no idea where Lux and Raven are, and there's no way I'm knocking on the guys' door for fear Kellan will answer, and I'll be forced to face him.

Yeah. It's taken several days, but I'm ready to admit that I was hurt—actually, more like devastated—by how easily he'd assumed that I'd be okay with some sort of bizarro friends-with-benefits scenario. I've been in the worst mood, so I've kinda kept to myself. I'm used to going it alone, anyway. And what difference does it make if I go back to being a hermit?

And that's when my inner voice cries. I really like having a few friends. And I'd really liked Kellan. *Fuck.* I hate this. I pause right on the stairwell, closing my eyes and trying to push him out of my head.

"Star? Can we help you?"

My chest jumps with a stuttered breath, and my eyes fly open to find Hawk standing beside me, looking at me curiously. "Oh. Um." I swallow and glance over my shoulder to see how much I still have to bring up. And that's when I notice Kellan and Maddox both standing on steps immediately behind me. "Uh." I turn my head swiftly back to Hawk, trying to control the quiver that seeks to take over my lips at Kellan's proximity. "Yeah. I guess I could use some help. Thank you."

Maddox clears his throat, "All that down there yours?"

I turn and nod at him. "Yeah. I replaced all my stuff that was damaged."

"That's good." Hawk reaches out, taking the box I was holding before I can protest. "I'll head up with this. Are Raven or Lux up there?"

I glance over my shoulder, noticing Maddox has gone down, picked up a bunch of boxes, and is on his way back up. Lux and Raven have most likely given up on the sad girl who refuses to talk to anyone. And I can't blame them. "Nope. I'm not sure where they are. I left the suite door open, though. I, uh, figured I wasn't going to be gone for long."

Kellan hasn't moved from the step below me, putting us eye to eye every time I look over my shoulder. Something about the steady way he's gazing at me makes my chest tighten. As Hawk takes off down the hall and Maddox follows, Kellan's voice rumbles, "You know, you don't have to explain why you'd leave a door open. No one thinks someone breaking into your room was your fault." He asks quietly, "Have you been staying in your room? I wasn't sure if—"

I don't let him finish, but nod and brush past him, taking the stairs down to the main floor to collect more of my packages. Kellan follows, then stands directly in my path, holding his arms out for the boxes. "You don't have to carry those up. We've got them." As he says this, Hawk and Maddox join us.

Hawk shakes his head and gestures to the stairs. "Seriously, Star. Go ahead up to your room. We'll take care of the heavy lifting."

"You'll have your hands full unboxing and putting everything away, anyway." Maddox smiles at me and pats my shoulder. For whatever reason, it strikes me as funny —he's always such a grouch. Not today, though.

A little bewildered, I blow out a breath, I nod. "Yeah, okay."

Up in the suite, all of my packages are neatly stacked outside my door, which is great, but also a little overwhelming. It'll be okay. I'll take care of this, and then I can move on and try to forget what happened. Hawk and Maddox edge inside, setting down the final few boxes.

"Thanks, guys."

Hawk nods. "Sure, no problem." Maddox gives a little wave, and they head back to their suite.

I know without a shadow of a doubt that Kellan probably took his time, wanting to be the last one up here. What does he want from me? To discuss how he made me feel like shit?

"This is the last one." Kellan appears at the door with a cautious smile.

My heart gives a hard lurch. All the words I thought I'd say to him have flown out of my head. This is going to suck. I turn around, exhaling steadily from between almost sealed lips, and use my new key to let myself back into my room.

"Can I help you bring everything in?"

I glance up to see Kellan awkwardly shifting from one foot to the other, his hand ruffling through his hair and tugging on it at the back of his head. He looks away for a second before meeting my eyes. "I know you're upset with me."

Is he for real? I shake my head, slicking my tongue over my lip. "I have a right to how I feel. I thought—" I grimace as I pull open a box, unearthing my new sheets and a duvet. *Shit.* I'm going to have to wash all this crap. "You know what, forget it. It's not important what I thought."

I stand upright again, staring steadily at him with an icy gaze.

"It's important to me," he mumbles.

"If I was at all important to you, even as a friend, you wouldn't have acted like a complete *dick* not two seconds after I came on your hand." I can't help it. My eyes have a mind of their own, flicking down to the very hand that made me come harder than I ever have before. *Shit. Don't look. Don't think about how good he made you feel.*

His mouth drops open at my brazen words, and I'm certain he's about to say something, but I don't let him. "I didn't even get to finish my sentence before you dismissed me. And I'm well aware I was the instigator that night. I know I asked you to sleep in the bed with me, then offered to give you a hand job, then practically begged you to touch me. Like a fucking desperate *idiot.*"

I'm full-on shaking, my stupid body betraying how upset I am, just like it betrayed me by wanting his touch. But I can't stop now. "I know it was all on me. But you could have said no, Kellan." My breath hitches, and at his stunned expression, I repeat it for him, only this time, I can't hold back four days' worth of frustration. My words come out in a shout that could bring down the roof. "You could have fucking said *no!* It would have hurt less. Instead, you got off, got me off, and then treated me like trash. Like what we did was something you could throw away as if it meant nothing."

Fuck. My face burns. The way my heart crashes around in my chest can't be good, and fuck, my lower lip is quivering. I bite down on it. Hard. Tears threaten to unleash from my eyes and run down my face. And he doesn't get to see that. I push my glasses back up the bridge of my nose, since they'd slipped a bit while I was screaming. *Fuck.* How much more humiliation can I handle in one day?

Over his shoulder, Raven and Lux appear in the doorway. *Oh, great.* Perfect timing.

Kellan's head drops back as he looks at the ceiling, a slight groan rumbling up from his chest, but he steps to the side so the girls can see into the room. "Maybe I should go," he grits out, his voice low. "We can talk later." His jaw twitches, then goes rigid. As if he's holding himself back because the muscles want to move. I can tell.

"Um. What's going on?" Raven's melodic voice usually calms me down, but not this time.

Lux's head is cocked way over to the side, her brow pinched so hard a deep groove runs down the middle of her forehead.

By their facial expressions and the way they're eyeing

him, I can tell they heard at least a portion of what I'd said. Because I'd *shouted* it. *Right.* I swallow down the lump of ugly embarrassment and mutter, "Kellan and the guys helped me bring my new stuff upstairs. Kinda like Kellan helped me out the other night." My lips twist. His lush green eyes plead with me not to take this further. But I can't stop myself from finishing as I cross my arms in front of me. "It was no big deal, right?" Pausing when he doesn't say anything, I can't help but prod for an answer. "Right, Kellan?"

Discomfort radiates from him. He's ready to leave. It's obvious. Goddammit, that's exactly the opposite of how it'd gone in my head. I thought he'd come closer. Get in my face. And then maybe, like in one of the smutty romance novels I have hiding in my e-reader, he'd take my face in both hands and kiss the fuck out of me. That's how it was supposed to have gone.

His eyes lock on mine, and his jaw works to the side before he quietly murmurs, "I wanted to tell you I was sorry. I handled everything fucking poorly."

My throat constricts as I stare at him. And before I can compute what he's said or respond at all, he slips past Lux and Raven, and is gone.

The girls watch his retreat. When they turn around, the looks on their faces would be comical if any of this were funny at all.

"What the fuck was that?" Lux shakes her head a bit. "Come on, we can talk and help you unpack. That way you don't have to look at us while you spill."

Raven taps a thoughtful finger to her lip as she surveys the stacks of boxes. "Do you need booze? Just because I've sworn it off for a while doesn't mean you can't have a little rum and Coke or something."

Lux pauses in a squat position next to a large box that she's commandeered. "Or cookies. I could make cookies if you want." Her brows lift, awaiting my response.

"Um." I wet my bottom lip and bring my fingertips to my temples. Gently massaging, I close my eyes for a second. "It'd be dumb to run after him, right?"

"Yep. No doubt. He needs to sweat for a bit, it sounds like." Lux stops to pull out my new laptop and sets the box on my very empty desktop. "So, are you two—?"

I sigh. "We aren't anything, honestly." I flop down on the unmade bed and begin to pry the tape off one of the smaller boxes.

Raven's unpacking a box containing all my brand-new toiletries, carefully pulling everything out and setting it beside her on the carpet in a pile. "Maddox wasn't so sure about that."

"Neither was Gage." Lux winces. "Kinda hard to keep shit on the down low when we live in each other's pockets." Then she shrugs, pulling another box toward her.

Raven stands up, then stoops over, collecting the products she's unpacked and walks them into the bathroom. As she opens drawers and tucks things away for me, she raises her voice so we can still hear her. "What happened in his bedroom? You had literally just told us that you were upset the guy you were dancing with wasn't Kellan. And the next thing I know, Maddox mentions that Kellan slept in there with you." She comes back out to join us, lifting her hands like she's cheering. "So, I was like, 'Yay!'" She frowns, digging into another package. "But then, it was more like—" She wrinkles her nose, sticks her tongue out, and gives me a thumbs-down.

I nod, mildly amused by her retelling, and set aside a box of office supplies on my desk chair. "I asked him to come in there with me. I couldn't sleep. Truly. And I dunno. We were both a little ..." I clench my teeth.

The pause in my explanation is enough to make both Lux and Raven glance up from the packages they're sorting through. "A little what?" asks Lux.

"Um." *Just say it. It's the appropriate word.* "Horny. We were horny."

Raven tries to suppress a smile and fails. Instead, she winds up grinning at me and blushing. "We kinda heard you shouting about getting each other off."

"Yeah." I let the word drop like a brick as my shoulders sag.

"So. If you both got off, what was the problem?" Raven shrugs innocently, but the way she's eyeing me, I know she gets it. Even when she follows up with, "I'm trying to understand." What she means is, she's trying to help me understand what's in my head.

"I was still ..." I look at them, my eyes getting big, willing them to understand me without having to explain. But they shake their heads, waiting, so I heave out an exaggerated breath. "I was still kinda having aftershocks, if you know what I mean. And I'm pretty sure his hand was still between my legs." More quietly, I finish, "He was already acting like we were two buddies helping each other out. A couple of bros who would smack each other's asses in the locker room after a good game. I dunno. I couldn't sleep after that."

"Weren't you sort of helping each other out, though?" Lux grits her teeth and ducks her head. "Sorry."

I swallow. This is what's been bothering me. "Technically." I cringe. "But I felt ... dismissed, almost? I don't know. Maybe I'm not explaining myself well enough. I didn't think that what we did together meant we were seeing each other or anything like that. I—" I shake my hands in front of me, as the truth stares me in the face. "I wanted him to like me, and I think maybe he just doesn't. Not like that."

"Like you were good enough for meaningless sexy times, but you're upset that he didn't want more. Or—" Raven holds up a finger. "Or he was unable to tell you that yet. That could be it, too."

ELEVEN

KELLAN

I sit down at the dining room table and rest my head in my hands. I'd known Star was upset with me and had been hiding away in her room, but I'd underestimated how badly she'd taken everything. I should have fucking known better. Bottom line. I had a good idea she liked me, and I let it go too fucking far.

The fucked-up part is that I do like her. I'm simply not ready to articulate it because it would mean sharing things with her that I'm not sure I'll ever be ready to explain. I'm fuckin' stuck.

"You all right, man?" Hawk sits down across from me, rubbing his hands over his face.

In answer I jerk my head a bit, then get up and go into my room, closing the door behind me. Hawk won't be offended by my silent exit. He gets me. Pulling out one of my many sketch pads, I climb onto my bed, propping my back against some pillows, and begin to draw.

Thirty minutes later, I have a rough sketch of the concept for the second painting in my series ready.

Shame. This time it's not Star's emotion, this one is about me and the way I felt after I treated her like I did.

FRIDAY, the guys poke their heads into my room before they head out for the night. It's been a couple days since Star laid into me, and we haven't spoken since. She's there, right across the hall, and I know it's not the worst torture imaginable because I'm well-versed in that, but it's still pretty bad and makes me anxious as hell. I'm constantly straining to hear her voice and wonder if I've simply done too much damage to the relationship we were forming. I'm unsure if we'll ever be on friendly terms with each other again.

I'm miserable. I want more. And I can't have it.

"You sure you don't want to come with us? We're just getting dinner. Maybe grabbing coffee somewhere after."

I roll my eyes. "I'm not putting myself through a Dr. Seuss date night with Couple 1 and Couple 2." Shrugging, I say, "It's cool. We can do something tomorrow. Hit the gym or watch a movie or something."

Maddox frowns. "Okay, man. Suit yourself. You gonna hang here?"

"Yeah, probably. I might head to the art cave for a bit. Maybe not. I've got plenty to do right here." I know they feel bad leaving me behind. But the thing is, we've never been the three musketeers. We've always had our own stuff going on and come together when we need each other. It's never been a big deal. But now that they both have girlfriends, things are a little different. Especially since it leaves Star and me as the awkward fifth and sixth wheels of our group.

An hour later, I'm in the middle of sketching at my easel, but not making a whole lot of headway. I don't know what's wrong with me other than my inspiration has kinda dried up, and my head is all kinds of clouded. And it certainly doesn't help that I got my grade back for my practice speech back yesterday—who the fuck grades a practice speech, anyway?—and I'm frustrated. I knew I hadn't done well, but fuck. I let out an annoyed sigh. Nothing is going right lately.

"Oh."

That startled, gasped syllable catches my attention, and I glance up. Star stands in my doorway, looking at me with curious green eyes. I thought maybe she'd gone out with our suitemates earlier since it's been quiet. Then again, Star's a quiet person. Except when she's yelling at me, anyway. A vision of her angry and shouting hits me right between the eyes. Before it's too obvious that I'm off in my head, I clear my throat and set my sketch pencil down. "What's up?"

"Sorry, I thought you went out with the others." She points over her shoulder. "I'm missing a chunky silver ring that I wear a lot, and I thought maybe I took it off here ... like maybe, um—"

"When you stayed here. Yeah. Understood." I drag in a deep breath as our gazes connect. "I haven't seen it, but I haven't been on the lookout for it, either. You're welcome to poke around wherever. I can, uh, help ... if you want."

"Okay. That'd be great." It's difficult to ignore that

she's perfectly still, her eyes fixated on the bed we shared last weekend.

My chest clenches as I attempt to steady my breath. I was such an ass. "Let's start in the suite since you were out there first."

We spend the better part of the next twenty minutes digging between couch cushions, scanning the floor, looking under furniture, and checking the kitchen area.

Star stops in the middle of the suite with her hands on her hips, looking around. "Do you mind if I take a look in your bedroom?"

"No, go ahead." And what's odd is I don't mind. I don't generally let people into my space. My high school girlfriend, Tammy, had hated that. But for me, my bedroom has always been the place where I hide, my sanctuary. And even though I've moved out of my father's house and away from the emotional and physical abuse, I still view this room like that even though I'm not in danger here and am slowly healing from the ordeal that was my childhood.

But Star ... it feels natural for her to be here. It doesn't bother me at all. And for now, I'm choosing not to think too closely about the possibilities of what that could mean.

I stand at the doorway and watch as she scans the room, her lip tightly caught between her teeth. After a few minutes, she shakes her head in dismay as she gets up off the floor from where she was looking under the bed. "I don't see it anywhere."

"I'll keep an eye out for it now that I know what I'm looking for."

She nods. "I appreciate it." Her eyes flick to mine. "Kellan?"

Her quiet tone catches me by surprise. "Yeah?"

She stands in the middle of my room, looking a little like she's going to be sick. "I wanted ... I wanted to apologize."

My brows dart up on my forehead. I'm completely baffled and positive my expression shows it. "For what?"

Star gives me a pained smile. "The other day. When I yelled at you. I was upset, but that doesn't excuse me shrieking at you like a crazy person. And then you said you were sorry, and I felt shitty. I wanted to come over right after and say something, but I wasn't sure it'd be a good idea. But I'm sorry. I really am."

An odd sensation washes over me, muddling my thinking. She's apologizing. I've apologized plenty to my father for not being the son he wanted. But through all the abuse, he never once showed an ounce of regret. Never once came to me and said he was wrong or sorry for what he'd done. And here's this girl—someone I've hurt—and she's full-on apologizing for her behavior when she was upset by something that was totally my fault. She had a right to say or feel however she wanted.

I don't know that I deserve the apology. But I cling to it like a lifeline and rub my hand over my chest, trying to keep the young boy inside of me in check. Staring at the floor, because I can't bring myself to meet her eyes, I nod. Everything I want to say is caught in my throat. My gut twists and burns. How is this girl able to so effortlessly yet meaningfully say those words to me? After the awful way I treated her?

In my peripheral vision, she pivots on her heel and slowly walks away. And still, I can't open my mouth to stop her. To ask her to stay so I can figure out how to express the tumultuous thoughts that reside inside my head.

My eyes slam shut as my jaw twitches. My inability to communicate what I'm feeling makes me ache. I spend the next several minutes pacing, my fingers interlaced over the top of my head. Gritting my teeth, I finally stop. And then I march straight from my room and out of the suite.

I take several deep breaths before I finally lift my hand, rapping my knuckles against the girls' closed door. "Star?" Somewhere within me, I find the strength to say her name loudly enough that she'll hear me. Then I stand there, waiting for interminable seconds, and wonder if I'm crazy to think she'll come to the door. Give me the time of day.

What am I doing? What am I doing? What am I doing? My bare chest heaves as the door opens a crack. She peeks out at me, all nervous and wild-eyed, then glances down the hallway. I don't know what she's looking for. There's no one else here. Only me.

My brow furrows. "Were you expecting someone else?"

"I don't know. I guess not." She has a very solemn look on her face, but pulls the door open a tiny bit wider. "Did you need something?"

"Um, I have a weird question for you." I eye her carefully, tilting my head to the side. This might be the dumbest thing I've ever done in my entire life. She's never going to go for it.

Her gaze sharpens, her focus intense. "Go ahead." She bites down on her lip and drags her teeth over it.

I don't necessarily need a model for what I'm working on, but— "I, uh, would you be willing to come sit in my room for a bit?"

Her face pales, and she blinks rapidly behind her glasses. "Yeah, I don't know about tha—"

I blow out a hard breath, interrupting. "I appreciated your apology, even though I hadn't expected it, and I know you didn't have to do that. Maybe I can explain—" I hesitate. Can I share why her apology had thrown me for a loop? I don't know. I give her a pained look. "It's for my art class, what I need you for. It's this entire unit on human emotion that we're working on. One of the weekly assignments is drawing a range of facial expressions." I breathe out. Breathe in. Wait. *Dumb. Dumbest idea ever.*

Her head cocks to the side as she studies me. "And what? You want me to sit for you? Like a model?" Her eyes dip down, and I swear she's looking at my chest. Or maybe my tattoos. My skin tingles with awareness.

"Yeah. We don't technically have to have one, but I'm having a little trouble without an actual face to look at. The assignment is one of the components for my final project for the semester."

"So. You're saying it's important." A ghost of a smile passes over her lips as her gaze lifts back to mine.

I nod, liking the way she's looking at me from under hooded eyes. "To me, yes."

She wets her lips. "So, if I were to do this, would you need me to wear anything specific, or just whatever?"

"I'll be sketching your face, so you can wear whatever's most comfortable."

"And how long do you need me for?"

Forever. That word spins through my head, unbidden. "Until I'm done." I give her a hopeful look at the same time my heart slams around inside my chest. I want a chance to talk to her again, to clear the air. And maybe I also want to stare at her for however long it takes me to do the sketches. I'll attempt to push aside the part of me that longs for things I'll never be fully capable of achieving.

"Yeah, okay. I was just getting ready for bed; planned to hang around reading." She shrugs. "Um, do you want me to leave my makeup on or can I wash my face?"

My gaze drifts slowly over her delicate features. Heart-shaped face, high cheekbones, cupid's bow lips, cute little nose ... Gorgeous eyes. "Clean face, please."

Star presses those perfectly luscious lips of hers together, almost like she's trying not to smile. "Give me five minutes. I'll be right over."

"Great." This is totally unlike me, but I'm strangely excited to spend this time with her. I don't usually find it easy to hang out with anyone but the guys. There's something intriguing about Star, though. I haven't quite figured out what makes her tick. But I want to. Getting a little lost in my head about what all of this means, I slowly back away as she closes the door.

In my room, I nervously pace, but I don't know why I'm anxious about this. It's Star. I'm comfortable with her. Fuck, if I wasn't, I never would have done squat with her in the first place. My brain chooses this moment to give me a slideshow of all the things she and I did together in my bed. Flashes of her hand stroking up and down my dick, her face as she'd watched me come, the way she'd felt and the moans she'd made as she fell apart. *Shit.* Until I opened my mouth and fucked it all up, we'd been good. Where would we be now if I hadn't tried to push her away? Suddenly, I want nothing more than to go back to where we were. But I know that's not possible. All I can do is proceed from here.

I take a couple deep breaths, willing myself to not screw things up again.

"Kellan?"

I turn around to find Star's cleaned her face of the minimal makeup she usually wears and has changed into a black tank top and dark-pink pajama shorts that match that chunk of dyed hair that frames her face. She hesitates a second on the threshold of my room, touching her fingertips to the stem of her glasses. "Sorry, I didn't know what to do about—"

"Your glasses?"

She nods, giving me a shy smile.

"What do you think?" I look away from her for a moment and stare at my very blank canvas because she looks so damn good. I don't want to admit this to myself, especially since it's too late now, but this could very well be mistake number two. *Fuck.* I definitely don't have it in me to push her away again. Not this time.

We're simply model and artist. I do this all the time. It's no big deal. *You sure are good at fucking lying to yourself.*

She shrugs, cautiously. "I don't feel much like myself without them. But it's okay. Whatever you need. It's your assignment."

"Tell you what. Let's start with them on, and then maybe I can try it both ways, and we'll see what we think."

She lets out a shuddery breath, her gaze roaming my room. "Um, where do you want me?"

I point to the stool that sits near my easel. A million bees buzz in my head, and to make matters worse, my stomach flips around like a competitive cheerleader.

She perches on the small stool. "Now what?"

"Well." I clear my throat, taking a seat on the chair in front of my easel. "I'm going to capture your natural expression first, so you can look right at me and relax."

She nods, folding her hands in her lap.

In all honesty, now that she's here I'm a little over-whelmed—but not in a bad way, more like I can't quite believe it.

"Tell me to shut up if this question bothers you. But why'd a simple apology make you freak out like that?" She clenches her teeth. "I mean, not freak out, but you kinda— Ugh. Sorry, me talking probably isn't conducive to what you're doing over there."

"It's fine. I'm just getting started." I've roughed in the shape of her face, trying to capture as many details as I can. "Um. I guess sometimes I get caught up in my head. I can't remember anyone ever seeking me out to apologize like that." I draw in a breath as I continue to move the pencil around the large sketchbook attached to my easel. "My family. They're pretty bad about things like that." A sigh works its way from me as I glance back at Star, whose brows have drawn together. "Relax, please."

She smiles sheepishly and smooths her features. "Sorry."

I nod with a slight smirk and continue working. After a few minutes, I'm done with the preliminary sketch and set the pencil down on the small tray at the bottom of the easel.

"So, your family—you aren't close?"

I can't blame her for asking. I gave her the in. Shaking my head, I grimace a bit and brace my hands on my thighs. "Nah. Not at all. My brother is a real dick most of the time. He's two years younger and always seems to do everything better than I do. Everything that matters to my dad, anyway. And my dad, he—" I huff out a harsh breath. "We don't have a relationship. Not one worth talking about, anyway. He's never thought that I was good for anything."

She frowns.

"Hold that expression." I snatch up the pencil and go back to work.

Star mumbles, trying not to move her facial muscles, "But what about your art?"

"To him? It's dumb. Useless. A pointless waste of time. He'll be pissed when he realizes I've declared art as my major."

"Oh, shit. He'll be mad?"

"Definitely. I don't give a fuck. It's not his life."

"Your mom?" Star's brows lift on her forehead slightly before she goes back to the scowling frown that I'm currently sketching.

My chest clenches. "I don't remember her. I was two when she died in childbirth with Jamie."

"Oh. I'm sorry."

I let a slow exhale pass over my lips and try to concentrate. "It's okay. I wish I'd known her, but that wasn't in the cards." I wet my bottom lip, then bite down on it as I draw in the frown lines on Star's forehead. "Anyway, saying you're sorry is not something anyone in my family is proficient at doing. Kinda sucks. But it's not like I expect anything from either of them." I scan the work I've done so far and nod. "Okay, take a break."

She nods, wiggling around on the stool as she brings her face out of the frown she's been holding. The longer she moves and stretches, the more my eyes are drawn down to the little shorts she's wearing—more specifically the lean legs that extend out of them. To distract myself, I get up, thinking I'll grab something to drink. "You want some water or something?"

"Um. Yeah. Water is good." And she smiles at me.

My gaze drops to her berry-pink lips. *Fuck.* I need a second to breathe. I stride from the room, crossing to the kitchen, and falter with my hand on the fridge handle because Star's followed me. I swallow hard, pivoting to face her.

She shoots me a hesitant smile before catching the corner of her lip between her teeth. God, she's close. Within a half-arm's length of me. "I don't know if this will make you feel any better. But my family is kinda bizarre, too. My dad took off when I was like eleven and a few years later, my mom married this absolute douche and—" She jerks to a stop, shaking her head and making that pink chunk of hair come loose from where she'd tucked it behind her ear. "It's just bad. But anyway, I was going to tell you that considering your family is full of jerks, you turned out mostly okay." She shrugs, a hint of a smile on her lips.

My brows draw together as I let a derisive, awkward chuckle loose. I grit out, "I wouldn't be so sure about that."

Her mouth opens, and she blinks several times behind her glasses, her wide eyes searching mine before she quietly says, "Maybe you should let the people who know you best be the judge of that. You're among friends here." She steps forward, and her hand ever so slightly brushes mine.

I scan her face. I wonder if she knows how effortlessly gorgeous she is. Her skin is creamy and smooth. And those eyes. Mine are green, too, but hers are so vibrant. Sparkling. And fringed by the darkest lashes. I'm sure the majority of people never see past the funky blue eyeglasses or the hair with the quirky pink streaks in it to the girl beneath—the one who looks at me like she sees right inside my damaged heart. And she doesn't care. She likes me the way I am.

My head's a mess, but my hand finds hers, and our fingers tangle together.

Why does this girl do this to me? All I want is to be close to her. But how the fuck do I do that without— *Fuck it.* Before I know what I intend to do, my other hand comes up and lifts her glasses to the top of her head so I can see her eyes clearly. That sea of green and the emotion churning within them nearly knocks me sideways, but it also spurs me on. My fingers slide over her smooth cheek before cupping it in my palm. Her skin is so soft. So beautiful. I stroke my thumb over her cheekbone, which sends my blood pounding through my head as my chest gets unbelievably tight.

I bring my face an inch from hers and breathe her in. My nose nudges hers. She releases a slow sigh. It's a sound of yearning that promptly makes me lose my mind.

My chest heaves with a tortured breath, then my mouth crashes into hers. I'm so full of want, the feel of her lips against mine practically sends me to my knees. And she's not pushing me away, either. She tilts her head to the side, and when I slide my tongue over the seam of her lips, she opens for me.

Shuddering with the need to know how she tastes, my tongue surges inside her mouth. I stroke and lick and suck, desperate to devour her. It's never been like this before. I've never wanted to consume someone like I do her. And what blows me away is how fiercely she returns my kiss—like she's been waiting for this moment all her life. The way she presses up onto her tiptoes and leans in, her breasts rubbing against my chest, makes me want to carry her off to my bedroom and do untold things to her.

It all plays out in my head, and it makes my dick swell in my pants. *Fuck.* She's so fucking perfect. I want to make her come all over my fingers again so I can suck them clean like I should have the first time we were together. The mere thought of being with her again makes me feel like my brain is going to explode.

I let go of her hand so I can splay mine across her lower back and pull her tight to me. Her hands find my waist, fingers sinking into the skin just above the waist-band of my joggers. *Good. Safe.* A ragged gasp escapes me, and I slide my fingers into her hair, holding her right where I want her. And I go back for more, sliding my tongue over her lower lip. She's like candy. God, I want to suck on her lips, on her tongue. I want to take things so much further.

Breathing hard, I pause for a second, staring into her dilated, glazed-over eyes. Does she feel the same way I do? Need for her courses through my system. Lust, I guess. *Fuck.* I go in for another feverish kiss, groaning. I wonder what her warm wet mouth would feel like on my dick, what it would be like to shoot my load down her throat as she sucks me dry.

Her body bumps against mine, and I know she can feel how hard my cock is as it's rubbing against her belly with our every movement. She whimpers, and her hands slide up my torso as we strain to get closer. I want her, I do. She makes me feel like I could actually do this. Like I could be like any normal guy with his girl. But—

Star's fingers graze my nipples, then drift upward, and I immediately tense, my entire body going rigid and stiff. My eyes fly open at the same time I tear my lips away and remove her hands from me, shoving her hard enough that she stumbles backward. It's like a bolt of lightning has come down and cleaved us in two. *Fuck.* My heart races frantically in my chest. *Shit. No.* Embarrassment and shame flood me.

Dazed and startled, Star fumbles for her glasses, which are still perched up on top of her head like a pair of sunglasses. Slipping them into place, her eyes meet mine. "Are you okay? What did I—?"

My jaw clenches hard, and I bend at the waist, bracing my hands on my thighs, willing myself to calm the fuck down.

"Kellan?"

Adrenaline rages through me, tremors racking my body. I need to make sure she knows this isn't her fault. My chest jerks as I right myself and try to breathe normally. "It's not—" I scrub my hands through my hair. The concern on her face, the confusion ... it's almost too much for me to take. I rasp, "This? This is *not* your fault. And I'm so fucking sorry." I begin to back away on unsteady feet toward my room, anguish filling my heart and making me ache.

"Kellan ..." Her voice quakes. She's definitely trying not to cry. Her eyes slam shut and her lips tremble. She takes in several deep breaths before her eyes flick open and pin on mine.

I shake my head, slipping into my room. As I shut the door, I hear her clear as day.

"Someday you're gonna trust me enough."

TWELVE
STAR

It's been days since Kellan kissed me, and I'm still reeling. It wasn't a little peck, either. It was all heat and tongue and want, and I couldn't get enough. That kiss had been building for a while, whether either of us wants to admit it or not. We were insatiable. I'd wanted the scorching sweetness to go on and on because it was everything I wanted—like maybe he was coming around to the idea that I'm someone he could be with, someone he could see as more than just the girl who lives across the hall. And everything was great. Until he pushed me away again. Literally this time. It'd happened so fast it made my head spin.

At least this time, he didn't go all *Bro, give me a high five*, and slap my ass as he shoved me out the door. *No.* He said he was sorry. And I know now how important an apology is to Kellan. But damn, it may have been easier to take if he'd brushed it off as meaningless again.

That's not what this had felt like, though. I'd gotten a

terrible sense that he's trying to protect me from something. Or maybe protect himself? I don't know.

He'd revealed a few things while he sketched that have me questioning who he is and where he's come from. Because from the outside, he looks perfectly normal. Good-looking, talented son from an affluent family, going to school at a prestigious university.

But there are little things that don't add up. First, there's the way he's terribly quiet and withdrawn, unless he has something to say. Then, some of the things he said about his family's dynamic—it's really off. It seems like he's the black sheep of their little family. And finally, there's gotta be some sort of physical intimacy issue. He's nervous to get close to me. And it's confusing. He'll let me touch his dick. He'll kiss me. But the second my hands came into contact with his upper torso, it was a no-go. That area is completely off-limits. And the poor guy had been absolutely mortified by his reaction. I'd seen the pain that resided deep in his eyes. It'd made my heart clench, and I'd wanted to weep. I'd stayed up all night worrying about him and continued to pretty much ever since.

I don't know if he heard me as he walked away, but someday he'll trust me enough. I won't push him, though; he'll need to come around on his own terms. And I'm not so dumb that I don't realize I have my own boatload of crap to deal with. I purposely didn't tell Kellan about Milo when we were sharing about our families. I couldn't. I'm terrified he'll want to know more, and with the way Milo has always reacted to people who get too close to me, I know it'd be bad.

I want whatever this is with Kellan. And that's a big problem.

"So, what do you think of that plan?" Raven nudges me, and I'm pulled back to the present where we've been waiting for our psych class to begin. Raven's inquisitive gaze is locked on me. Lux leans forward when I don't answer and cocks her head to the side, her gray eyes full of amusement.

Oh, shit. I've been in la-la land the entire time they've been discussing plans for this weekend. I close my eyes for a brief second. "I was, uh, I was thinking about something else. Repeat, please?" I shoot them a closed-mouthed smile.

Raven laughs. "Oh, man. You've been totally in another world. Ever since Friday night."

"And holed up in your room again, too. You can be honest. Did something happen with you and Kellan? You've both been acting so weird." Lux bites her lip. "Are we wrong? We stopped in the guys' suite before we went to bed on Friday, and Kellan was in one helluva mood. He mentioned you sat for him. Like he sketched you or something?"

I blow out a breath through pursed lips. We still have ten minutes before our psychology lecture starts. "You guys can't say anything."

Both of them sit up straighter, and Lux puts her hand over her mouth for a second before blurting, "Oh my God. We're right?"

"I mean it. This is like a girl thing. You can't talk to Hawk and Maddox about this because ... well, you know." I bite my lip as they nod and urge me on with hand gestures. "He did use me as a model. And then we got to talking ... and he told me some not-so-great stuff about his family. The guys may know about that, I don't know." I let out a hard breath. "And then ... he kissed me."

Raven lets out a little squeal and claps. "I knew it. That's great." But her face falls when she notes my lack of reaction.

"It's not great?" Lux eyes my confused expression warily. "He's a little prickly. Like a porcupine."

"The kiss was *really* good. But the minute I tried to touch him, he shut down." I rub my hand over my forehead and wince. "Oh, man. I shouldn't have told you that."

"We won't say a word, promise." Raven frowns and pats my back.

"I'm confused. And it's not exactly the first time he's made me wonder what on earth he's thinking, either. So it's a little frustrating." *Hello, pot—meet kettle.* I know full well my actions confuse the hell out of everyone, too. I chew on my lip, eyeing both of my friends. They're quiet, letting me have my say, which I appreciate. "It's entirely possible he's got things going on that I'm not prepared for." I exhale loudly. "I've gotta pee before class starts. Watch my bag?"

In the bathroom, I stand at the sink, attempting to collect myself. I didn't actually have to go. I just needed a minute to think. Maybe I shouldn't have hinted that I think there might be something wrong. I let out a sigh and shake my head. That was probably dumb. I dig in my pocket for my ChapStick and stare at my stupid self in the mirror while I apply it. I can't take it back now, so I'll have to deal with whatever happens. Maybe I need to make it super clear that they shouldn't bring anything up. Both Raven and Lux know Kellan pretty well, if only because they've spent more time in the guys' suite than I have. I hope they won't say anything.

Down deep, I know it doesn't matter if Kellan has something he's keeping from me. I want him, all the same. That kiss sealed my fate.

My phone buzzes a couple times, and I pull it from my back pocket. Frowning, I note that class starts in one minute before I glance at the texts.

Lux: Come back quick.
Lux: Raven's freaking out.

Shit. What the hell? I hurry back to the lecture hall. At the top of the steps in the back row, Raven and Lux are right where I left them, but it's obvious Raven is crying while Lux tries to calm her down before class starts. I take the steps two at a time, racing back up to them. I perch on the seat beside Raven, my body turned toward her. "What the hell happened? I was only gone a minute."

Raven sniffles into a tissue. "He said I was covered. Why are they asking why I haven't paid on my payment plan?"

Lux pulls a *yikes* face, then grits her teeth, whispering low to me, "Some guy from the bursar's office came in and asked to speak to her. He said there was some sort of problem with her scholarship, and she needed to come to see them directly after class to straighten things out."

"But didn't Professor Riddick take care of all of that? He said he'd adjusted it to a full scholarship. We all saw the email."

Raven shrugs. "He did. I don't understand." Her lips tremble and a tear runs down her cheek.

"We'll go with you. Right after class." I pat her knee. "It'll be okay. No one is going to take our Raven from us. Got it?"

Her sad eyes meet mine, and she nods slowly, as if she's having trouble trying to convince herself of the truth.

Lux rubs her hand over Raven's back. "And you know damn well Maddox wouldn't let anything happen. He'd probably offer to cover you until they got things straight. You know he would, as much as you're against that."

Raven nods, and I can tell that's reassured her, at least a tiny bit. But then her face crumples. "W-What if it's Spencer causing problems again?"

I scowl. *No way.* "That douchebag is probably scared enough of what's about to happen when he has his court appearance that he wouldn't dare do anything more now. He's not even allowed on campus. I hope his ass lands in prison. He's already in so much trouble, he wouldn't want to add to it." *Would he?* My gaze flicks from Raven's to Lux's. They both shrug, then Raven starts crying again. She's breaking my heart. *Oh, man.*

"Do you have any more Kleenex for her? I only had one left in the package I keep in my bag." Lux squeezes Raven's thigh. "Hey. It's okay. We'll get it figured out."

She speaks in low tones as our professor calls the class to attention, and I dig around in my bag.

A moment later, I find my stash of tissues ... but also something else. Another fucking matchbook. I don't touch it. Trying to remain calm, I hand Raven the package of tissues before I whisper over her head to Lux, "What did the guy look like who came by to talk to her?"

Lux's eyes narrow. "Um. Dark, kinda inky-black hair. A leather jacket. I don't remember much else. Why?"

I press my lips together. "Just curious. I'm betting this is all some screwup."

THIRTEEN

STAR

When we get out of class, our trio moves as a unit with Raven between Lux and me, but it turns out that getting her out of the building is all that will be required of us. Maddox waits at the bottom of the steps and when Raven spots him, she leaves us behind and takes off running. As soon as she reaches him, he folds her into his arms, his head tucked down near her ear. I can tell immediately that he's saying the right things because her body visibly relaxes. Fuck, he's good with her. For her. Now that they've gotten everything sorted out, anyway, because it was definitely touch and go a few weeks back.

"I texted him." Lux raises her hand to wave, and just by the expression on his face, we know he's got her, and we won't need to visit the bursar's office with her today.

"Good move. He'll straighten things out for sure." I don't know what to make of this because I can't think of any way the guy they described earlier isn't Milo. That fucker thinks he's pretty slick. And this is how it always begins, too, with something that's kind of upsetting, but will blow over quickly. Something that no one will realize was a warning but me. *Fuck*. A shiver runs down my spine, and I glance at the people moving around us, going in different directions; kind of like ants scattering to where they need to be next. He's here. Somewhere. Is he watching? "I'm going to head back to the dorm. You going that way?"

Lux shakes her head with a smile. "Nope, I'm meeting Gage at the library. We've got another one of those horrific partner assignments due."

My insides twist and curl in on themselves. I don't want to be alone. "Oh, okay. No biggie. I'll just head back on my own, then." Giving Lux a bright smile, I hike my bag up over my head, seating it crossways on my body, ready to head off on my own.

She clears her throat and points across the quad. "Or not." I follow her gaze. "There's Kellan. You should talk to him. You deserve a chance to straighten things out."

My heart does a weird little hiccup as my eyes follow him. "But I don't know what to say to him. He was really upset."

She lifts her hands in a classic *I don't know* gesture. "Maybe tell him you think talking about what happened would be a good idea." Pressing her lips together, she raises her brows at me. "Good luck. And no. We won't breathe a word. Promise." Out of nowhere, she grabs me in a fierce hug. "It'll be okay. Now go catch up with him." She throws me a wink and takes off in the direction of the library, while I turn my gaze back to Kellan's retreating form.

My teeth clamp down on my lips and a swarm of

butterflies invade my belly. I wonder if he'd want to finish his sketches. Maybe we can start there. And if I'm with Kellan, I'll be safe enough. I give one last furtive glance around me, looking for Milo's signature leather jacket and dark hair anywhere in the vicinity. Seeing none, I take off at a run across the quad. "Kellan! Kellan, wait up!"

At the sound of his name, he stops in his tracks and pivots, slowly walking backward, eyeing me warily as I run.

I stop right in front of him, not exactly out of breath, but my lungs are definitely making my chest rise and fall quickly. "Hey. Um, I was hoping we could talk."

He swipes his thumb over his lower lip, apparently thinking. "Are you going back to the dorm?"

"Yeah"—I nod—"you?"

His eyes roam over me and light my body up everywhere they land. "Yeah. I'd rather talk in private, if that's okay with you."

I tilt my head, taking in the way his strong shoulders have drooped and the shifting he's doing from one foot to the other. "Of course it is."

His swallow is visible, and he's no longer meeting my eyes, but rather, staring off over my shoulder. He draws in a deep breath. "Yeah, okay. Let's go."

Walking side by side, we head toward Royal Bridge. I don't think I'm crazy to sense that Kellan is anxious. *Shit.* I didn't mean to suggest we dig deep into his psyche and figure out why he reacted the way he had. Of course, I'd love to know, but— I can't think about that right now. I turn my head, studying Kellan's profile. "So, this isn't what I wanted to talk about, but I was curious if you wanted me to sit for you again. You know—for your project? I wasn't sure if you finished the rest without me or what? Or when it was due. Or—"

"I thought you were the quiet, introverted one," he mumbles, but then slyly shoots me a teasing wink. I swear, I feel the blush work its way from my toes all the way to my cheeks.

"Oh. Uh. Sometimes when I get nervous, I talk a lot. I also tend to embarrass myself by being a little blunt." I heave out a breath, my lips twitching into a smile. "You know, kinda like right now."

"You haven't embarrassed yourself ... yet. But why are you nervous?"

"I—" My face feels so freaking hot. "Um." *How do I even say this?* "All of our interactions have been a little odd. Like, not normal."

"Maybe you shouldn't try to fit a couple of square pegs into round holes."

I scrunch my face up. "That sounded a little dirty. But I think I know what you mean."

He clears his throat and smiles. "I haven't finished the sketches, to answer your question. We can do some more if you're up for it after."

After. After we talk. After— My brain zings around in anticipation of being alone with Kellan again. "Oh. Okay."

We walk along in silence for several minutes, crossing the bridge and strolling up to our dorm. Despite the way he gently teased me minutes ago, Kellan's jaw grows more and more tense the closer we get to our destination, and he keeps looking at me out of the corner of his eye. I'm definitely not the only one who's nervous.

As we let ourselves into Duke Hall, we move swiftly through the foyer and up the stairs. At this point, it's like some weird challenge. Will he offer to tell me what's going on in his head, or will I have to be the one to ask? I wet my lips as we approach the suites, and Kellan bobs his head in the direction of his.

"We can talk in here." He unlocks the door with a quick twist of his key and holds it open while I precede him into the room.

It's strange to think it's only been a few days since I was last here and Kellan was kissing the breath out of me. My toes curl in my boots, and my thighs quiver the tiniest bit in their knit stockings. I bite my lip as I spin around in time to see Kellan close the door behind us and lock us in.

My brows draw together. I've never seen any of them lock that door while they're home. Not until they hit the sack.

Kellan has a strange look on his face, but as if I'm being pulled by a magnetic force, I cover the distance between us without a second thought. Standing right in front of him, I tip my head back, curious if I can discern what he's thinking. The muscle in his jaw still twitches, and his chest rises and falls faster and faster the longer we stare at each other. His eyes are half-hooded when he whispers, "Can I trust you? Like you said?"

The question catches me by surprise, and I frown, much like I had while he was last sketching me. "What's going on, Kellan?"

He shakes his head, hesitation clear on his face.

"Answer the question. If I ask you to do something for me, can you handle it?"

He may not be certain of me, but I know in my heart I'd probably do most anything he asked. And I'll prove it. "Of course I can."

His voice sounds raw and gritty as he continues. "No questions asked right now. Okay?"

A ragged breath steals past my lips because he's slowly eliminating the space between us. "Yes. Okay."

He takes my hands in his, and before I see it coming, he's reversed our positions and has backed me up against the door. In one strong hand, he firmly secures both of my wrists, pinning them over my head.

I blink, a rush of air escaping me.

"I need you to do exactly what I tell you to. Okay? Hands above your head at all times. Whether I'm holding you there or not. This is the only way this can work for now." *No touching. Got it.* And without time to think further on it, I nod my understanding. The second I do, his mouth is on mine, and his groan is an intense rumble at the back of his throat. It has a jolt of arousal streaking all the way down my spine, unleashing a throbbing in my pussy. This is. *Whoa.*

He devours me with slow, steady licks and strokes. I'm burning up, even though we've just gotten started. The length of his body secures me to the door, and his free hand grips my hip. I squirm against him and suck his bottom lip into my mouth. He attacks right back, kissing deeper and deeper still.

There's something about the way he has my wrists pinned, how my breasts are brushing against him that drives me out of my mind. I've never experienced anything like it before. I moan, bucking my pelvis into the long ridge of his cock that is currently restrained by his jeans.

Nipping at my lip, breathless, Kellan glances down. "That skirt. Are those tights under it or ...?"

I shake my head. "Nope." I prefer thigh-high stockings. And this pair is cute and warm and has elastic around the thigh opening. They stay up great. And, oh shit, whatever is about to happen between us, I get the feeling that it's going to happen with my stockings and combat boots *on*.

Kellan's hand gathers the material of the plaid schoolgirl skirt I'd worn today, pulling it up and out of his way. He buries his face in my neck, licking the spot where my pulse thrums wildly at the same time his fingertips trail up my inner thigh over the stocking.

I suck in a breath when they meet my bare skin. A delicious shiver rolls through me as those fingers move so terribly slowly. Up, up, up. Intently, he watches me as I lose my mind while he continues to stroke just shy of where I want him—and he knows exactly what he's doing and how it's affecting me.

"I'm going to touch you, Star. Play with you. Drive you right to the edge where you won't know whether you're coming or going." He exhales sharply and squeezes my wrists in his hand. "You doing okay with this?"

I nod, and the absolute truth falls from my lips. "I like it."

"Good girl. Hands stay up. I'm taking off your

sweater." He releases his grip on my wrists and removes his hand from under my skirt.

I don't know what it says about me, but I like his praise. A lot. A wave of heat rolls through me, and I bite down on my lip as he lifts my sweater over my head and drops it to the floor.

A low rumble sounds in his chest as he looks at me. "Fuuuck." I'm in a lacy black bralette, and it doesn't leave a whole lot to the imagination. His gaze is steady, and my nipples grow tight in response, becoming peaks behind the material. They feel hot. Like I'm on fire and the flames are only going to burn hotter until he soothes them with his mouth.

"Please," I beg, only it sounds like a whimper. And from the way his smoldering green eyes connect with mine, I think he likes it.

He bends a bit, his tongue darting out to wet the lace. The moisture seeps through to my skin, causing another jolt of pleasure to shoot downward and make my legs tremble. He licks at the same nipple again, and I let out a strangled moan. With every swipe of his tongue, my back arches, trying to get more and more of the wet, wicked sensation. "Yeah. You like that, don't you?"

I nod, so lost in what he's doing to me, I can hardly think.

Switching to the other side, he starts the same process all over, turning me into a writhing, wanton mess. My nipples are so taut they ache, and there's a corresponding pull deep inside my body. "Kellan," I gasp. "Please, please, please."

"Are you begging?"

I nod fervently.

"What do you want?"

"Your mouth sucking on my breast and your fingers sliding inside me."

"One thing at a time." Kellan tugs on the cup of the bralette, and my entire boob pops right out. He gives a satisfied grunt and greedily takes my nipple deep inside the wet warmth of his mouth. My back bows when he sucks and swirls his tongue around and around. And while his mouth is busy, his fingers tug the lace from the other breast before testing its weight in his hand. He toys with my nipple, pinching and twisting, and it's a miracle I haven't moved my hands from where I've anchored them above my head.

He lets my nipple go with a wet pop, then kisses a drugging path across my skin before inflicting the same exquisite torture on the other side. He's worked me up so much I can feel my heartbeat between my legs, and my panties are wetter than wet. I rub my thighs together.

He releases my nipple, moving up to huskily murmur in my ear, "You want me to take care of that?"

I bite my lip and nod. "Yes."

He flips my skirt up as he sinks to his knees in front of me. "I need you to promise one more time. No matter what. Hands above your head."

Kellan could ask me to eat a jar of pickled pigs feet, and I'd do it at this point, so long as he keeps going. I swallow hard. "Promise." But— I thought he was going to use his fingers on me. I'm— I glance down as his nose nudges my mound through the matching lace boyshort panties. Oh, God. I don't think fingers are the only part of his plan anymore.

He inhales raggedly, running his hands up the front of my thighs. My heart is pumping so damn hard, and somehow, it's diverted all blood to my pussy because I feel so swollen and wet down there, it's almost embarrassing. I don't know how I'm not creating a puddle on the floor.

Kellan growls, "Taking these off, too." He hooks his fingers in the waistband of my panties, then peels them down over my stocking-covered legs. He somehow manages to get them over my boots and off. I'd have offered to help, but *hands up.*

I try to imagine what he must see. Boots and thigh-highs. Bare pussy concealed by my skirt until he pushes it back up. Boobs jutting out of my bra, supported by the lacy bralette underneath. Kiss-swollen pink lips and flushed cheeks. Oh, and arms over my head. *Holy shit.*

His big hands grip the juncture of my thighs, thumbs sliding over each of the tendons down there. He's so fucking close to touching my pussy, I'm about to come unhinged. I pant. I writhe against the door. It's probably not pretty. "Fuck," I whisper. And as soon as the word has left my mouth, he leans in, his breath coasting over my bare skin.

"You. You were meant to be worshiped, Star." With one hand, he finally touches my pussy, his fingers sliding through my arousal. "So fuckin' wet." He pushes two fingers inside me, leisurely pumping for several seconds, almost seeming enthralled, before he removes them and puts them directly into his mouth. He sucks hard on them, moans a little, then effortlessly lifts one of my legs and positions it over his shoulder. And then his mouth is on me, and all thought falls out of my head. I can only feel. His tongue flicks over my opening, licking lightly then with more determination. "You're dripping for me."

"Oh, God." My head knocks hard against the door as it falls back, but my hands stay up over my head.

"Look right here. I want you to watch me. I want you to see how much I'm enjoying this."

My thighs quiver at his words, and I can feel moisture seeping from me, I'm so turned on.

He must be fired up, too, because he's growling and groaning and feasting on me. His wicked tongue laps over every inch of my skin, then he uses his hands to hold me open while he lashes and sucks on my clit.

Every time I think he's done, he dives right back in. He adds his fingers again, gliding them through my folds, petting me as I throb out of control for him. Those fingers stroke into me and a third rubs over the ultrasensitive bit of skin between my opening and my ass. I shake, wondering how much longer my leg is going to support me, but at the same time, I know I'll fight tooth and nail to remain right where I am, if only he'll keep doing *that*.

Sizzling heat washes over me, and my vision tunnels as I stare at him working me right to the brink of insanity. There's a coiling sensation in my lower belly that tightens and tightens until I'm certain I'm going to snap. Instead, I tip my hips forward, practically standing on my booted tiptoe, totally at Kellan's mercy. With my hands up, I'm literally in a position of complete surrender. "Oh, God. Oh fuuuck. Kellan. Kellan. Fuck."

The rumble that comes up from his chest and vibrates over my clit sends me into orbit. I'm Star, living among the stars. It's the most surreal thing, how my body flies out of control, shaking and pulsing on his mouth and fingers. The muscles inside me rhythmically squeeze as he continues to stroke my pussy, and his tongue softly slides over all my engorged flesh. I tremble hard, watching him adore me.

"You're beautiful, you know that? Every fuckin' inch of you. You came so hard." He kisses my inner thigh with a sigh. "We'll be doing that again."

Just then, the sound of close footsteps interrupts the blissful state I'm in, sending me into a panic. "Oh shit!"

Kellan's up off the floor in a flash, banging on the door next to my head. "Give me a sec."

I slap my hand over my mouth, my entire face hot. One of those I-can't-believe-this-is-happening laughs spills from me, and I scramble to pick up my sweater off the floor.

"You can pull yourself back together in my room." Kellan stoops to pick up my panties and slips them into the front pocket of his jeans with a naughty wink.

A wave of heat rocks through me, and I'm pretty sure my eyes are big like saucers, the pupils wide. They always look crazy when I'm aroused. "You're bad!" I hiss, one hundred percent amused at this different side of Kellan.

He shrugs, a smile stretching his cheeks. And it's so infrequently that I've seen a real, true smile on Kellan's face, I decide to ignore the fact that he just stole my underwear.

"What's going on?" We hear Maddox through the door, then something that sounds distinctly like Raven has smacked him and a bunch of whispering.

I shuffle into the bedroom with my sweater clutched to my chest and shut the door. After I put my boobs away and tug my top back over my head, I put my ear to the door to listen.

"Dude. Who do you have in your room?" Maddox's voice is plenty loud enough to hear.

"It's Star. Don't you dare fuckin' embarrass her."

"Why would I do that?" Maddox's voice sounds a bit surly. But that's kind of his natural state, so it doesn't necessarily mean anything.

"Is she okay? Maybe I should go in there?" Raven's voice is filled with uncertainty.

I clench my teeth and shake my head, not that Kellan can see me.

"She's fine. She's just washing her face. We're doing another modeling session so I can finish that assignment I've been working on."

"Cool, but why's it smell like se—"

"Don't fuckin' say it. I'm warning you. Not unless you want me to tell you what Raven sounds like when she—"

"Heeeey," comes Raven's laughing voice. "Don't bring me into this."

"Fine. Got it." Maddox groans playfully. I can imagine his hands in the air. Kind of like mine were just a few minutes ago.

I stifle a laugh at that thought, and head for the bathroom. I may as well go ahead and wash my face like

Kellan suggested I was already doing. Maybe I can do a cool water rinse and not feel like my face is scorching hot like I've gone and dipped my entire head in a vat of lava.

The second I get into the bathroom, I'm greeted by a mirror that shows me just how much I enjoyed what Kellan did to me. My hair is a tousled mess, especially at the back where I'd thrashed around against the door. From chin to forehead and ear to ear, my face is flushed a color that I think should be coined orgasm-red. There's even a little abrasion on my chin from Kellan's kisses. And oh. *Oh no.* My nipples are still standing erect like I have little pencil erasers stuck on there. Placing my hands over my breasts, I close my eyes and try to breathe calmly for a count of ten. But it does no good because I imagine Kellan's hands and mouth on me.

Oh boy. I'm in big trouble.

FOURTEEN
KELLAN

Star emerges from my bedroom a few minutes later, her head held high and her cheeks a rosy pink. Looking around, her mouth tugs into a frown. "Where'd Maddox and Raven go?"

"They took off to get dinner." I shrug, hoping it was right of me to assume that Star and I still need more time alone, because I was the one who'd suggested they make themselves scarce.

Her tongue darts out, slicking along her lower lip, and like a starved man, my eyes follow. "Oh. You didn't want to go with them?"

Without a word, I shake my head and reach for her hand. Tugging her closer to me, I clasp her chin with my fingers. My face hovers inches away, our breath mingling. She looks deeply into my eyes, and I can't help myself. I brush my lips over hers two times, and then again before thrusting my tongue into her mouth. She kisses me back, all heat and longing, her tongue curling with mine. And without me asking, she keeps her hands low, gripping my waist.

A few seconds later, as we're gasping for breath, she moans, "I can taste myself on you." She licks into my mouth with more fervor than before.

My cock swells in my jeans, and a low groan vibrates in my chest before rumbling out. I can't remember ever wanting someone so damn much. I've pushed girls away for so long. *Fuck.* Thoughts of all the things I want to do with her swirl through my head like a tornado. I want her mouth on me. I want my dick in her pussy. I want ... fuck. *Everything.*

But she deserves at least a few answers from me. After all, I made her promise to do as I asked, and she'd agreed without question. I don't know why or how she's able to accept what I need from her. I exhale roughly. *Fuck.* I'm such a goddamn mess. But I want her. My mind is full of what it would be like if she were mine. I'm ... obsessed. Strong word, but that's what this is. I can't stop thinking about her.

Fuck, how am I already in this deep? It's both terrifying and exhilarating. I stamp a final kiss to her mouth. "Come on. We'll talk, I'll draw."

She follows me willingly right back into my bedroom and seats herself on the stool to the side of my easel, just like she had yesterday. "I'm excited to see the finished product, by the way. I don't know if I'm supposed to be looking, but— You're so talented, Kellan." A soft smile curves her lips as her gaze moves over the sketches I've already completed. "Are these what you'll turn in, or will you work on them more?"

I sit down and take a deep breath, eyeing her. *Focus, Kellan.* But fuck. It's hard with this girl sitting here showing interest in something that means the world to me. "Honestly, it's up to me. These are pretty basic right now, so I'll either use these to help me with something a little more detailed, or I'll go back and add to these. It really just depends on how I feel when I look at them." I shrug. Star's watching me like I could do no wrong. Like I'm something special. Fuck, it's messing with my head. "Okay, let's get started so I have more to work with. Can you give me a surprised expression?"

Her brow furrows, then she laughs. "Um, yeah." She arranges her face carefully, those pouty lips forming an O with her cheeks sucked in and her brows lifted.

"Good." I pick up the pencil and quickly sketch the shape of her face before speaking. "Can I be honest with you?" I rasp, glancing at her for a quick second before returning my gaze to the sketchpad.

"Um, yeah. I like honesty." Her voice sounds a little wary, but I know I should say something.

"I feel like I owe you an explanation for what I asked of you earlier. And I know this is what you wanted to talk about." Pausing, I try to collect my thoughts, but it's no good. "I-I'm not sure where to start." My chest clenches hard. *No. Not now.* I clear my throat, hoping to ward off any more stutters. My eyes flick to the side, noting that Star continues to hold her surprised face, only now it's slightly more realistic. "I ... uh." I stop, gritting my teeth. *Dammit.* I fiddle with my pencil like I'm prone to do when I'm thinking.

"Kellan, I'm not dumb. I get that you only want to be

touched in certain ways. And that you're a little nervous around me." As I watch, she tucks her hair behind her ears. It's totally a stall tactic—like she's trying to decide whether or not she should say something more. "So, what if ..."

I draw in a breath, my eyes finding hers. My heart is pumping hard enough that I reach up and rub my hand over my chest. I'm wearing a shirt in my room, which I never do. It's like a fucking security blanket because I'm afraid to have a repeat of my meltdown. It's probably dumb to worry about it. Star'd done so well keeping her hands right where I asked her to earlier. But self-protection habits are hard to break.

"Maybe we should concentrate on something else for now." She catches her full lower lip between her teeth and raises her brows.

"Like what?" The words come out all gravelly and rough, and my breath hitches while I wait for her to explain herself.

Her eyes never leave mine as she slowly spreads her legs until she's straddling the stool, one booted foot planted on either side. I can't help it. I break that eye contact when I notice her hands beginning to slide up her legs, catching the skirt and dragging it upward, inch by tantalizing inch. "Well. You still have my panties. So I'm guessing you like the idea of me bare under my skirt."

I'm fuckin' mesmerized as that skirt keeps moving higher and higher. My gaze flicks to hers, then back down as she reveals herself to me. She's well-groomed, I'd noticed that earlier, with only a tiny landing strip of pubic hair present. The rest of her is pink and perfect—

and swollen from our earlier play. An idea slams into me. "Would you show me how you like to touch yourself?" Saying those words makes my dick harden behind my zipper. This could be either the best or the worst idea I've ever had.

It would seem I've thrown her a little. Star blinks a few times behind those sexy glasses of hers as she considers my question. She points at the sketchpad. "You're not going to draw—" She pauses on a hard exhale and licks her lips. "You know. I mean—?"

My voice is hoarse when I answer, "Just your face." My brows rise fractionally, as I reiterate my request. "Can I draw your face while you masturbate in front of me?" I point at the other sketches I've completed. "This one would be desire."

She stares at me, and I swear her pupils begin to dilate at the idea of it. "Yes." Without further prompting, she slips one hand between her legs.

For several moments, I can't help but stare at the vision in front of me—the hot girl in my room sitting on my stool sans panties, legs spread open and touching herself. I'm kind of surprised I'm handling this as well as I am because my heart is rioting in my chest, sending blood pumping straight to my dick. *Fuuuck.* Getting myself together, I murmur, "Okay, eyes on me. As much as you can. Don't worry about anything else." I sketch as quickly as I can, my pencil flying over the paper. Blood rushes from my head as I glance alternately at what she's doing to herself and how it's affecting every nuance of her expression. *Fuck.* The word keeps popping into my head —but seriously. *Fuck.* It's practically like a chant at this point. I could draw her like this forever and never get enough. *Fuuuuuck.*

Willing myself not to let my fast-growing erection embarrass me, I focus on what's happening in front of me. Star seems to have a pattern going—she dips two fingers down, slides them inside her pussy, then brings the slick arousal up to her clit. Her fingers rub over it, mostly in circles, but sometimes side to side as well. She's working herself into a frenzy, and her face is so beautifully expressive, I'm getting some great images. And yeah, more than one, I've drawn several now. Teeth sinking into her lip, desire-filled eyes burning into mine, then a gasp and lips parting gently. And it's too bad these are pencil sketches, because I'd love to show that pink flush that she gets on her cheeks when she's sexually excited.

Wanting something more, I flip to a fresh page, and draw on a larger scale. I work feverishly, all while my dick is so fucking hard behind my zipper, it seems like it could burst through at any moment. And my balls—fuck, they ache, the heaviness a constant reminder of how bad I want Star, need to have my dick right where her fingers are currently pumping into her body. Yet, I push on, not willing—or able, really—to stop. Not until she comes.

This. Is. Everything. She's falling apart right before my eyes, and fuck that's what makes it so goddamn hot. As requested, she's trying her damnedest to keep watching me, but that doesn't stop her chest from heaving with each panted breath or her pelvis from rocking against her hand as she chases her orgasm. I pause for a second, my gaze falling to her pretty cunt again. Her arousal floods her fingers, moisture coating her from engorged clit to her tiny puckered asshole.

Fuck. One day I'm going to have all of her. I will touch her everywhere humanly possible, with my fingers, with my lips and tongue, with my cock. I'll learn her body like no one before me ever has.

I press my left hand down over my erection, gritting my teeth at the almost unbearable need to whip my dick out and take care of things right alongside of her.

That'd be hot. *Shit.* I blow out a breath. And just as I'm thinking about actually following through, Star lets out a breathy whimper. She's trembling all over, and her fingers work furiously over her clit.

I set my pencil down. I'm unsure if she's aware of my movements at this point, she's so caught up in what she's doing. "That's it, baby. Just a little more. You're so fuckin' beautiful. I love watching you."

"Kellan. I'm gonna come. Like now. Right now," she gasps.

As I watch, her body slows before her muscles clench, and she cries out. I can only assume from the way her eyes have glazed over and her jaw has fallen slack that she's experiencing a seriously intense orgasm. "Shit. That's ridiculously hot," I whisper as she begins to come down. I turn in my seat and drag the stool—a piece of furniture that I'm never going to look at the same way ever again—toward me.

She stares, and it's almost as if she's not quite here with me yet. Circling her wrist with my hand, I draw her fingers from where they'd been pressed against her clit up to my lips, then suck them into my mouth. As I lick them clean, my tongue swirls around and around, and the heady flavor of her floods my senses. What I'm doing gradually brings her focus back to me, and after blinking a few times, she chews on her lip. Ever so slowly, I release her fingers from my mouth, and set her hand on her thigh. "Have I mentioned how good you taste?"

I don't know how she blushes when her cheeks are already pink, but she does. "No."

I slide the pad of my thumb over my lip. "I'd eat you for breakfast, lunch, and dinner. All my fuckin' snacks in between, too. You're better than Twizzlers."

A naughty look slides over her features. "What if I said I wanted to taste you, too? Would that be okay?"

A pained groan rips up from my chest, surprising both of us.

"It's okay if it's not." Her brow furrows.

"That's not it. I'm so fuckin' hard. Watching you like that"—I scrub one hand through my hair—"was insane. I couldn't keep my eyes off you." I shift, glancing over my shoulder at my sketches. "I was drawing so fucking fast—I wanted to capture and remember every detail of the way you looked."

Star stands up directly in front of me. "Tell me if I do anything you don't like." She begins to lower to her knees.

"Wait." My breath heaves out. "Let me turn back around." I shift on the seat, facing my easel again. I tug her in front of me.

"Are you going to draw—?" Her lips twitch.

"I don't know. Maybe." I'm so fucking worked up about where I know this is going, it'll be a miracle if I don't immediately nut and embarrass the hell out of myself.

She gets on her knees in front of me, and I shuffle my legs open a bit wider to accommodate her. "Um." She slowly runs a hand over my erection. "Is this a jumbo marker, or are you happy to see me?"

I don't know how I keep my cool, but I lean to the side, dig into my pocket, and whip out my ever-present marker. "Funny, it's actually a Magnum Sharpie. You might want to keep checking for something else in my pants, though."

Star huffs out a laugh as her hands go for the button of my jeans, flicking it open and pulling down the zipper. I moan in relief as the pressure on my dick is partially released, then lift my ass and shove the jeans down along with my boxer briefs. My cock springs forth like it's been anxiously waiting for this moment. My breathing is ragged already, and she hasn't touched me yet. But damn, she's looking. And because she is, it feels like all the blood in my body is pulsing right there in my dick.

"Definitely way bigger than any Sharpie I've ever seen." With a twist of her lips, Star grasps the base of my cock in one of her hands before slowly leaning in and flicking out her tongue to catch a bead of pre-cum glistening on the tip.

I shudder with pleasure as her velvety soft lips envelop me, and she sucks gently on the crown of my cock. Her mouth is insanely wet, and I begin to think I might die right here. "Fuuuck." I huff out a breath, and she smiles around my dick before sliding me slowly into her mouth. Inch by inch, she takes me in. I'm not stupid—

I know I'm not a small guy. But fuck, the way she's swallowing my length is impressive.

Working me with her hand and mouth, I know it won't be long before I blow. I mean, the last time I got head was more than two years ago. It's been me and my hand ever since. Tammy couldn't handle my issues. Didn't understand why I wouldn't take my shirt off, why I wouldn't let her touch me in return in all the ways she wanted to. She got angry with me the last time we were together because I told her to stop what she was doing. I'd almost had a panic attack right there in her fuckin' pink princess bedroom because she simply didn't get it. I didn't have my tattoos yet. And there was no way in hell I was taking off my shirt in front of her. And maybe that wasn't her fault. I don't know. But seventeen-year-old me wasn't anywhere near capable of explaining my hang-ups and definitely not able to voice why they existed in the first place.

So, the feel of Star's warm, wet mouth sliding up and down my cock is very welcome, and fuck, she knows what she's doing. "Your mouth, Star. Fuck."

She peeks up at me from under her lashes. I can see the hint of a smile on her lips, even though her mouth is full of my dick. *Holy shit.* My body is giving all sorts of involuntary twitches, and I can't help but thrust forward into her mouth as she licks and sucks me. I'm wound so fucking tight, I could come at any moment. Jolt after jolt of insane pleasure streaks down my spine, making me hard beyond belief.

With a wet pop, Star comes off my dick, her lips pink and swollen. "Were you going to draw? I want to see what happens." The light of mischief in her eyes makes me want to give it a try.

My voice rough, I rasp, "I have a feeling this isn't going to go very well, but I'll try." She waits until I pick up the pencil and flip to a clean sheet of paper.

She bites her lip as she strokes her hand up and down my shaft, waiting for me to begin.

My throat bobs with a hard swallow. *Fuck*. Her mouth isn't even back on me yet, but I can't concentrate enough to do shit, so I hold the pencil to the paper and let my every jerk and tremor appear. She lowers her mouth over my cock once more, flicking her tongue along the underside. I flick the damn pencil across the paper in a matching motion. She moans around me, and dazed, my arm lowers, dragging the pencil along with it. I look down at her and thread my fingers through the hair at the nape of her neck, relishing in the sensation of her head bobbing to take me deep into her hot, wet mouth.

When I hit the back of her throat three times in a row, I clutch the pencil so hard it snaps in my hand. She smirks around me as it drops to the floor with a minor clatter. I can't help myself, I'm too engrossed in everything she's doing to me. I grip her head with both hands now, glad to be able to concentrate fully on her. I don't know what the fuck I was thinking. I was never going to be able to draw jack shit. Not when her mouth is on me. Not with the little sounds she's making as she sucks me, filling my ears like they're playing on a stereo at full volume. Groaning at the overwhelming need to come, I try to control the thrust of my hips, but only have a modicum of success.

Star pauses to look up at me, her eyes watering at the corners, and I swear I've never seen anything that I liked so much as the image of my dick in this girl's mouth. My lips part as I feel my orgasm barreling toward me, and I plunge deep into her mouth. And she takes it, eagerly. Over and over.

I have a sudden flash of what it would be like to have my dick pounding into her tight, slick pussy and heat roars through me, sending my heart pounding into over-drive. Making unintelligible sounds, I give myself over to the sheer bliss of what Star is doing to me. My balls pull up, and cum rockets down the length of me, spurting into her waiting mouth. My dick pulses hard, my head dizzy with the explosive nature of the orgasm.

Star swallows, looking up at me through dazed, glassy eyes. I haven't come so hard in, well ... ever. She releases my cock from her mouth, and I cup her cheek, staring at her in wonder. After a moment, I groan, seeing my cum at the corner of her mouth. I have a bizarre need to nudge it back into her mouth, so I do with my thumb.

Her hands move to rest on my thighs, and she gazes up into my eyes. I bend at the waist, pressing my lips to hers before my tongue swipes over her lip. She hums, opening her mouth for me. And I lick right inside, uncaring that she just swallowed. If it's good enough for her, it's good enough for me. I groan at the taste of me on her tongue. I savor this moment of intimacy between us.

How much will she be able to handle? Will she understand? Or will she gradually lose interest like Tammy did if I can't be what she wants me to be? It makes my chest throb and ache to think I may never be able to give Star everything. I close my eyes against the idea that my past might tear her away from me.

But then she laughs, and my eyes fly open. And I see why. She's twisted around so she can see what I put on paper while she was sucking my dick. I can't help but laugh, too. "Sorry. That wasn't nearly as good as when I was watching you. I wasn't able to concentrate on anything, not even on an idea of what I wanted to draw. It was all I could do to hold the pencil in the general direction of the paper."

I get up from the chair—which I will never look at the same way again either—and yank my pants back up, tucking my dick inside.

"To be honest, I'm impressed you got that much. But I want to keep it. Can I?" She stifles a laugh, which only makes me want to tickle her, which I do for a quick second. It's just enough that she lets out a loud shriek.

I tug her back to my chest, holding her tightly to me, and kiss the top of her head. A rough whisper is all I can manage. "It's yours. It's what you did to me, so you can keep it if that makes you happy. I'll even sign it." I don't know how this thing with Star and me will work, other than to take everything one day at a time and hope that what I can give her is enough.

FIFTEEN
STAR

There's no denying it. I've been kind of in my head about Kellan. Not in a bad way, more in an I'm-all-caught-up-in-the-newness-of-him-and-me way that has me unable to focus on much else. All of yesterday afternoon and into the evening, I'd felt like we were in this cozy little bubble together. And I loved it. I want to know the real Kellan, the one he hides from everyone else. He's shown me bits and pieces, but I want the whole thing. There's something addictive about the way he makes me feel when I'm with him. And when I'm not, his bruised and battered heart calls out to mine. He's all I can think about. I'm smitten.

After my eight o'clock history class, I hang out at the library for an hour and manage to get some of the assigned reading done. Glancing at my phone, I pack up and head over to meet up with Raven and Lux at the Bean like we'd briefly discussed this morning.

I have a pretty good idea that coffee with the girls is going to turn into a barrage of questions about what's up with me and the often-brooding, strangely quiet artist across the hall. *Especially* after almost getting caught—literally with my underpants down—in the suite by Maddox and Raven yesterday, followed by the walk of shame this morning. And it couldn't have just been a matter of me sneaking out. *Nooo.* I actually passed Hawk and Lux lounging on the couch in the guys' suite, then Maddox and Raven, who were making coffee in our kitchen. To their credit, each of them had kept their mouth shut, however I do anticipate some questions once the girls finally get ahold of me today. And the thing is, I'm okay with it. They're fast becoming the best friends I've ever had. There's no reason *not* to keep them up-to-date on the developments of whatever this is between Kellan and me. I've been plenty nosy about both of their relationships. It's my turn now.

I wonder what the conversation was like among the guys this morning. There's no way Kellan's going to get the same curious treatment that I'm about to get. I can only imagine that the guys' way of discussing this sort of thing is much different. But if these were average dudes, I'd think he'd get stuff like, "Hey, did you bang her yet?" or maybe "You two fucking now?"

But actually, if I know these three, I'd bet there's been no verbal conversation at all. Maybe a smirk or a knowing nod. Considering how well they know each other and what a private guy Kellan seems to be, this seems the most likely.

I take a deep, fortifying breath as I approach the main door of the Bean. Dodging a few people coming in my direction, I sidestep, then catch a bit of blurred movement in my peripheral vision. I turn my head and squint, making an attempt to focus a little better. Unfortunately, sometimes my glasses don't help as much as I think they should. But even though my eyesight isn't good enough to tell me who's over there leaning against a tree, my breath whooshes out. I swear it's him, but it's difficult to say for certain because his back is to me. Black leather jacket. Super black hair. He exudes that confident posture I'm all too familiar with. My heart rate spikes. He's hanging out like he somehow fucking belongs here.

My eyes bug out of my head as he pushes away from the tree, turns, and starts coming in this direction. Oh God. *Oh shit.* It's gotta be him. I lunge for the door handle just as someone pushes the door open from the outside. In a panic, I slip past them and into the coffee bar. For a moment, I stand stock-still, unable to move. A violent tremor rolls through my body.

"Star! Over here." Lux's voice jolts me from my daze, and my eyes flick over to the table that she, Hawk, and Raven have commandeered. It takes everything I have to shake off the pure terror racing through my veins and make my feet move in their direction.

Lux has swiveled around in her seat, leaning toward Hawk. Their backs are to me, but Raven sees my face and gets up, giving me a hug. "You okay?" she whispers.

My eyes flick to hers, and I give her a look that I hope she reads as *I'm fine.* I follow it up with the smallest smile.

Raven clears her throat and nods before tapping the side of a to-go cup that's clearly meant for me. "I had them make your mocha the way you like it."

"Thank you." I let a ragged breath pass my lips as we sit down and wrap my hands around the warm cup to conceal the trembling. Feeling Lux's and Hawk's curious gazes on me, I shoot them a fake-ass grin. *Act normal.* But how do I do that? I'm ninety-nine percent sure that was Milo out there. What. The. Fuck? I swallow hard, pursing my lips together.

Hawk clears his throat, perhaps sensing—though incorrectly guessing the reason for—my distress.

It's a safe bet that he thinks whatever is on my mind has to do with Kellan, and I need a minute alone with the girls. It's not. That's not it at all. But how would I begin to tell these people about my psychotic stepbrother?

As Hawk rises, he asks, "Does anyone need anything else? I'm going to get some of those egg bites. I need fuel." He raises his brows when we remain silent. "Nobody? Ooookay."

Great. My nerves have gone and infected the entire group.

He winks and gets up, tapping Lux on the shoulder and leaning down to whisper, "This had better not be one of your I-don't-want-anything-to-eat-but-I'll-steal-whatever-you-bring-to-the-table shenanigans."

Leave it to Hawk, who I had first pegged as a complete asshole, to try to cheer us up with a wisecrack. It's not my fault, really, that we initially thought he was a dick. He'd tortured my friend. But since the truth about their past has come out, I've realized he's a genuinely nice guy. Lux is lucky to have ended up with the good twin. Not that she should have had to go through that with his brother, but that's not my point. *Shit.* My brain is totally out of focus. It's a struggle to pull myself back to my friends and our conversation. I blink a few times and readjust my glasses.

Lux gives Hawk a goofy grin. "Could be that we'll eat all your food. I guess you're about to find out. Order wisely." I'm fairly certain Hawk's smart enough to bring back enough for each of us to have some. That's how this entire thing with them has been working lately. This guy loves to take care of her, and us by extension. It's freaking adorable. And convenient for Raven and me. And also makes me want that for myself. I have no doubt that if Maddox were here it'd be much the same story. He's so ridiculously different when he's around Raven, like really, truly happy. My eyes roam over my fair-haired friend. She seems just as absorbed with him—the happiness positively shines from her eyes.

Once Hawk wanders up to the counter to place his— our—order, I suck in a breath. "So." I shoot the girls a tight smile before I focus on Raven. "No Maddox this morning?"

Raven shakes her head. "Nope. He's got classes back-to-back. I'll meet him later." She doesn't miss a beat. "Did something happen with you and Kellan?" She frowns. "Your expression when you came in here ... you seemed a little freaked out."

I bite my lip. My stomach twists at the mere thought of bringing up Milo. "Nah, I'm good." I take a deep breath. "I'm sure you're wondering about me and Kellan ..." And just like that, their attention is diverted. Not to mention, the second I start thinking about Kellan, a little smile tugs at my lips, despite all the Milo bullshit.

Lux's eyes take on a conspiratorial light as she leans in. "Rae told me that it seemed like maybe you all were hooking up when they got back to the dorm yesterday."

Raven's eyes meet mine, and she gives a dainty shrug of her shoulders. "Sorry? But not actually. Ever since you told us you wanted it to be him dancing with you, I've been waiting for you two to figure things out."

My cheeks heat. "I never intended for it to be a secret. We were just a little caught up yesterday."

"A little?" Lux snorts with laughter.

Raven's lips twitch. "Did you hear what Maddox said through the door?"

Oof. And now my face flames red. "Um, yeah."

"What did I miss?" Lux glances first at me, and when I don't answer, at Raven.

I roll my eyes to the ceiling. "Let's just say it was obvious when they walked in that some sexy times had been happening in the living room."

Flustered laughter bursts from Lux. "Oh, God." She covers her mouth with her hand as she giggles.

Raven bites down on her lip, looking over at me, and I can tell, she's trying to hold back some laughter of her own. "Kellan is so quiet. I have to say I've wondered what he'd be like in bed. Sorry if that's weird."

"I don't know yet. Things are moving along, though." There's no denying it, stuff is definitely slowly happening between me and Kellan—both on physical and emotional levels. It makes me feel good that he's letting me in like he has. He's like a puzzle I'm dying to put together. Some of what he says, though, it does make me nervous. There's definitely more he hasn't yet shared with me. But whatever it is, I want to be the one who's there for him. Not that he has to get over whatever it is, but I'd like for him to trust me with it.

I close my eyes for a brief moment while I let out a swooning sigh. The way he touches me is something else. He's reverent but adventurous. Careful but commanding. And surprisingly talkative during all of it. Almost as if he wants me to know how much I turn him on and how much he likes what we're doing.

I want to know everything about him, including whatever deep darkness resides inside his wounded soul, and what it was that put it there in the first place. I give an involuntary shudder. My brain has been working nonstop, sorting through the delicious complexity that is Kellan Murphy.

And in the midst of my little daydream, my gaze catches on someone walking in front of the coffee shop, jerking me away from my indecent thoughts. I suck in a breath. Just some football player wearing a black jersey. Not a leather jacket. My eyes shoot around the room, then toward the windows at the front of the shop. *This is my safe space. I am safe here.* I allow myself to breathe a little. And as long as my stepbrother doesn't march his ass through that door, I'm okay.

I jerk myself from my thoughts and back to my friends and take a quick sip of the coffee to hide my minor freak out and force myself to smile. "Yeah. We're having fun." I purposefully wriggle my eyebrows, which makes them both laugh. "I did sleep over there, but it kinda happened naturally. It's not like we planned it. We hung out on his bed, listening to music. And I fell asleep."

Which is odd because I never do that. It's very rare that I let my guard down with anyone.

Hawk returns to the table and slides two plates of delicious-looking egg bites to the center. Lux grabs a napkin and dives right in. Instead of immediately going for the food, though, Hawk gives me a smooth grin, his brows raising. "I heard part of that conversation." It's almost like he wants my permission to speak before saying anything ... which I appreciate, actually.

What is he about to say? Do I want to know what Hawk is thinking? Who am I kidding, of course I do. My lips twitch in anticipation. "Go ahead, Hawk."

He leans forward, bracing his hand on his thighs. "I don't want to interfere or get in the middle of the girl talk." He hesitates, eyeing me carefully. "But I will say this—Kellan's been in a better mood lately. And that dude is super cautious about who he lets close to him. So, take that however you want to. Only you two know exactly where you're at with"—he smirks—"whatever it is you're doing."

Lux smacks him in the chest with the back of her hand.

He laughs. "Right. Or *feeling*. My girl seems to think there are feelings involved."

I can't control my smile. "I appreciate your input, actually. Thank you for sharing that with me."

I can't stop myself from glancing toward the front of the coffee shop again. My palms are sweaty, and my heart races, making my chest tight. *Shit.* I'm about to lose it. It was so dumb of me to let Milo see who I hang around with and who my friends are. And Kellan. *Oh, God.* The last time I let a guy get close, my stepbrother took care of him pretty quickly. Wayne was a nice guy, so when minor threats didn't scare him off, Milo ran his car off a damn road. When I think about how much worse it could have turned out, it makes me sick to my stomach. Thank goodness Wayne wasn't badly injured. There'd been no way to prove that it'd been Milo, though. And it wasn't long after that Wayne decided I wasn't worth risking his life for. Can I blame a high school kid for not wanting to stick around? I'd guess he wasn't so interested in the relationship ... probably just the sex. And Wayne was a catch, so I'm sure there were plenty of willing girls waiting to take my place. I'd tried not to pay attention.

Raven's looking at me expectantly. *Shit.* What did I miss? "Sorry. I was off in my head."

"That's obvious." Lux smiles. "She asked if you think there's something there. Feelings. You know, like"—she elbows Hawk—"this one suggested."

"Oh. Um." I flick my eyes over to Hawk, who's shoved one of the egg bites into his mouth and is sitting there quietly chewing away, watching me with an interested look on his face. I'm no idiot. He will totally relay this information to Kellan, if he sees fit. But there's no reason to lie. "I like Kellan. A lot. More than a lot. Despite the mixed signals he gives off sometimes. And I know there's plenty he's simply not ready to share with me."

One brow goes up on Hawk's forehead at the same time Lux and Raven exchange a quick glance. I calmly lift my shoulders to my ears and drop them. Hawk totally knows what I'm referring to. I see it in the way he's observing me. "It's okay, my feelings aren't a secret. You can tell him. I don't care. I don't see how he *couldn't* know at this point." Hell, I care about him enough that the whole Milo sighting earlier is wigging me the fuck out. Especially now that I've admitted it out loud. I like this guy. Like, a lot. I blow out a careful breath and hide my nerves behind my coffee cup as I take another swallow.

Raven leans over and pokes Hawk's arm. "Since you're in a sharing mood ... Has Kellan said anything?"

He shakes his head, wetting his lips. "Okay. One, just because I'm sitting here, doesn't mean I'm revealing the inner workings of my bro's head. And two, Kellan isn't so much a man of words as he is of action. I've never seen him have a girl inside our suite, let alone the inner sanctum of his bedroom. The fact that he's invited you into his room more than once is major. He's private about his space, even with us. So, take that information however you want."

Lux grimaces at him and teasingly sticks out her tongue. "Gee, thanks for the insight."

"I'm telling you ladies as much as I can without breaking trust with my friend." He clears his throat, locking eyes with me. "Keep in mind, trust is huge for him." He slaps his thighs with his hands, and begins to stand, but then jerks to a stop. "Shit, did Lux tell you about the note we found under the suite door this morning?"

My stomach rolls over. "Note?"

"Yeah. It said *Hey, did you ever wonder what your girl*

does when she's not with you? She had fun riding me tonight."

"Who was it aimed at?"

"No idea. There wasn't a name on it." The muscle in his jaw twitches hard. "I dunno. Anyway, it's weird. And all three of you girls were with one of us last night."

Raven laughs. "Between this and the strange guy telling me that my room and board hadn't been paid yet ... kinda weird."

I draw in an unsteady breath. "I guess I missed catching up with you about it while I was with Kellan yesterday. So, the entire bursar's office thing was crap?"

"*Total* crap. I was so upset, Maddox had to speak to them for me. But they were able to verify that everything's a-go for my scholarship. I don't have to pay anything anymore. And they had no idea who we were talking about when I described the guy."

I shift uncomfortably in my seat. Do I tell them? I don't know what to do. They're going to be pissed. I feel like a complete asshole that I've kept this from them. I'm positive he's been responsible for everything crazy happening around here—the fire alarms, my handsy dance partner, the destruction of my room, the scholarship confusion, and now this note? This is all typical Milo behavior right before he goes in for the kill.

Lux fiddles with something in her hand. "This is the second one of these I've found in our suite." She tosses a matchbook onto the table. "Odd, right?"

SIXTEEN
STAR

The second Lux drops that matchbook on the table, I bolt out of my seat so fast I knock over my chair, stunning my friends. Despite their shouts to come back and tell them what's wrong, I shoot out the door of the coffee bar and take off, sprinting as fast as my feet can carry me. And I'm damn fast, so if I don't want anyone to catch me, it isn't going to happen.

I head for the library, determined to hide out for a while. Inside, I climb the stairs to the third floor and find a spot where I can see anyone who might be coming my way. I'll totally just chill here until it's time for my one o'clock art class later.

My mind reels thinking about how Milo had just appeared out of nowhere, leaning against that tree, not thirty yards from me. A violent shudder shakes my body to my core. I'm completely overwhelmed with everything this means. *I knew.* I knew before I'd ever seen him that he was here. There'd been way too many things that pointed to it. But damn, was it too much to expect I could come to Shadow River and not have him follow me? My eyes crash shut. I can't believe this is happening. I need to talk to my mom. Maybe I can convince her this time. Maybe things will go differently. Nothing about this situation is good.

With a sigh, I dig into my bag for my sketchbook so I can work for a few minutes on my art assignment. *Shit.* I poke around, but it's not there. I must have left it back in my room. Glancing at my phone, I note I barely have enough time to go back to fetch it before class. So much for getting any of the assignment done.

Ten minutes later, I jog up the steps to Duke Hall. Outside, I grasp my ID and scan it, then yank the main door open. Giving a cursory glance around the lobby, I'm glad to find I'm alone. I suppose at this rate, Milo could be anywhere. I'll have to be on guard at all times now. I take a deep breath and climb the stairs to the second floor, fumbling for my keys as I hurry down the hall. At our suite, I slip the key into the lock and let myself in, then move directly to my room.

When I jam the key into the lock and begin to twist it, the door pulls open from the inside, yanking me forward by the neck and sending me to my hands and knees. I gasp aloud at the impact. Pain shoots from my kneecaps up my thighs.

In shock, I don't register at first what's happened, only understanding that the breakaway safety feature of my lanyard has actually worked. The key is still in the lock, the nylon lanyard dangling from it in two pieces. Wincing, I swallow and for the first time, I look up to figure out what the hell just happened. Warning bells clang in my head, sharp and true, the way they always have.

Black combat boots, holey jeans, black leather jacket. Matching blacker-than-sin hair, and eyes so deep and dark, I swear they belong to the devil himself. *Milo*. I shriek and scramble to my feet, automatically backing away with my heart up in my goddamn throat. *No.*

"Hey, pretty Star," he grits, his voice deeper than the last time I spoke to him. He steps out of my bedroom, stalking toward me as I back my way into our suite's common living space. He eyes me like I'm something he'd like to snatch up and hide away until he's ready to play with me. Because that's how Milo's always looked at me, as his plaything. He rakes his teeth over his lower lip, tilting his head to the side. "I like the pink in your hair. That's sexy. Did you do that for me?"

I suck in a terrified breath as my brain tries to wrap around the fact that this psychotic asshole is standing so close he could reach out and grab me. He's broader than he once was, has way more muscle, and he's a lot taller, too. And that means if I couldn't fight him off before, I'm going to have one hell of a time of it now. I pivot, knowing my only option is to try to run from him.

Moving lightning fast, he's on me, yanking me hard, his fingers clawing into my bicep. I know he's going to bruise me. He pulls me to him, wrapping his arms around my middle, and lifts me clear off my feet, crushing me to his chest. "Now, where the fuck do you think you're going, pretty Star? I thought you came home early so we could get reacquainted."

What does he mean I *came home early*? Oh. Shit. Of

course. He's probably hacked into some university computer system. I bet he knows my entire schedule. He probably knows all of our schedules, considering he's been able to creep in and out of here, leaving us notes and matchbooks and who knows what else. *Fuck. Fuck. Fuck!* I struggle against him, but his arms only cage me tighter. My breathing is shallow and fast. I have to get away from him.

I squirm and twist, kicking into his shins with the heels of my boots. "What the hell are you doing here, Milo?" I shrug my shoulders this way and that, trying to dislodge his hold on me.

"Star. First, you know I always do whatever the fuck I want." His voice is deadly quiet as he whispers in my ear. "And second, have you forgotten how I get off on it when you struggle?" I go limp, hoping it'll make him drop me, but he barks out a devious chuckle. "I can hold you with one arm, sis. You're always going to be smaller than me. More vulnerable. I can do whatever I want to you or with you. And you never know when I'll follow through and make good on my word—you know it wasn't a threat but a promise."

Fear races through my veins. One of Milo's favorite things when we lived in our parents' house was to sneak into my bed and talk about how good it will be for me when he finally decides to fuck me. He gets off on the entire stepbrother-stepsister dynamic.

Clutching me to him with one steel-banded arm, he digs into his pocket before he brings something up in front of my face. My breath hitches when I focus on the matchbook in front of me. I freeze.

"You've never liked my fondness for fire. Not when I burned down that tree out back and blamed it on a lightning strike. Not when I set the cat's tail on fire."

I shudder. Poor Kismet had run around, making the most awful noise until he dropped dead. It was horrifying. I cried for a week afterward, but I've never gotten another pet since. No way. And somehow Milo had convinced his father that the cat simply walked too close to the fireplace. Such bullshit.

"Why do you think you can get away with whatever you want?" *Keep him talking. Maybe he'll forget about the matchbook.* I make every attempt to keep my eyes from drifting to it, but it's hard. He keeps waving it in my face.

"Easy. Because I'm Raymond Frank's son. And I can do no wrong. That's what he's always told me."

Milo's right. He's the same smooth-talking devil he's always been, able to convince everyone that he's a shining example of what a young man should be. He must be, as Raymond Frank's son, right? No one has ever understood that he's a ruthless, conniving psychopath except me. Not his dad, not even my mom, who is supposed to be on my side. He gets something in his head, and he makes it happen, then conveniently has excuses and alibis that seem plausible to everyone but me.

Milo manipulates those around him and possesses not a single ounce of empathy for anyone else. He doesn't feel guilt or remorse for a goddamn thing he's ever done to me or anyone else. Add to all that a penchant for fire-starting, and he becomes one hell of a scary dude.

I won't let him see that I'm terrified and about to piss my pants. I gasp, "I'm done. I'm done being scared of you." And even though my voice is unwavering, I know he sees right through me.

His wicked laugh makes my blood run cold. "Try telling that to someone who will believe those pretty lies." His hot breath wafts over my face as he maneuvers me to my back on the ground. He straddles me, clamping both of my wrists in one wickedly strong hand over my chest, and somehow still holding the matchbook in the same hand pinched tightly between his forefinger and thumb. I try to buck him off me, but it's no use. He knows it, and I know it. "You're only going to wear yourself out doing that."

I watch as he pulls a match from the book and passes it over the striker, so close to my chest I'm afraid he's going to catch my shirt on fire. A tiny flame flares to life. He smirks, staring at it, and watches until it gets down to his fingertips before finally blowing it out. My chest stutters as I hold back a sob. "Please, Milo. Stop. Whatever you're doing."

He flicks the burned-up match remnant on the floor next to my head. I squeeze my eyes shut. The low rumble of his voice results in another sob from me. "This is fun. Will I drop it on you or not?" Another match strikes to life.

The acrid burning smell fills my nostrils. I open my eyes just in time to see him flick the lit match away from him. It lands on the floor near my shoulder. Thank God, it goes out instead of catching the carpet on fire.

He does this over and over again, and the craziest fucking part is that the fire has him so entranced, he's hardly paying attention to me. Sucking in a breath, the second he strikes another match to life, I wrench free and ram two fisted hands into his groin as hard as I can, then punch him square in the jaw. His head snaps to the side and he gasps, both in surprise and pain, so I use the moment to my advantage. Twisting hard to one side, I dislodge him from above me using every ounce of strength I have. The sicko flops to the side when I push my way free, cupping his dick with both hands and groaning like he's dying. His face is etched with agony— an agony he totally deserves. Fucking *asshole*.

Never has my heart thundered so hard in my entire life. I waste no time scrambling to my feet. Milo makes a grab for me, but I pull free, then bolt toward the door, not giving two shits that he's still moaning and acting like he's dying. He bellows his displeasure at my escape. I doubt he's going anywhere fast because I was vicious with that blow to his man parts. I take off, knowing if I can get far enough away, there are plenty of places I can hide. With my heart racing, I dart down the stairs where there are witnesses lounging on the couches in the lobby, should I need them. *Go, go, go!*

I burst through the main door, not bothering to waste time looking over my shoulder. I have to assume he's got his eyes on me. I tear down the steps and only pick up speed from there. I feel an overwhelming need to run. To hide. Somewhere he can't see me. Somewhere he'll never think to go.

SEVENTEEN
KELLAN

For the last two hours of my art studio time, my hand has flown effortlessly over the canvas, sweeping the paintbrush where it needs to go, my chest tight. It's almost as if my head knows what I'm painting, and my hand is simply the vehicle holding the brush. I'm hardly watching what I'm doing, just reloading with the appropriate paint colors and go. It may be the easiest thing I've ever done. And the most significant. Because this is me, on a canvas. The churning gut, the tortured soul, and the unfathomable pain that had resulted in my behavior toward Star that first night in my bedroom, and the shame that washed over me as I pushed her away, knowing I wanted her, and unable to come to terms with what it could mean. That's what I'm expressing on this canvas.

When I first sketched out what I wanted to do for this piece, I'd been deep in my head, attempting to untwist all the torment and anguish inside me. I want to be normal for once. I want to be able to give Star what she needs from me.

Somewhere along the way, this girl has sunk into my skin and soothed the fractured pieces inside me. I pause for a moment, sharply drawing in a breath as I set my supplies down to take a break.

"Phew. *Lust* is coming along very well." Ryleigh laughs, fanning a hand in front of her face. "Are you doing okay over there?" she asks, slipping over to my station from hers. She plops onto a chair, and when I don't immediately respond, she cocks her head to the side. "You've been awfully quiet today. You know, quiet for Kellan, not for other people. So, *super* quiet."

I gesture to the canvas. "I think so." My head drops back on my shoulders, and I stare up at the ceiling for a few moments while she studies my work. I never have liked being around when people are observing something I'm in the process of working on. Hell, I don't like showing it when I'm done half the time either. I've had to get over it and grow a thicker skin, though, because part of the process with these more advanced art classes is that we're always looking at everyone else's work. It's fuckin' agonizing.

"It's stunning, Kellan. Powerful. Moving. I hate it as much as I did the first one."

What the fuck? I blink, scowling as I force my gaze to hers.

She laughs, shaking her head and grinning. "Calm down. I meant that when I looked at your first painting in the series, I had a very visceral reaction to it. An over-whelming sense of fear just poured from every brush-stroke. I can't even explain why or how I knew what you were doing. Because it's abstract. You wouldn't think it would reach out and punch you in the gut like that, but it did. It blatantly screamed *fear*. I immediately got it."

A sheepish look crosses my face. I should have known better than to think Ryleigh would mean she disliked my work, though I do think she'd tell me if I were on the wrong track. She's helpful like that. And brutally honest.

She winks at me, then allows her gaze to drift back to the piece I've been consumed by. "This one, though ... It's like it's clawing at my heart. I'm trying hard to come up with what I think this means to you, but I'm—" She hesitates, shaking her head. "It's not that I'm not getting it." She chews hard on her lip, a deeper line forming on her forehead the longer she stares. "I think it's more that I've never experienced something like this, never felt quite this way. It's a complexly layered emotion. Just completely raw. Anguish, almost. When I look at it, I feel this soul-deep conflict. Whatever this is." She turns a bit on her seat to face me, her brows pinching together. "So ... what is this, Kellan?"

I blink rapidly, then mash the heels of my hands into my eyes, rubbing hard before tearing them away to meet her questioning gaze. "It's the way I felt about myself after—"

Her brows draw together, and then she glances around. "It's okay, we don't have to discuss it here if you'd rather not."

I run my hand through my hair, wondering what she'll make of this. "No, it's not that." I don't think anyone's paying us any attention anyway. "Um, so Star and I—"

Her brows shoot up on her forehead so far they're

above the rims of her glasses. "Wait, are you telling me all three of you guys are dating all three of the girls in the suite across the hall?" She gives me a look; it's amused but disbelieving.

"Yeah. That's probably one of the reasons this can't possibly work. And I had actually wondered if maybe we'd just naturally gravitated toward each other because of hanging out together so much, but ... no. I definitely have a thing for her." I try to clear my throat, finding a huge lump caught there the longer I talk. I grit my teeth and run my hand over my jaw. I can tell by the look on her face that she's curious but also concerned. Probably because I'm acting like a freaking weirdo. "Fuck. I'm just going to say it."

"Yep, spit it out. You'll probably feel better." Her lips twitch a bit.

"The first time Star and I fooled around, I acted like I didn't want her like that. Like she meant nothing to me." I swallow. "I made her feel like shit." I breathe out a hard exhale.

"Kellan—"

I hold my hand up, shaking my head. "It was my choice to handle it like that. And we've come a long way since then. At least I think so. But that,"—I point at the painting—"is supposed to be shame and the intense feeling of disappointment in myself."

"Oh, shit." Ryleigh remains unmoving, simply watching me.

"Yeah. Combine that with an unhealthy dose of hellacious upbringing and abuse, and you've got yourself a winner." I shake my head. "Anyway. I like her. A lot. But I don't know how to navigate an actual relationship with anyone when my past keeps getting in my way. I've got a couple hang-ups from when I was younger that have come right along with me into adulthood. I'm—" I run my hand over my mouth. "I'm scared because I've never felt this close to anyone before and am afraid I'm going to fuck it all up. She understands that I have very intense issues surrounding physical touch and"—I grimace— "intimacy, I guess. But it seems like she's okay taking it slow. I worry I'm going to get attached to her and she'll leave. Fuck. I already *am* a little obsessed."

Ryleigh blows out a stream of air through her pursed lips. "That was a lot to unpack. And I have a feeling you hide this shit from people. Am I right?"

"Obviously."

"In fact, that may have been the most you've said to me ... like ever."

"Maybe." I smirk at her.

"So, I guess my advice—you are looking for advice, right?—would be to be honest with her about whatever those hang-ups are. Be clear up front. That might not even mean explaining all the details, though, the closer you get, the more it's going to make sense to tell her what you're dealing with up in that brilliant noggin of yours."

I catch the corner of my lip with my teeth. "I think Star understood that if things were going to happen between us that it had to be on my terms, but—" I groan. "I want to be a fuckin' normal guy for once. Is that too much to ask?"

Ryleigh cocks her head to the side. "Eh. But you wouldn't be the person you are today without your life experiences, Kellan. All you can do is work with what you've been given. And if she's the right girl for you, she'll understand. Really, are any of us 'normal'? Or do we just hide our shit from each other?" With a press of her lips together, she pokes her finger at the bridge of her glasses, moving them back into place. "And I happen to think you're pretty cool. Obviously, so does Star." She raises one arched brow at me, waiting for me to agree.

"Yeah." I blow out a hard breath. "Okay."

"All you can do is be honest with her, take things slow, and try."

"I gue—" A commotion makes me stop mid-word.

"Kellan?" Star's panicked voice greets my ears from the far side of the room. "Sorry. Sorry. Do you know where Kellan Murphy is?"

My eyes meet Ryleigh's wide ones. "Over here." I move swiftly toward the door, a lump rising in my throat. "I'm right here." I duck and weave through everyone's artwork. We're spread out all over the damn room.

"Kellan?" The way she chokes out my name again is like a dagger to my heart. She's close to breaking down. I can tell.

When I finally catch sight of her, my heart misses a beat, then thuds hard. Her hair is untamed, her face deathly pale, and her eyes are wild and scared. What the fuck happened? I catch her to my chest without a thought and hold her tightly. Her fingers clutch at the back of my shirt.

Breathe. You can handle this. You have a shirt on.

She's not touching your scars. My throat tight, I rasp, "I'm here, I've got you. I've got you, Star."

She shakes her head, unable to speak for several seconds as her body quakes against mine. "I'm sorry. I'm sorry," she gasps out.

There are curious stares and whispers from my fellow classmates, and I feel the immediate need to protect her from their prying eyes as she breaks down. I hurry with her toward the far side of the room, winding our way to where Ryleigh and I have our stations.

From somewhere behind me, I hear Ryleigh. "Nothing to see here. Carry on, people. You've got three paintings due next week. I'm sure you've got better things to do."

Finally reaching my private corner of the room, I help her sit in the chair that Ryleigh had been sitting in moments earlier. I squat down in front of her, touching a few fingers to her chin, and tip her face to mine.

"K-Kellan, he w-was in my room. W-waiting for me." The stutter in her voice twists my gut, and because I'm so thrown off by it, I almost miss what she actually said.

I draw in a careful breath. "What are you talking about?" From beside me, Ryleigh holds out a bottle of water out toward us. "Thanks." I take it from her and loosen the cap before placing it in Star's hands.

She uncaps it and lifts the bottle to her lips, the shaking of her hand visible. "I have something to talk to you about. But maybe I should wait and do it all at once. It's something I should share with all of you. Because he's making sure all of you are involved. He's quietly poking at everyone I'm close to, just to prove he fucking can."

"Whoa." Ryleigh's face colors. "Sorry. I'm sure you didn't intend for me to weigh in. But what the hell?"

Star's gaze flicks over to Ryleigh, almost like she's only just realized Ryleigh's observing. Star gives her a small smile and heaves out a breath. "Don't worry about it."

"Who are you talking about?" I softly breathe out the question as my heart thunders in my chest, thinking about what Star's told us so far. Someone's got her all kinds of freaked out. In my mind, I flash through so many instances where her fear has been downright palpable. The fire alarms. When she thinks someone is following her. The dude that was feeling her up that she thought was me. And immediately following, the disaster we found her room in. And then there's the other stuff. The odd note under our door, the miscommunication about Raven's scholarship, the matchbooks that keep popping up all over the place.

"My stepbrother." She tucks a few pieces of hair behind her ear. "He's psycho. That's the short story."

Stepbrother. I automatically bristle. "You didn't mention him when we were talking about our families." She's telling me that someone who is close to her instills a level of fear in her that inspired me to paint that terror I'd seen in her eyes. I glance at Ryleigh, then at the painting in question. Her eyes widen, but she clamps her lips shut.

I clear my throat, trying not to fly off the handle like every nerve in my body is telling me to do. "Did he hurt you? Touch you?"

Star is clearly rocked by whatever transpired. She closes her eyes at the same time her right hand runs over the bicep of her left arm, then to the nape of her neck. "I, um. He yanked my door open while I was trying to unlock it. My keys—" She pats her chest where her lanyard would normally hang. "Shit. He might have my keys, Kellan."

"Don't worry about that right now." He's obviously been able to pick the locks just like Hawk and Maddox, so whether or not he has her keys is kind of a moot point, and the locks are only there to maintain an illusion of safety. In reality, these girls are sitting ducks if this guy wants to come into their suite. Moving to the side, I brush her hair away from her neck, wincing at the abrasion on her nape from the lanyard cord. "Okay, so the lanyard pulled and broke when he yanked the door open."

She nods. "Yeah. I landed on my knees, and then when I tried to run, he caught me by my arm before I could get out of the suite." Tentatively, she brushes her fingers over her arm again.

"Can I see?"

Her teeth sink into her lip, and she exhales hard through her nose, but she pulls up the sleeve of her shirt. She looks away, and I flinch when I look down at the spot she'd touched.

"Oh, shit." Ryleigh's exclamation is soft but exactly what I'm thinking.

There's already the beginnings of a bruise forming just above her elbow. He marked her skin. With everything in me, I want to whisk Star away from here until I know this asshat has been taken care of. "What else." It doesn't come out as a question, but more of a gruff demand as more and more of my control slips.

A shuddery breath passes through her lips. "H-he had me on the floor, straddling my stomach." She takes several shallow breaths as I grip her thigh and squeeze. "H-he—" She pauses to blink back tears, but then a fierce look slides over her face. "He had my wrists in one of his hands, and he was lighting matches and flicking them to see where they'd land. He thought it was fucking funny until I got my hands loose and slammed them into his man junk." The muscles in her jaw twitch as she holds herself still, staring into my eyes, waiting for me to respond.

Fury flashes through every inch of me, and I can't help it, I have to look past Star while the anger snaps and crackles inside me. He meant to instill fear in her, that much is clear. And if he hurt her while he was at it? He didn't fucking care. Who knows what would've happened if one of those matches had landed on her and caught her clothes or hair on fire. Or touched her skin. My chest rises and falls in jerks. Burns are no fucking joke. I should know. I carry scars over most of my shoulders and the upper part of my chest and back. It seems like my asshole father and her crazy stepbrother have something in common.

"Kellan?" Ryleigh's quiet voice interrupts the chaotic tumble of thoughts barreling through my brain.

I suck in a breath, blinking as my focus moves toward the sound of my name, then immediately shifts back to Star. Her eyes are pinned on me. "I'm sorry. I'm really sorry."

My brows dart together. "What?"

"You look so angry. But I didn't know where else to go, and you make—"

When she doesn't keep going, I exhale harshly, still feeling like I'm about to lose my shit. Now that I know even this small detail of what she's been dealing with, I view Star in an entirely new light. This girl. How long has this been going on with her stepbrother? And what else is he capable of? "First, I'm angered by what the fucker thought he could get away with—not with you. Never with you. And second ... I make what? What were you going to say?"

"You make me feel safe." Her murmured admission sinks deep into every tortured corner of my mind. In that moment, I know without a shadow of a doubt that I will be that safe place for her, no matter what. If I can shelter her from the storm that is raging around her, I'll consider myself successful.

Out of the corner of my eye, I note the swooning gesture Ryleigh makes before she turns around and goes back to her painting. "Do you want to go somewhere so you can fill me in on everything that's been happening? There's a lot of stuff suddenly making more and more sense to me."

After a moment's thought, Star shakes her head. "Can we wait until I have everyone together? I don't want to have to keep rehashing everything, and I could honestly use a distraction because I've been on the verge of freaking out all afternoon." She grits her teeth. "Is that awful?"

"No." I rise out of my crouched position and hold out my hands to her. "I get it." I draw her to a standing position and into my arms. Her hands find my waist, holding on tightly, and her cheek rests against my chest. My heart thuds a bit at the contact, but this is nothing I can't handle, much like when I've held her in bed. This isn't the type of touch that will set me off. We stand perfectly still for several moments just breathing each other in.

"Oh," she gasps.

I glance up to see what's caught her attention. Her gaze is fixed on the two paintings I've been working on. "What's this? They're beautiful. And a little scary."

I chuckle softly. "Um. Remember that project I told you I was working on? These are the big pieces for the show that's coming up."

"But what am I looking at? It's abstract."

I clear my throat. "Our assignment was to create a cohesive three-painting project centering around emotion ... And I'm sure some people will probably use a color scheme or similar brushstroke patterns or even the same subjects or models to satisfy the professor's requirements."

"Well, that's cool."

"Yeah. But look at Ryleigh's." I point out what we can see of her work from here. "Her themes for each painting are connected. So, I think—I assume, anyway—that people will get that it's a themed set. She's going to title hers *Love*, *Lust*, and *Hate*."

Star's mouth drops open. "Wow."

"Pretty cool, right?"

She nods, then spends time looking over mine again. "So, wait, what are yours, then?" Her brows tug together as she studies the two mostly complete paintings.

I wet my lips. "I don't want to spoil it for you."

She jerks her head back to look up at me and blinks a few times as our eyes lock. "Does it have to do with me?"

"Most definitely."

"And ... do you know what you're doing for the last one yet?"

"That depends on you."

EIGHTEEN

STAR

Being with Kellan makes me feel better, but I honestly don't know what comes next. I'm sick to my stomach with worry. What if everyone blames me for bringing this psycho to our door. *Literally.* That's why I'd asked Kellan to distract me earlier. I'm at the point where I know what needs to be done, but I'm scared to death to actually reveal everything.

"What do you think? Ready to head back to the dorm? I can paint all day, but it feels like you're running away from this. And that makes me worry for you."

My eyes flick to Kellan's. The entire art class has abandoned their paintings. The class has been over for well over thirty minutes. "Um."

Kellan shakes his head and gives me a few more minutes by taking his paintbrushes over to the sink. Once he's done cleaning them and his hands, he comes back to where I've been leaning against the wall watching him. He rests one forearm above my head and clasps my chin with a few fingers. He tips my face up to his, and stares steadily into my eyes. "No one is going to blame you. And I think we need to get to our friends so you can explain the situation with your stepbrother before it blows up. Am I wrong to think this is going to get bad?"

Slowly, I shake my head, my lips curving downward.

Kellan dips his head closer, and for several seconds, we're still. Simply breathing each other's breath. He skims the pad of his thumb over my bottom lip, and my gaze drops to his mouth. I want it on mine again.

I need to know that my huge mess isn't making him second-guess this thing between us. It's kind of funny to think like that because I'm unsure what we're doing. Kellan doesn't tell me how he feels with words. But his actions—that's something else altogether. His body tells me everything he doesn't—or can't—with words.

Kellan's mouth lowers to mine, and he catches my lip in his mouth and sucks gently before his tongue swipes over it once, then plunges into my mouth. He devours me, moaning as he slides his hand to my nape and readjusts the angle. On a ragged breath, he comes up for air, and pins his gaze on mine, our noses touching. "I won't let anything happen to you. I swear it."

His solemn vow hits me right in the chest, warmth cascading throughout my body. Our green eyes connect. I know he means it. And if I ever had a question about his feelings for me, it's gone in that instant. His lips crash over mine and with me pinned to the wall by his greedy kisses, his hands wander. He teases my nipples, then his fingers glide over my ribs and down to my waist before he grasps a butt cheek in each hand and firmly squeezes my ass. He groans, lifting me in his arms. My legs lock around his waist, but I suck in a nervous breath, having a moment's panic when I don't know what to do with my hands. "Kellan?"

Between nips and licks, he growls, "My hair. Put them in my hair."

So I do, desire crashing over me as I thread my fingers through his wavy locks and tug his mouth back to mine. My heart beats so damn fast, I'm afraid it's going to erupt from my chest.

I suck in a breath as his erection nudges me between my legs. We've done a lot of fooling around, but this is the first time this kind of contact has happened, and I'm dying for it. I fervently wish that there wasn't so much clothing between us. We grind together like two addicts chasing their high. I wouldn't stop if an entire classroom of students walked in on us right now. I'd keep going and going because a rush of pleasurable feelings shoots and pulses through me. My swollen pussy throbs with every brush of his hard cock, and I can't help but think what it would be like to feel Kellan moving inside me.

I whimper, quickly losing control. I can't remember ever feeling like this before. I want to tear our clothes off and crawl inside him. I want to be so deeply connected no one could ever tear us apart. At that thought, my chest shudders against his on my next breath.

Kellan presses me hard to the wall so his hands can move. He's got them all over my ass, and his fingertips brush along the seam of my jeans between my cheeks. His lips ghost over my jaw, then find my neck, pressing open-mouthed kisses where my pulse flutters like mad. He rocks against me, over and over until I know if he keeps it up, I'm going to come. I gasp out, my voice rough, "Don't stop. Whatever you do, don't stop doing exactly what you're doing." I moan as each thrust of his hips drives me higher.

He nuzzles his lips at the side of my neck just below my ear, then sucks the lobe into his mouth. His breath in my ear sends a jolt straight down to my clit. Continuing to rub his dick on me, he whispers, "Like this?"

My mouth falls slack as waves of heat slide through me. "Oh, God. Y-yes. Kel-Kellan." It's so intense, my eyes practically roll back in my head. "Kiss me."

He sucks my lip into his mouth before growling against my lips. "You're so fuckin' beautiful when you fall apart." It makes my heart give a little jump when he pauses to look into my orgasm-dazed eyes.

"Is someone still here?"

"Shit." Kellan clears his throat. "I'm here, Professor Zara. Just finishing up."

Her footfalls come closer. I was kinda hoping she'd leave without checking on Kellan, but that's not what's happening.

He presses a firm kiss to my lips before we unwind our entangled limbs while he sets me down. He blows out a hard breath, giving me a look that can only be described as *crazy eyes* as he pushes a hand to his hard-on. "Fuck."

I stifle a giggle, and motion that he should grab his messenger bag that's sitting on the floor. He grabs it and slings it over his head, the bag landing in front of the monster dick trying to escape from his pants just as his prof makes her way past Ryleigh's paintings and comes into view.

"Sorry, I didn't know you had anyone with you."

I give her a little wave. "I finally made Kellan show me what's been keeping him so busy. I'm his friend, Star."

"Ah." She nods. "The muse." She gives a little wink and pivots on her heel. "Carry on, Kellan. And turn off the lights when you're done."

We wait until we hear the slam of the door as it closes, then promptly burst into laughter.

"That was hysterical. Is she always this laid back?" I wrinkle my nose, laughing some more as I wipe tears from my eyes.

"Yeah, actually." Kellan shrugs, holding his hands up.

My heart feels all fluttery that he's spoken to his professor about me. "I'm your muse, huh?"

"You already knew that."

A smirk teases my lips. "But I didn't know everyone else knew, too."

Kellan slides his hand over his jaw, looking me up and down. "Let's get outta here. I know she said we could carry on, but I'd rather we carried on somewhere else."

I grin and look around us, readjusting my glasses. "Oh, I dunno. This could be totally hot." Just when I'm about to suggest we finish what we started, my phone vibrates a few times in my pocket. And then again. And again.

"Maybe next time." He hooks an arm around my shoulder, but I can tell his mood is swiftly deflating. He brushes his lips over my temple. "You'd better check in with Lux and Raven. You don't know what state Milo left the suite in. They could be worried."

I breathe out. "Right." No way would the asshole

have taken the time to pick up the bits of burned matches off the floor. Hell, maybe the suite door was standing wide open when they returned.

As Kellan and I walk down the steps of the art building, another text notification sounds, and I thumb my phone open to have a look at everything, my eyes drifting over the entire thread of messages. *Shit.* I should have texted them to warn them before they got back. That was totally stupid of me. I grit my teeth, regret sinking deep.

Lux: Hey, are you both okay?
Lux: I'm at the suite. It's open.
Raven: Oh, shit. WTH?
Lux: I've no idea what's going on.
Raven: Is Hawk with you?
Lux: No. He's at practice.
Lux: Star's door's open, too.
Lux: And there are freaking burnt matches all over the floor in the living area.
Lux: I'm trying hard not to, but I'm freaking.
Raven: Mad and I are on the way.
Raven: Go wait downstairs on the couches.
Raven: What class should Star be in?
Lux: Leaving to go down now.
Lux: Art, I think.
Raven: So, hopefully with Kellan.

I glance at Kellan, my brows pulling together hard, a frown edging its way onto my lips. "I was stupid. I should have said something."

"They're upset?"

I exhale hard and rub a hand over my cheek. "Upset. Worried. I don't blame them. It's not like Milo would have shut the goddamn door or picked up after himself. There are probably burns in our carpet and bits of matchsticks left all over. He went through an entire matchbook."

"Milo." Kellan's teeth positively grind together as he stiffens, drawing me closer to his side. "Fuckin' Milo." He shakes his head as I lean into him while I quickly tap out a few messages to the girls.

Me: Yes. I'm with Kellan. We're coming.

Me: I will tell you everything when we get there.

Me: I'm so sorry.

Lux: Are you almost home?

Raven: We're freaking out.

Raven: Are you okay?

Me: Crossing the bridge now.

Me: I don't know how to answer the second question.

Lux: Oh. Shit.

Almost back to the dorm. Almost time to spill my dirty, dirty laundry and my guts and everything else all over the place. I can't believe it's come down to this, but it's way past time that they knew. I'll be beating myself up for a long time for not saying anything sooner. All I can do now is to admit to the shit show that's likely to ensue from here and apologize.

Kellan squeezes my hand, his fingers laced with mine. "Are they okay?"

"Um, they're freaked out. You'll see why when we get up there."

"Well, I can fuckin' imagine, considering what you told me about his attack earlier."

"Yeah. That's exactly what this was." I wince, then sigh heavily, wishing I could make all of this go away. "Why can't my mother or his dad ever see him for what he is?"

We've only gotten halfway up the stairs to Duke Hall when the fire alarms blare, their angry wails piercing the quiet afternoon.

NINETEEN
STAR

I jump a mile at the shrill sounds, and my heart shoots up into my throat, leaving plenty of room in my chest cavity for the impending sense of dread and fear to fill me. *No, no, no. Get me away from here.*

Kellan tightens his arm around me and grits out, "What the fuck." It's not a question, simply a disgruntled statement. Because seriously. *What the fuck.* I don't realize my body's gone rigid until he tugs me forcefully away from the building. "Back up. Here they come."

We continue to move in reverse, our eyes locked on the dorm as we stare in horror. This is no alarm pull. The main doors are flung open and smoke billows out. I can't take my eyes from the uproar as Duke Hall residents come pouring out of the building in various states of dress. Granted it's only like four in the afternoon, but some of them are already rocking their pajamas, staying in for the night. My breathing is shallow as my gaze latches onto the flicker of light visible through the haze of smoke. Wait, not light. I think it must be flames. Without a doubt, this is all my fault.

"This is effing insane," one girl says as she passes by us, arm in arm with her friend.

Sirens fill the air once again—along with flashing lights and lots of action as the fire trucks and other emergency personnel pull up. I blink. He did this. I know he did. Is he watching? I whip my head frantically in one direction and then the other, while attempting to keep tabs on the door. We haven't seen Lux, Maddox, or Raven. And I'm about ninety-nine percent sure they're inside the building. At the very least I know Raven told Lux to wait downstairs for her. But did the three of them go upstairs? Are they trapped in there? My body quakes with fear.

Some guy practically snarls as he exits in a towel, completely covered in suds. "I swear to God, whoever keeps doing this shit, it's not funny."

I clutch Kellan's hand, both of us staring at the doorway, waiting for our friends to emerge. But a minute or two later, there's simply no one else coming out, and I begin to panic for real.

"They're here somewhere. We just missed them," Kellan murmurs. I didn't have to say a damn word. He knows I'm freaking out in earnest now.

Another few students walk past us, their conversation plenty loud enough for us to overhear. "Some idiot threw a lit match in a trash can. It went *poof* and caught fast because there was a bunch of paper in there."

"Seriously?" His friend whips his head toward him.

The first guy shrugs. "That's what I heard."

Yeah, sure. Some random idiot with a match ... or one particular psycho. My phone buzzes in my hand, and I choke back a relieved sob when I see it's Lux.

Lux: Are you here? There's a fucking fire on the first floor.
Me: Where are you?"
Lux: We had to go down the back stairwell.
Lux: We're behind the building.
Lux: Maddox didn't even let Raven grab her phone.
Lux: (she's a tiny bit pissy)
Me: We'll come to you. Don't move.

I let out a strangled breath I hadn't realized I'd been holding. "They're around back—Raven, Maddox, and Lux."

"Right." Kellan nods, stroking his hand over his chin. "Hawk would still be at practice for a while yet. Let's go." He puts his hand on my lower back and ushers me forward, giving all the craziness a wide berth.

Rounding the building, I spot Raven's white-blonde hair almost immediately and pull free from Kellan to run toward her with my arms outstretched and a stupid-relieved grin on my face.

"Oh my God, this is insane," Raven shakes her head, squeezing me tight.

Lux's eyes are wide and nervous as she comes in to make it a group hug. "Does this have anything to do with our suite being wide o—"

I clench my teeth together as they release me, my

gaze pinging between them, and then up to Maddox's dubious stare. "Maybe. Yes. I don't know. *Yes.*" I huff out a breath before rubbing my hands over my cheeks. I can feel them reddening and think it may take a giant block of ice to stop the burning embarrassment at this point. "I'm going to explain. All of it. I can't keep it in anymore. Not when this shit keeps happening."

Stunned silence meets my declaration.

Maddox's face is a grim storm of emotion. "Yeah. You're going to need to expand on all that. I want to know what we're dealing with. I'm done being unprepared. I found another one of those I-fucked-your-girl notes—and it was in my goddamn room this time, on my fuckin' pillow, signed by that motherfucker, Spencer." He stops to rub his hand over his brow. "Except we know it's not him. Someone seems to think it's fuckin' funny to bring up past hurts and use them to jab at us." His gaze flicks to Lux's, but she squeezes her eyes shut.

"Don't." Lux's face has turned ashen.

Maddox lets out an exasperated groan, and tugs Raven under his arm. "I'm sorry, Lux, but if this has to do with Star, then she needs to know everything."

I swear, I'm going to keel over on the spot, this is all making me so ill. Kellan has stepped close, though, placing an encouraging, supportive hand on my back. "Tell me," I murmur.

"When Raven and I told Lux what we found, she checked Hawk's room, and his note was even worse than mine—it was signed by Landon. Whoever is doing this knows enough about our lives to stick it to us when he wants to."

To my mortification, my body begins to shake uncontrollably. I bring both hands to my face, staring in horror at the best friends I've made here, and try to form words that will make this okay, but there simply aren't any. I don't know what to say or how to act. And I hate that this is all crashing down on my friends' heads. Milo obviously thinks messing with them will make me sit up and pay attention to him. And he's right. I'm watching every sick, twisted move he makes. I bite down hard on my lip, so hard I wince, but I don't stop.

In my peripheral vision, Kellan directs a swift jerk of his head toward Maddox. The low rumble of his voice leaves no room for argument. "It's not her fuckin' fault." Kellan turns me to face him, holding me by my shoulders. "Hey. Look at me." When I don't immediately meet his eyes, he shifts, moving his head, until I do. "Star," he rasps, *"not* your fault."

My lip wants to wobble, but I hold it firm and slowly nod my understanding before meeting everyone's gazes again.

Lux looks a little numb, and I'm sure the sheer insanity of supposedly receiving a note from her deceased ex-boyfriend—the guy who tried to rape her—hadn't gone over well. I can't say I'm super excited about what Hawk will have to say about the turn of events either. And I absolutely feel for Maddox and Raven, who've just been through hell and back with Spencer. They're still waiting to hear whether Spencer takes a plea deal or whether the case will go to trial. Raven had kept some of the scarier details of what Spencer had done to her to herself, and now that we know everything, I get why Maddox is so growly. He's protective of her, and I appreciate that more than he knows.

I'm a little afraid that's what's happening with me—that I'm keeping too much shit to myself—and I'm too damn terrified to open my mouth and bring down Milo's wrath on myself and these people I've come to care about. What's happened to date is only the beginning, unfortunately. I know Milo too well to believe he'd stop at petty notes or a trash can fire.

"I'm sorry. I'll get you up to speed." I glance around for what feels like the thousandth time in the five minutes we've been standing here.

Kellan's arms loop around my middle from behind, lending me his strength. He rests his chin on my shoulder. "What do you guys think about getting pizza at that place off campus? We can talk there. And Hawk can meet us as soon as he gets done with practice."

My stomach churns. It's time to finally tell them about the guy who's been fixated on me for four and half years.

TWENTY
KELLAN

A half hour later, eight of us are squeezed into a large rectangular booth at Pizza Pie. At first when Lux asked if it would be okay to have Matty and Ryleigh join us, I thought it'd be a bad idea to involve more people. But after thinking it over, Ryleigh is the one person outside of my immediate friend circle who I trust. I can't think of how it could harm anything. And frankly, maybe more eyes are better with this sort of thing. Because I don't want a repeat performance of today's events.

"So, we're truly talking about a real-life psychopath, then?" Raven looks astonished, lips wrapping around the straw to take a sip of her Coke.

Slowly, Star nods as she meets Raven's eyes across the table. "Yes. He fits almost all the characteristics of one. He manipulates and does what he wants without a drop of regret or any remorse at all. And he's so slick, he has people fooled. Everyone's been under the impression he's practically perfect. He dresses well. He gets good grades. He excels at sports."

Lux's eyes are wide. "But he's kinda crazy from everything you've said. Your poor cat." Some of the shit Star has told us this guy has done is just pure insanity. How many kinds of demented do you have to be to set fire to an animal?

Star nods, a sad look on her face. "Even after I anonymously gave the school a heads-up that he had planned to set the place on fire, no one believed it ... until he tried to do it." She lets out a heavy sigh that I feel right down to my bones. She's dealt with this asshole for way too long.

On the other side of Star, Ryleigh sets down her pizza and wipes her hands on the napkin sitting in her lap. "Can I ask how long you've known he was like this?"

"A long time. And that's hard for me to admit. Our parents married when we were freshmen in high school. We were kinda tossed together at first. We both like computers a lot and were in the same grade, so our parents thought we'd get along well. Turns out, it's more like I'm the good hacker to his bad hacker." Her eyes flick around the table. "The whole Spencer deal is current, public knowledge. But he probably had some real fun digging around to figure out that leaving you guys a note about Landon would hit hard. He'd have been ridiculously thrilled to find something that juicy to use against you."

Maddox grits his teeth, sliding a look past Raven and Lux to Hawk at the far end of the table. "Fucker doesn't know who he's messing with, does he?"

"You can say that again." Hawk clears his throat. "So, what I want to know is how bad is this going to get? You said something about him being let out of a psychiatric ward?"

"Yeah. He's eighteen now, but he was a juvenile when all of this started. The agreement that they came to, since he was caught in the act of setting the fire was that he be evaluated by a mental health professional. That doctor advised that he be placed at a facility for juveniles where his behavior could be monitored, and he could be appropriately medicated if necessary." Star wets her lip and releases an unsteady breath. I hate that this is so unnerving for her. But it's necessary. I reach for her hand under the table because clearly neither of us has much of an appetite. Our breadsticks sit on our plates, untouched. "I don't know the specifics because I chose to look the other way. I was just so relieved he was gone."

Maddox growls. "This guy sounds like a real piece of work."

"You don't know the half of it. He's great at the buildup, too—when he's decided he's going to fuck with someone specifically." Star sneaks a look at me out of the corner of her eye before she continues. "Um. I started dating this guy our junior year. Wayne. Super nice guy. Milo got it in his head that he didn't want me to date him —anyone, really—and started messing with him. At first it was dumb stuff like threatening notes in his locker, stealing his belongings, and then it started to escalate. Wayne's car was keyed, then he got accused of cheating on a test. And then there was *the letter.*" The way she says it sounds ominous. My heart begins to thud painfully in my chest. I have a feeling I'm not going to like what she's about to say.

The entire group stops what they're doing, giving Star their full attention. "It said something about how Wayne had no business touching 'his' girl. It crashed through Wayne's bedroom window, wrapped around a baseball, going like eighty miles per hour." She hesitates. "Did I mention Milo was the star pitcher on our high school's baseball team?"

From the end of the table, on the other side of Ryleigh, Matty groans. "What a shit."

"It gets worse. When Wayne refused to stop seeing me, his car was run off the road. After that, Wayne broke up with me. Milo got his way. I don't know whether Wayne spread the word or what, but I flew solo the rest of the way through high school." She shrugs, dejectedly. "Maybe it was for the best, though. Milo is dangerous, and he can do no wrong in his dad's eyes. And my mom goes right along with it. He's like the golden child. I've been dealing with this bullshit for years."

Hawk narrows his eyes. "But wait. How did you know it was him who was doing all that crazy shit?"

"Most of it, he directly told me it was him. He got off on taunting me by taking responsibility for it and then threatening me with bodily harm if I said anything. He made it clear he'd make me regret it." Star's fingers clamp down hard on mine. I can tell by looking at her that there's maybe a little something she's holding back, but she continues before I think too much about it. "That's why I kept quiet for so long. I truly thought he would follow through with his threats." My girl looks down, blinking rapidly, before she quietly says, "I was positive he'd hurt me. And now that he's out ... not only does he *have to* know it was me who ratted him out, but I also got to attend Shadow River, which was his top-choice school until he got caught and fucked everything up for himself."

"Shit." Raven nudges my foot under the table "I'm so sorry, Star."

There's a murmur of agreement from the group before Star responds. "I'm sorry I kept it from you. I've been nervous from day one. I kinda knew he'd be out some time after his eighteenth birthday, which was in late August." Her eyes flick to Hawk's. "When you were sneaking in at the beginning of the year, I kept thinking you were him. And there was one time that I swore someone had been in my room." She sighs heavily. "You didn't—"

"No." Hawk doesn't let her finish. "I never so much as touched the doorknob." He shoots us a distressed look. "I only ever busted in to see Lux. Promise."

"Then I'd say we'd better assume he's been in and out of there and watching from the start." Star winces.

I can't fucking believe what she's been through. But we'll put a stop to this somehow. "The question is, how are we going to deal with him?"

When we get back to campus, the fire department has cleared residents to return to the dorm. It wasn't a huge fire and had been contained to a large trash can. The closer we get to our suites, the more nervous Star seems. I let everyone go upstairs ahead of us, drawing her to a halt. I pull her back against me. "You know you're staying with me, right?"

She shivers in my arms. "Are you sure?"

I press my lips to her neck, mumbling, "Um, yeah. There's no way you're staying alone."

I feel her deep breath as she relaxes against me. "Okay. I'll get some stuff from my room."

Outside her suite, we stop again. Or rather, Star does. She's hesitating big-time.

"You nervous to go in there?"

"Maybe a little." Her breath hitches before she quietly says, "Do you think they blame me?"

"I think they probably wish you had said something sooner, but there's nothing we can do about that now. No one thinks you're responsible for his actions. Come on. Let's get your stuff."

From the looks of things, the other two girls have already cleared out, the suite completely abandoned. My gaze lands on a few charred marks on the carpet. I close my eyes for a moment, to calm myself. But fuck, I can tell from the marks on the floor right where he had her pinned between his legs. Anger blooms in my chest, hot and thick. "Fuck," I mutter as I look around.

Star stands beside me, unmoving and staring at the same spot on the floor. "He— He was going to do things to me. I know it." Her gaze flicks to mine, and my brow arches in question. "When I struck him, his dick was hard."

I heave out a breath. Goddamn, I don't want to think about that because it'll drive me insane. "Let's not give him this kind of power. Get your things. You don't have to think about it anymore tonight."

"Okay." The worry I see in her expression yanks at something so deep inside me, it almost brings me to my knees.

I catch her chin with my fingers. "Hey. You're safe with me."

"I know. But I'm scared. He's messed with the others. What happens when he comes after you?"

My jaw twitches. "Then he won't know what hit him. Because I'm not scared of fuck all, Star. Not a damn thing. And I will protect you with everything I have." I mean it when I say it, but she swallows, then nods before heading into her room to collect a few things without saying anything. I don't know if my protective streak freaked her out or what. Too late to take it back now, though.

I wait at the doorway, hands catching the door frame above my head and silently watch as she moves around the room, pulling out a small bag, then quickly stuffing assorted clothing inside. She ducks into the bathroom for a minute, and while she's in there, I notice her key and lanyard are still dangling from the lock. I guess that answers the question of whether or not he has her keys. Not that it matters, seeing as how the creep seems as adept at breaking and entering as Maddox and Hawk are. Star's ever-present travel-size can of pepper spray taunts me as it dangles from the lanyard. I huff out a laugh. Who knew back then that I'd soon be waiting to take the same girl who sprayed me in the face with this stuff to my room to spend the night? Who knew I'd have all these urges and feelings? One thing is for damn sure—I wasn't ready for Star St. James. But maybe I could be. And more importantly, I think I want to be.

After another minute, she comes out of her bathroom with a toiletry bag and tucks it in with her other stuff. She takes a second to glance around, then shrugs. "I guess this is it. I can always come back over if I need more stuff." She huffs out a breath. "Not that I expect you to put up with me forever."

I take the overnight bag from her, as well as her backpack when she picks it up. "You're not staying here until we're certain it's safe for you to do so. And so long as that fucker is out and about, I'm afraid you're stuck with me."

I don't know if it's the part about not staying in her

room or that it's with me that's making her brow lift like that.

Shooting her a calm smile, I shrug. "What? Ask Hawk or Maddox if Lux or Raven are staying here."

"Okay, so maybe you have a point."

"Besides"—I give her a playful scowl as she locks the suite behind us—"I thought we were getting on just fine in the art studio earlier."

There it is. A smile lights up her face. "Yeah, okay. Let's go, Casanova. You've convinced me."

Inside the suite, our friends are behind closed doors already. I gesture first to the TV, then the kitchen. "Do you want to watch TV or need something to drink?"

She shakes her head. "No. I'm good. We could probably use some rest. Can we sleep in tomorrow?"

"Yeah. No classes for either of us until after lunch, right?"

"Right. I freaking live for my Tuesday and Thursday class schedule."

I take her hand and tug her along with me as I march to my room. Inside, I shut the door behind us and lean back against it. "You can have the bathroom first."

She nods, gives me a quick smile, and takes her overnight bag from me. I can't keep my eyes to myself as she scurries in there, closing the door behind her. She looked so damn good in the jeans she'd been wearing today. But— Fuck. She's about to sleep here. In my bed. With me. I'm amused that she thinks I'm getting any sleep at all tonight, because at this point, I highly doubt that's going to be possible.

I rub my hand over my chest, wondering what

protocol is here, having her stay with me after we've messed around several times. I don't know what she expects. And then I immediately feel like the biggest idiot ever because I know this girl likes me. I lace both hands on top of my head. *Fuck.* This is brutal.

The bathroom door clicks open, and Star slips out. She's wearing a pair of loose pajama pants with little computers printed all over them and a plain white T-shirt. Her face is clean of makeup, and she looks so damn sweet, especially with the way her cheeks have picked up a rosy-pink color. The thing is, I know she can also be plenty sassy when she wants to be, not a shy bone in her body. Not when you know her. I clear my throat, gesturing to the bed. "Make yourself comfortable. I'll be out in a few."

Drawing in a breath, I let my mind wander as I brush my teeth. And, of course, like it has intermittently all evening long, despite the seriousness of the earlier conversation, my thoughts go directly to how good it'd felt to dry fuck Star in the art room. I don't know what would've happened between us if Professor Zara hadn't interrupted. Would we have fucked right there in the classroom? My brain is close to detonating at the mere thought of it. I want her so badly it hurts.

I'm overheating, burning up at the thought of Star and me together like that. My dick is so fucking hard, I don't know how I'm going to manage to walk out into my bedroom and not have her notice. I don't know what else to do but take a few seconds to breathe and splash some cool water over my face. *Can I handle this?* I sigh. I haven't a fucking clue. But there's no sense in hiding from her in the fucking bathroom all night.

When I open the door, Star's already turned off all the lights except for the dim lamp on the nightstand. She's sitting up in the bed, scrolling through something on her phone. "Um. I hope you don't mind ..."

My brows draw together, looking her over for some clue as to what she's talking about. That's when it hits me like a sledgehammer to the chest. She's wearing one of my shirts. A slow smile stretches my lips before they twitch with amusement. "Are you asking if you can wear my shirt?"

She nods, pulling her legs up to her chest under it. Bare legs, which were encased in cute pajama pants when I went into the bathroom earlier. But those are now on the floor next to the bed, along with the T-shirt she'd had on.

I swallow hard but hide it by reaching back and grasping my shirt at the collar and pulling it off over my head. At the edge of the mattress, I hesitate, noting how she's watching me like a hawk, her eyes skimming over every single one of my tattoos as if she's cataloging each one for further study. My hands make quick work of the button and zipper of my jeans. And fuck, that zipper is like a wild animal screaming in the night as I pull it down. It shrieks, *Hey I'm mostly naked and getting in bed with a hot, sexy girl.*

We might be about to do some things together that could cause some problems, like they have for me in the past. I know from the way Star moved against me earlier that she wants more. But I need to figure out how to do that without completely fucking losing it.

"Kellan? Are you ...?"

How long have I been standing here staring at her? My eyes flick to hers. She can't know. I clear my throat. "Am I what?"

"Nervous?"

Oh. I scrub one hand over my jaw, studying her as she studies me, then shift that hand to the back of my neck tugging on it. "Not really." I wince at the lie. "Maybe."

She pats the bed, slips her legs out from under my shirt, and scoots over to give me room. "We've slept in the same bed before."

"I know ... but the first time you snuck out because I was too busy being an asshole. And the second—" I huff out an embarrassed laugh as I climb in with her. "You fell asleep." After a brief hesitation, I murmur, "This just seems ... significant."

Her brows lift, but she scoots down into the bed, rolling to her side to face me as she takes her glasses off. "Can you put these over there?"

I reach out and take them from her, twist, and set them onto the nightstand. From there, I flop onto my back and cover my face with both hands. There's no way around this. *Fuck it.* My voice comes out as a low, raw rasp as I say the words I've been so fucking nervous to share. "I'm a virgin."

It's so quiet, I swear the sound of my thundering of heart fills the room. My dick has been swelling since the moment we stepped into this bedroom together and lying here side by side isn't helping matters. My palms are all sweaty and my skin feels tight, as if it won't be able to contain me much longer. *Nope, not nervous at all.* I take several deep, steadying breaths, but it doesn't help much. My face heats with embarrassment. And the longer I hide from her, the worse I feel. I draw my hands down and turn my head toward hers.

She's wearing a soft smile. There's not even a hint of surprise on her face. "Kellan, are you gonna stay over there, or are we gonna do something about it?"

I let out a quiet laugh as I roll onto my side to fully face her. "I wanna fuckin' kiss the hell out of you. I-I—" I pause to gather my scattering thoughts. "I want more, Star. I want all of you."

"So, what's stopping you?" She's the picture of calm, in direct opposition to the tumult inside my head.

"I just—you remember what I asked of you the other day, right?"

"Of course I do." She huffs out a breath. "I've never questioned it." She slips a finger under the waistband of my boxer briefs, skimming across my lower abdomen before she pulls the band out far enough that it snaps a bit when she lets go. "If you want to have sex, we'll need these off."

My breath hitches at her words. *Oh, hell. Is this finally happening?* Will she be able to handle what I need from her? Touch is such a hard thing for me—and it's difficult to explain to someone else without going into the sordid details of how my father tortured me. I've never expected anyone to understand my triggers. But somehow, I have a feeling Star might get me without knowing my entire story.

My cock twitches in my boxer briefs, and I'm fairly certain the pre-cum leaking from me is making a nice wet spot on the front of them. Hard to tell since they're black, but I know it's there. *Fuck, I want this.* But deep inside, there's that part of me that is so fucking scared to get too close to someone. To let anyone see the real me, to share the ugliness that I was brought up with, the pain inflicted by my own family. There are things I don't know if I'll ever be okay with.

She sits up, kicking the sheet and duvet from us. Catching the corner of her lip with her teeth, she whips the T-shirt she stole from me over her head. My gaze immediately drops to her full breasts with their dusky-pink nipples and the smooth expanse of her stomach. She's got the cutest fuckin' belly button I've ever seen. I allow my eyes to roam a little farther south until they come to a full halt at a tiny pair of red boyshort panties. I groan, my mind flashing back to her bringing herself to orgasm right in front of me. She'd been so fucking pink and wet, I'd almost come just watching her fingers work her clit. And the look of ecstasy I'd captured on paper? Fuuuck. It was so unforgettably hot.

I drag in a pained breath as my gaze travels down her bare legs all the way to her little toes, nails painted in a dark, deep color, like the night sky. *Fuck.* I'm itching to touch her everywhere, and I fully understand I want to do things to her that I'm specifically asking her not to reciprocate. But everything about her calls out to me, tells me this is right. She's the one. I stare into her eyes, questioning in the only way I know how. *Please understand me.*

Softly, she whispers, "Take control, Kellan. Do what you need to do."

I sit up quickly and shift around, pushing her back to the mattress. I crawl between her legs and grasp her wrists in my hands, holding them firmly on the pillow above her head. I pause for several seconds, looking into her vibrant green eyes. Her back arches, and her taut nipples graze my chest. Fuck. It feels so damn good, I can't resist lowering a little, letting our bodies brush again. She gives a satisfied moan, not breaking eye contact. And in this moment, I know for damn certain that I want to be looking into her eyes when I enter her body.

My breathing ragged, I bring my mouth closer and closer to hers. I want to put it all over her body. Touch every inch of her. But I'll gladly begin with her sweet lips. My tongue trails lightly over the bottom one, getting a taste of her before I sweep into her mouth with a groan. I kiss her fiercely. Passionately. Meaningfully. With everything I am.

And this girl, she meets me lick for lick and stroke for wild stroke. Our tongues tangle and twist and curl. Every nip and rub of her lips makes me hotter for her. She sucks my lip into her mouth, and I groan aloud. Hesitantly, I lower my body to hers, blood roaring through my head, and lust pounding through my veins. The skin-on-skin contact throws me for a loop, my chest going incredibly tight. *Fuuuck.* There can't possibly be anything better than the feel of her soft, warm skin on mine and her body straining toward me.

But then, I prove myself wrong as my hips rock,

bringing my cock into contact with her panty-covered pussy. Fireworks shoot off in my head, and to disguise how overwhelmed I am, my lips leave hers to seek out her neck. She gasps when I bite softly, then grinds herself upward, rubbing against my aching dick.

A jolt of electricity zips straight down my spine. "Fuck. You feel so good," I grit, need rushing through my body with every desire-filled touch. Her legs have dropped open, bent at the knees, and she's pushing her feet into the mattress to provide leverage to rub her pussy up and down on my cock. It's the most sublime thing I've ever felt. *Yet.* Because there's more. I know there's more. I shudder at the knowledge that tonight I'm going to have it all.

"Do you want me, Kellan?" Star's question comes out on a breathy gasp. Her eyes connect with mine.

"God, yes," I grunt.

"Then take me. You don't always say everything you're thinking. But I need you to show me. I need to know." She looks up at me from under hooded eyes. "I want to feel you moving inside me."

If I try to reply, my voice will be hoarse, so I nod. Releasing her hands, I move down her body, taking the time to drop kisses in unexpected places and to run my tongue over her. The scent of her skin gets to my head and drives me mad. I slowly torment all the hidden places that I doubt many others know about. She gasps when I lick the valley of her breasts and moans when I put my lips on the side of her waist, nibbling lightly. I want to learn every little thing about her. What makes her whimper and what makes her sigh.

When I get to her panties, I don't immediately take them off, but instead, bend at the waist and run my nose right down the front. It's like a punch to the gut. A soft growl rumbles in my chest. The heady scent of her arousal is going to turn me into an animal. I push her legs wide, studying the tendons that disappear under her boyshorts right at the apex of her legs. I lick one, then trail my tongue under the hem of her panties, making her squirm.

I hope she understood what she was giving up when she told me to take control because this is the only way I can see this working—at least for now. But her eyes are on me, never wavering. And I make sure mine don't break contact either as I rub the flat of my tongue over her pussy through the underwear, making her shudder. "Do you want my mouth down here?" I can already taste her, and I'm jonesing for more. She's like a drug habit I don't ever want to quit.

"Yes. Show me how much you want me."

Kneeling, I hook my fingers into the waistband of her panties and tug them down as Star lifts her ass to ease the way. My heart thuds heavily in my chest as I peel them off her legs and get another look at all her glistening pink skin. My dick throbs impatiently, but I want this first. I lower my head between her legs, immediately licking through her folds before I close my mouth over her clit to flick and suck until she's writhing on the bed.

Breathless, she moans, "Please." And just as she says it, I slide a careful finger inside her warm, wet heat. I slowly circle, paying attention to what she feels like and more to the point, what I do that makes her toes curl.

"Please what?" I growl, removing my finger so I can lick at the arousal that seeps from her. "Dear fucking God, you taste so good. I wanna put my cock in this pussy." I dip my tongue inside her and kiss her the same way I would her mouth. I'm insatiable.

Star's legs tremble, and I know she must be close. Lifting my head, I meet her lust-filled gaze. "Condom. But I'm making you come first. There's no way I'm going to last this first time. I know I haven't done this before, but it's not like I haven't been paying attention." I lean over, stretching to open the nightstand drawer, and grab the unopened box of condoms I'd put there way back in August, never thinking they'd get used. I tear into it and toss one on the bed. I lose my boxer briefs at lightning speed. Kneeling there, fully exposed, my breath catches, and my hands shake a bit.

Her brow furrows. "Are you okay?"

I nod, swallowing as I remove the condom from the packaging.

Star pushes to a sitting position and places her hand over mine. "Let me." She takes it, pinches the tip, and rolls it on me. My hips jerk at her touch.

"Fuck." Heavy breaths pant from me. "Sorry."

Her head tilts to the side while staring into my eyes. "Why don't we go back to what you were doing? And then when you're ready ... we're ready. You can go fast or slow, I don't care. And I'll keep my hands to myself unless you tell me otherwise." She leans back onto her elbows with her legs still spread before me.

My jaw clenches tight. She's so fuckin' perfect. "I wanna make sure you come first."

"Not arguing with that." She shoots me a devious smile and drops her legs open even wider. "Make me come, Kellan. I want to watch you do it."

She lets out a little whimper as I rest one hand on her inner thigh and push two fingers into her pussy. I stroke them in and out of her a few times before bending to lick circles around her clit.

"Oh, God. Yeah. Keep doing that." She wets her lips and her green eyes crackle with an inner fire as they watch my every move. It's so fucking hot, knowing she's watching me eat her out.

And I do—I feast on every delicious bit of her, plunging my fingers inside, imagining it's my dick. *Holy shit, she feels good.* I hope I'm not about to fuckin' embarrass myself.

"Kellan." She drops to her back and bites down hard on her lip as she peers at me. "Can I ... can I put my hands in your hair again? Like at the art studio?"

I glance up to find her hands are tightly fisted under her chin. The memory of her fingers clenching my hair has pre-cum leaking into the condom. "Yes," I rasp.

Star hesitantly brings her hands down, threading her fingers through my locks as I swipe my tongue over every inch of her engorged flesh. She sucks in a breath and tugs on my hair as I flick over her clit, then moans when I use the flat of my tongue to apply pressure and a bit of friction.

I can tell from the way her pussy is grinding against my face that she's chasing that elusive high, so close she can taste it. I let her keep using my mouth and tongue, and I gotta say, the way she's so uninhibited, rubbing herself on me the way she wants to—it's so goddamn sexy. It tells me a hell of a lot about what she needs.

Gasping out, her body stills for a moment, and her eyes glaze over. Her pussy squeezes rhythmically on my fingers over and over as she comes. "That's it, baby. You're so fuckin' beautiful." I remove my fingers and crawl up her body.

Our breaths mingle, chests rising and falling fast. Through the haze of her orgasm, we lock eyes. Urgently, she whispers, "Fuck me, Kellan. Please fuck me now. I'm still sensitive."

Fuuuck. I could explode on the spot hearing her beg like that. Quickly moving into position, I brace myself over her, noticing she's already moved her hands above her head. Watching her for cues, I line up with her pussy and push into her velvety warm heat. Sensation after sensation swamps me. "Fuuuck," I growl aloud. I never thought this would happen.

"Oh, fuck." Star's eyes are wide, and she lets out the mother of all moans. Holy shit, her body is squeezing the hell out of my dick. *Tight, tight pussy.* And she's still pulsing from her orgasm. My brain goes into overload. I take both of her hands in mine, threading our fingers together, and slide back until I'm almost out of her body, then slam forward again.

From there, I can't stop. I fuck hard, filling her body with my eager cock as my hips snap against her ass over and over again.

Star shudders beneath me, throwing her head back, her entire body quaking. "God, ye—"

I cut off her shout with a hot kiss, my body

completely taking over from all sane thought in my head. My brain is no longer in control. I would do anything to keep feeling like this. My lips devour hers, and I pound into her, her cries of pleasure filling my head. I never want this to be over. She feels so fucking good. I'm skin to skin with her, and it feels right. It's almost too much for me to comprehend. She's meeting me thrust for thrust, her body moving in rhythm with mine as I squeeze her hands tightly in mine. Kiss her hard.

Heat surges through me, and my balls begin to draw up. *Oh, fuck.* "Gonna come." There's no more vulnerable feeling than this. It's like I've gone numb everywhere else, the rush of intense feeling focused right on my dick as the orgasm streaks through me. I come hard. Harder than hard. I think my brain is leaking out my ears. My cock pulses as cum jets out of me.

Breathing raggedly, I kiss the side of Star's neck before pulling my head back to look into her eyes. Her face is flushed, lips a bit swollen. "You okay?"

Star's hands grip mine hard, and her legs squeeze my waist. "You fucked the hell out of me." She heaves out a breath with a smile. "I'm good. But are *you* okay?"

I stare into her eyes. "I think so. Maybe. That was—" I shake my head as I grip the condom to pull out of her. "Intense." Giving myself a shake, I climb from the bed. "Be right back."

In the bathroom, I dispose of the condom and give my hands a wash before I look up into the mirror. Grabbing the back of my neck, I tug hard on it. *Finally.* I blow out a breath, resting both palms on the counter. As usual, my eyes drift over my tattoos and everything they hide.

Sixteen roses. Sixteen scars. She's going to ask. I'll have to explain.

I don't know how long I spend staring into the mirror, but I'm pulled from my ruminations when there's a light tapping on the door.

TWENTY-TWO
STAR

"Kellan?" He's been in the bathroom for more than ten minutes. I stand outside the door, chewing absentmindedly on my lip. "Everything okay?"

Just when I've resigned myself to the idea that I'll have to go back to my suite if I want to pee anytime soon, the door opens.

Kellan in all his naked glory is definitely something to behold. He's all lean, sculpted muscle, smooth, inked skin, and one beast of a cock that he used rather impressively for his first time tonight. Is that what this is about, though? Is something wrong? Was it not good for him? Did *I* do something that triggered him? He had my hands in his the entire time we were having sex. I've told him before I'm not an idiot, I know he doesn't like to be touched. And I think I've figured out why, though I will never say anything unless he brings it up to me because I respect his privacy too much for that.

I may not have touched his chest or shoulders, but the missionary position we were in put me really close to him. And even without my glasses and the rather frantic nature of our coupling, I think I know what the problem is. His tattoos are a camouflage of sorts. They're hiding something. And it makes me sad to think what that could be. My brain can't even comprehend.

I suck in a breath. The idea that someone could hurt Kellan is crazy. Except— My hands begin to shake. What if ... My eyes crash shut. I don't want to consider the direction my brain has run in, wild with speculation.

He has a funny look on his face, but then he seems to shake himself free of his thoughts. His brows furrow as he rubs a hand over his jaw. "Sorry. I'm good."

"That's okay." I point behind him. "I need to use the bathroom." I give him a little smile. I haven't a clue what he's thinking, and I'll admit, that has me worried.

"Fuck. Yeah. Sorry." He steps aside to let me past, then crosses to the bed, and just kind of stands there in front of it with his hands laced on top of his head. I try not to gawk at his rear view since he's clearly torn up about something but *shew*. His tush is to die for, complete with those sexy little dimples above each butt cheek. I exhale sharply, shutting myself in the bathroom. I wish I knew what was on his mind because I have no idea whether it's me, him, or us that's causing his inner turmoil. Or something else entirely.

A few minutes later, I exit to find Kellan sprawled across the bed with the lights out. I can't tell if he's asleep until I get closer. His jaw twitches, lashes fluttering as his eyes open. "Hey." There's a rough quality to his voice that I've heard once or twice before. Usually when he's a little upset about something.

"Kellan, if I did something wrong, you'd tell me, right?" Tears prick at the back of my eyes at the thought that I could have caused him pain. Would he? Or would he hide it? *Shit.*

"Come here." The command in his voice settles bone-deep, and I can't help but comply. "I'm fine, baby." He pats the bed as he rolls to his side. "Scoot back here."

The way he says *baby.* Oh, God. It makes me ache with the need I have for him. Because I do need him. He's become the one I want to go to when I have a problem, which was highly evident after the Milo incident. Kellan had been my first—and only—choice of who to run to. I climb into the bed, allowing him to spoon me from behind. Maybe I should ask him about the tattoos.

He briefly kisses me right at the juncture of my shoulder and neck. "You'd tell me if there was more to this thing with Milo, right?"

I freeze. *Oh, God.* "What do you mean?"

He breathes out a sigh, the escaped air feathering over the side of my face. "You seemed on-edge tonight while you were talking to everyone."

"With everything that's been happening, I've been in a constant state of alertness since August."

Kellan finds my hand and laces his fingers through mine. "You think he was in your suite as far back as that? That he's been ... plotting this entire time? Playing some fucked-up game of cat and mouse?"

I huff out a breath. "You don't know Milo like I do. He can be devious." My chest constricts, and I squeeze my eyes shut, biting down hard on my lip. "Promise me you'll be careful."

"You don't need to worry about me. But I'll worry about you. Are you sure you don't want to report this to someone? I mean, there was a fuckin' fire downstairs. The psycho threw lit matches at you."

I sniff. "I know. But you don't—" *Ugh.* He doesn't get it.

His lips press to my shoulder as he lets go of my hand to allow his palm to coast up and down my arm in a soothing manner. "Talk to me, baby." The soft, sweetness of his voice brings forth the tears I've been holding back. They slide down my cheeks, and my body trembles against him.

"I meant it when I said he's a literal psychopath. I wasn't throwing that term around lightly. He's so manipulative, so smart, and such a good planner that he'll have an alibi, a million reasons why whatever he's done couldn't have been him. If I were to report it, he'd have someone somewhere willing to swear he was a hundred miles away when it happened."

My voice must have gotten kinda shrill because Kellan holds me tightly and makes little shushing noises as he strokes my hair back from my face. "I'm sorry. I believe you."

I let out a shuddery breath and nod. "Sorry. I get a little worked up when it comes to Milo. I should have known better than to think the hell I've been through in dealing with him was over."

"So, let me make sure I understand what you've said." He wraps his arms around my torso and brushes a kiss over my jaw. "With the Wayne thing, Milo said you were 'his girl' and that obviously wasn't true. And the only thing anyone ever caught him doing was something he didn't manage to pull off because you secretly warned the school."

"Yep."

Kellan bristles. "Okay. Well, he'll find out damn fast that he has no claim to you. But he has it out for you, too, so we'll be extra vigilant. If I catch him anywhere near you, I'll have to break his face."

We're quiet for a few moments before I whisper, "I hate that it has to be this way."

I feel his shrug against my back. "I'd hate to see him hurt you, so I guess we're even." Kellan's warm body behind me and the way he nuzzles his face against the nape of my neck make me feel a little dizzy. His big hand coasts down my arm, landing on my waist where he gives it a momentary squeeze before sliding over the swell of my hip. "Are you tired?"

A small smile tugs at my lips. "No. You?"

"Nope."

"Um. You could draw."

"Nope."

"Listen to music?"

"Sure, but I'd rather try to take your mind off things. Maybe we can distract each other." His hand drifts down over my stomach, caressing my skin, and his fingers brush lower and lower with each pass until they dip between my legs. Circling my clit with the pads of his fingers, he whispers, "Does that feel good?"

I nod, feeling his dick rapidly hardening behind me. It's sliding along my pussy with every slow, steady thrust of his hips. I breathe out a sigh. This is probably a comfortable position for him. Rear entry. "Feel free to tell me to be quiet and enjoy myself. But was it okay earlier?"

He lets loose a startled chuckle. "Are you fuckin' kidding?" His swallow behind me is audible. "It was like a dream. Thank you."

"Okay. I'm glad it was good for you." I move my ass purposefully against him. "Um. Condom?"

"Definitely." He loosens his hold on me, allowing me to lean far enough to snag the box of condoms on the nightstand and pull one out. I pass it back to him and lie back down. The packaging makes a crinkling sound as he opens it. After a moment, his hand finds my pussy from behind, and he strokes his fingers inside me. I've just felt the nudge of his cock at my entrance when I think of something better.

"Hey. Can we try something else?"

Kellan huffs out a quiet laugh. "Pretty much anything we do is going to be new to me."

I chew on the corner of my lip. "This spooning stuff? That's good sleepy sex. But neither of us is sleepy, right?" I want to know what he'll do when he realizes what I want.

"Right." He clears his throat. "So, we save that for later."

I sit up and give him a tiny smirk. "I'm game for as many times as you can go." Taking a deep breath, I lock eyes with him over my shoulder as I get on all fours. I'm rewarded with a look of shock but also one of unbridled excitement.

Kellan blinks a few times before blowing out a hard breath and scrambling to kneel behind me. "Fuck, fuck,

fuck," he gasps out. "Tell me right now, do you specialize in doing things that you know are going to make me come like a motherfucker? Because I—" His words fall off, and when I look back at him, it's to see him studying me—the very most private parts of me. He squeezes my ass with both hands, alternately kneading my skin and spreading me open wide for a better look. "Yeah. Fuck."

I can't stifle the laughter bubbling out of me, but I try. "Are you okay back there?"

"Yeah. Sorry. It's like all my best sex fantasies are coming true." He slips a finger inside me, rubbing the pad of it on my front wall. I shiver involuntarily. "Good?"

A moan passes my lips in response. "What'd you do, study female anatomy while you were busy not having sex?" I rock back, letting that finger rub against me in the best way.

"I pay attention. Listen a lot. But you knew that." He continues to play with me, and I'm really getting into it when he bites one of my ass cheeks. Not hard. Just enough to get my attention. The soft slide of his velvety tongue over the same spot makes me whimper.

"Ahh." My back arches, and Kellan groans in response.

"You're so fuckin' wet, I could slide in there right now, but I'm afraid I'll come on the spot. This view back here is something else."

And the next thing I know, both his hands are on my ass cheeks again, spreading me open, and his tongue spears inside me. He takes his time fucking me with it, then finds my clit with his fingers. I'm a mess, languidly rocking back to meet his mouth and making all these little mewling noises that I'm damn sure have never come out of my mouth before, but oh, God. He's so good at this. I let him keep going until I'm so out of control I'm right on the edge. "Kellan ..."

"Tell me you want it." He slaps my ass.

My eyes practically cross. The sting of the slap burns through my skin, but then he's rubbing away the pain in a way that makes me so hot I might melt right through the bed. "I want it," I pant.

"What is it you want again?"

"Your big dick." I shift my ass higher in the air.

"Good girl." His cock notches at my entrance, he grabs me by both hips, and drives forward, plunging deep.

"Oh, fuck." I grasp the sheets in front of me with both hands. He's immediately thrusting hard and deep. But faster, I need faster.

And as if he hears the inner workings of my mind, his body curls around mine, shuttling faster and faster into me. His cock strokes over the same spot inside me that his fingers had, and I can tell I'm going to have one hell of an orgasm.

His hand reaches around, and he lets me rub my clit over his fingers. I like how he does that. The only other guy I've ever been with—Wayne—didn't have a clue, and he'd do some weird shit that I think he must have learned from watching a movie, and I was too embarrassed to tell him so. But with Kellan ... I'd tell him if there was something he could be doing differently. The honest truth, though, is that I love how he touches me, how he fucks me. And this is only the beginning.

Our skin slapping and us moaning and panting together is so hot I want to record the sound of it so some day when I'm old and gray, I'll remember exactly how good this felt. "Faster, Kellan."

His hips snap against me four more times before he uncurls himself from me and kneels upright, grabbing my hips in his hands to thrust forward. "Fuuuck," he hisses. The telltale huffed exhales from behind me and the way his body drapes over mine tells me he's done. I kind of figured he might blow pretty quickly from behind me. I smirk a little, not even minding.

"Be right back. Don't you fuckin' move."

My body jumps at the command in his voice, my brows shooting up on my forehead, though he doesn't see my surprise because he's already in the bathroom.

Not more than thirty seconds later, he's back, his eyes assessing me.

"What are you doing?"

"Thinking about how I want to eat your pussy." He slides his thumb over his lower lip, then nods. "Come to the edge of the bed for me. On your back. Ass right at the edge."

His eyes burn as he watches me move into position, causing a wave of heat to wash through my body. I lie back, propping my feet on the mattress. "Like this?"

He shakes his head as he approaches. "No." Grasping my hips, he pulls me toward him, not leaving anywhere to put my feet. He kneels between my legs, slides his hands from my ass along the back of my thighs, and pushes them open, holding them there.

"Oh. Oh, God." My heart is stumbling all over itself,

doing a wicked dance inside my chest. Never once have I experienced oral sex after the main event, and I definitely didn't expect this from Kellan.

While I've been trying to get all that straight in my head, Kellan's gaze has locked on my very excited lady parts. He mumbles, "Fuck. My dick was just in here. Do you know how hot that is to me?" His chest heaves right before he leans in, lapping at me like a starving man. He uses his entire mouth to explore—licking, kissing, and sucking before moaning low and long as my body responds to the attention.

I'm getting wetter and wetter by the second as he greedily devours me. When he sucks on my clit in just the right way, I feel this throbbing sensation followed by a gush of arousal. I've never experienced that before. And fuck, I'm coiled so tightly down low in my abdomen, I know I could go off at any moment.

"Baby, play with your breasts for me. Do you do that when you're alone?" Kellan's husky voice knocks me sideways, and my nipples tighten at the suggestion.

"Y-yes. When I masturbate." I hold a breast in each hand, firmly tugging on my taut, needy nipples. "It makes me come faster."

He grunts his approval as he watches, then slides two fingers inside me, covers my clit with his mouth and sucks hard. It's like he's trying to pull the orgasm right out of me.

I moan his name as the tension inside me unfurls and takes flight. My body is racked by powerful contractions, and I can't stop the movement of my pelvis as I rub my pussy against Kellan's face. My head drops back onto the bed, dizzy, as I begin to come down. "What the fuck was that?"

"Like a solid thirty seconds of orgasm. You girls are fuckin' lucky, if you ask me."

I laugh, the feeling of euphoria still very much with me. "Yeah, but it takes a little more to get us there."

"Yeah, but multiples." He smirks at me. "Can I try again?"

TWENTY-THREE
KELLAN

Five minutes later, Star's eyes are rolling back in her head as her pussy pulses on my tongue. Her flesh is so swollen and wet, and I keep thinking about my dick sliding in there and what it feels like to come while inside her body. She tastes so fucking good, too. I want her again, but I'm afraid she'll think I'm some sex-crazed lunatic. So, instead, I crawl over her, kissing her softly. "Let's try to get some sleep."

Dazed, she stares into my eyes and nods. "Yeah, okay."

"You feel good?" I whisper as we settle in together, cuddled up in the middle of the bed.

"I do." She peeks over her shoulder at me. "Do you?"

"Uh-huh."

Quietly, she asks, "No regrets?"

My brows snap together in confusion. "What? Fuck no."

I can feel her silent laughter. "Just checking."

"Well, no need. That was kinda mind-blowing for me."

Her body relaxes against mine. "Thank you for trusting me, Kellan."

Emotion swamps me, and I can't speak, so I kiss the side of her neck and draw her closer. I have no idea if she understands how this has rocked me. I didn't think I'd ever find someone I was comfortable enough with to let go—and like she said, someone that I could trust enough. Because I definitely do trust her. And man, I'm fucking glad it was her that has helped me sort some of my shit. I can't adequately describe what I feel for her with words. What the two of us have together has sunk into my skin, my blood, and my very bones. She's making me believe I could live a normal life. That I don't have to feel so alone. Without anyone to love me for so long, there's been such a void in my life. And she's filling it with her self-assured sassiness, her intelligent, inquisitive mind, and her bold, beautiful heart.

For several minutes, she's quiet, and I think maybe she's fallen asleep. I breathe in the soft fruity scent of her shampoo and relish the warmth of her naked body against mine. I'd resigned myself to the fact that I'd probably never have a close relationship with a woman. But with Star—she's made it work for me. Now that I've had her, I know I'll never let her go. It's the what-comes-next part that's scary for me. That final step. But for me, a necessary one.

"Kellan?"

"Yeah, baby?" I rasp, choked up from everything that's been running through my head.

She lets out a long, slow breath. "How long have you had your tattoos?"

My breath hitches, and I swallow past the growing lump in my throat. "I got most of them on my eighteenth birthday."

She's silent again for about a minute, then her voice shakes a tiny bit when she asks, "The roses?"

Shit. Yes. All fucking sixteen of them at once. "Yes." My heart squeezes in my chest.

"I never thought of this until now ... Did you design the tattoos?" She laces her fingers with mine, squeezing gently before pulling our joined hands to her chest.

My voice still rough and scratchy, I answer, "Yes."

"They're like a big *fuck you* to your dad every time you walk around shirtless."

I never thought of it that way. But she's totally right.

"Kellan?"

"Yeah?"

"You really hate your dad, don't you?"

I let out a ragged breath. "Yes. I fuckin' do."

TWENTY-FOUR
KELLAN

Despite how late it'd been by the time we fell asleep last night—this morning?—I wake up right at seven to a naked girl in my arms and morning wood. I don't know whether it's the fact that my body is alive with holy-fucking-shit-I-had-sex energy or whether it's that my brain only wants to give me a slight reprieve from worrying about our conversation about the tattoos ... or it could also be that I'm concerned as hell about this situation with Star's idiot stepbrother. Whatever the reason, I'm wide awake.

Last night was ... fuck. It was the best night of my life. And I don't think I'm crazy for thinking that the sex was actually good, even though it was my first time. She made it easy for me and didn't ask a single question until after we were lying together, spent. And even then, it's not like she directly asked me *What the fuck, Kellan?* It was more like she knows what I'm dealing with is hard for me and is respectfully letting me take things at my own speed while giving me the opening to talk about it if I want to. She's pretty fuckin' special.

I guess I shouldn't be surprised that she has an idea that it has something to do with my dad. She's whip smart. Not only intelligent, but quick-witted, the kind of person capable of putting things together with the barest threads of information.

So, I don't know whether I should be more worried about the seemingly inevitable discussion that we'll have about my past—I do feel it's coming—or the fact that her psycho stepbrother is gunning for her. And much like I've kept my secrets all this time, I'm afraid she has, too. I think his threats are way scarier to her than she's letting on. She'd been so matter-of-fact about it at dinner ... and I'm fucking positive she'd made a concerted effort to hold it together in front of everyone. The only outward clue of her anxiety had been her death grip on my hand when we dug a little too deep for her liking. And *fuck* this Milo asshole. Anyone who would set a goddamn fire in a dorm that is home to hundreds of students as a simple warning is insane. He needs to be stopped.

We can't afford to ignore his antics anymore or brush him off as a nuisance. I do believe Star when she says he's a genuine threat. Dangerous. I'm hoping for some time to discuss with the guys how they want to handle this. Because we have our ways ... and the girls probably don't want to be aware until we're done. The trick is finding the bastard since he isn't a student, even though he's been creeping around campus for months now.

As Star wakes up and stretches, her ass brushes right up against my dick. All coherent thought goes right out of my head. "Morning," she murmurs, her voice rough with sleep.

I groan as my cock perks up further at the sound of her voice. "Morning."

She glances over her shoulder at me, her lips twitching in amusement when she catches onto my predicament and at the same time she shifts, grinding more meaningfully against my erection.

Each of her movements brings the most delicious torture with it. I kiss the side of her neck, cupping her breast and playing with her nipple. My voice husky, I whisper, "Two can play at this game." My hand drifts over her body, and I dip my fingers between her legs to find her pussy slick with arousal.

"I'm just going to grab one of these." She reaches for a condom and hands it back to me.

Maddox's deep booming voice cuts right through the calm of the morning. "Lovebirds, I hate to do this to you, but we have a problem." He raps his knuckles hard against the door. "Time to wake up and meet the bullshit of the day."

"Fuck," I whisper. Then louder, "Yeah okay, we hear you. Be right out." I heave out a frustrated sigh. "I guess we need to go see what the hell is going on."

"Maddox wouldn't be pounding on the door for nothing. But I don't want to know. It can't be good." Star's face pinches with worry.

"Nope, he wouldn't. And maybe not. But we'll deal with it. Together."

"I hate that we haven't even heard what's going on, and I already have this sinking feeling in my gut."

Five minutes later, we've managed to brush our teeth, pull some clothes on, and stumble out into the suite's living area. We're greeted by four concerned faces.

Without a word, Lux points at the table. Beside me, Star gasps, covering her mouth with her hands as she stares at the clear evidence that Milo was inside this suite within feet of all of us last night. The huge pile of match-books he's left for us is alarming. A clear warning.

My heart tugs, knowing how upset Star has to be. I reach for her to pull her into my arms, but she flinches and tugs herself away.

"I'm sorry, guys." With a shaking hand, Star pulls her phone from her pocket, thumbs it open. She draws in a breath and exhales slowly. It looks to me like she's looking for something, like maybe a particular contact in her phone. I have no clue what she intends to do until after staring at it for a few seconds, she taps on the screen. The phone's been set to speaker, and we wait while it rings a few times before someone answers.

The voice is female. "Star? I wish you'd stop calling us like this."

Oh, fuck. I think that's her mom. My gaze flicks around the room to each of my friends, who are listening in stunned silence. "I-I'm sorry, Mom. Um—" I'll be damned if I don't show her some support. I put my hand on her back so she knows I'm right here. Her body trembles, but she doesn't pull away.

"Spit it out. Your stepfather is getting ready for work, and I have a personal trainer coming in five."

Her ragged breath is the only audible sound in the room. "Mom, did you know Milo is here?"

"Where? Milo's working in Freeport. I told you that.

He's got a swanky apartment, brand-new furniture, the works. And now that he's got the job there at that tech company, he's all set. Screw college. Turns out he didn't need it."

Star shakes her head, and after a second stares up toward the ceiling, like she might be trying to stop herself from crying. "No, Mom. I mean he's here. He's been on campus at Shadow River." She turns away, putting her back to the rest of us. "Mom, he's been following me and is up to his old tricks again. There was a fire in our dorm last night."

"That's crazy. Don't be silly, honey. What would he be doing at Shadow River? He's getting his life back together. This whole debacle was ridiculous. He says to this day that he wasn't going to start that fire at the high school. That it was a joke. A misunderstanding."

Star huffs out a disturbed laugh. "When are you going to wake up, Mom? Why do you think he was kept in that psych ward after the evaluation by the doctors? He's not right in the head, and now that he's out, he's threatening me." She sucks in a quick breath before adding, "And my friends, too."

A deeper voice barks through the phone. "Star. You're upsetting your mother. You need to grow up and stop fabricating tales about Milo. He's never done anything to you. Nothing at all. Now stop this."

Star bristles at his words. She glances over her shoulder at me. Her jaw is clenched tight. "No, Raymond. Stop being blind to the fact that your progeny has mental issues. He's dangerous."

"I thought I told you to call me Dad."

One breath after another heaves from Star. Finally, she blurts, "If you were ever anywhere near a father to me, you would have protected me from him!"

There's a harsh gasp on the other end of the phone. The call ends.

None of us dare say a word for several seconds, and Star's visibly shaking now, though whether it's because she's upset, angry, or a bit of both, I'm unsure.

It's Raven who finally speaks up, softly whispering, "Are you okay?"

Star turns around, shaking her head. "They've never believed me. Not once. Not even when I told my mom—" She cuts herself off, an embarrassed cry ripping from her throat. "I'm sorry. I need to ..." Blinking rapidly, she heads back into my room.

Lux grimaces. "I feel so bad for her."

Rubbing my hand over my jaw, I groan. "I don't know what she meant by that." A couple of confused looks come my way, and I clear my throat, my voice low. "I'm worried there's more at play here than a crazy stepbrother pulling a bunch of asshole stunts."

Maddox grits his teeth, glancing at the pile of matchbooks. "I hate to say it, but that whack job is fixated on her—maybe he has been for a long time."

"I'm nervous for her." Raven looks like she's going to keel over. My jaw clenches. She literally just went through so much shit herself, so I can understand her upset.

Lux fidgets next to Hawk, and he pulls her close to his side, kissing the top of her head. He clears his throat. "So, what are we going to do about this? We can't have this guy terrorizing Star or the rest of us, for that matter."

At the opening of my creaky door, everyone's attention diverts to Star, who's got her bag and backpack. "I'm going to go. I'll stay in our suite by myself. I'm done dragging the rest of you into my shit."

There's some murmuring from our friends behind me, but all I can do is stare at her, seeing all the same fear that I painted on the canvas sliding across her features. She's terrified. And there are so many things I could say. Should say. But all I can get out is, "Star. Don't. Go." The words scrape over my throat and out of my mouth.

Her sad eyes reach into me and tear at my soul. "No, Kellan. Out of everyone, you're the one who least deserves to be mixed up in this. I don't want to be another source of pain."

And just like that, the girl I'm falling for walks out the door, taking my heart and everything I thought we'd been building toward with her.

TWENTY-FIVE

STAR

My heart is so heavy. It's one thing to know that my mother has the wool pulled over her eyes and my stepfather thinks his son can do no wrong, but I hadn't realized how shitty it would feel to have my friends hear them react like that. That phone call was nothing short of humiliating.

Because what's wrong with me? How am I the one supposedly spouting lies? Whether my friends are wondering why I'm not believable or they're simply sad for me that this is the family I'm stuck with, I don't know. But what I do know is that I don't want any of them in harm's way. I need time alone to figure out how to deal with Milo. Maybe there's something I can track down. Put my hacker skills to good use.

HOURS LATER, I give a look around from where I've been hiding in a remote, seldom-used computer lab on the top floor of the library. I'm due in Computer Science 159 in thirty minutes, but I wish I could keep at this for a while longer, keep digging. I think I found something, but I want plenty of evidence to back it up. First semester exams are coming up in a few weeks, and I can't afford to start skipping class now. What I *want* to do is curl up in my bed all day—but wait, I can't do that either because who the hell knows if I'll be safe in my own goddamn room. With a resigned sigh, I gather my book bag and take off for class.

The new Integrated Science and Technology building is the farthest from the quad and all the original academic buildings. I hurry along the sidewalk between the language and history buildings with my head down. I have zero desire to see anyone at all.

As I enter the ISAT building and take a right toward the lab, out of nowhere, a hand clamps around my bicep and yanks me through a doorway and into a seldom-used stairwell. I suck in a breath, already bracing myself. Milo's got me firmly in his grasp, his fingers digging into my upper arms. His face is inches from mine as he sneers down at me. "Hey, sis. Funny you'd be right here when I want to talk to you."

A troubled laugh bubbles from my mouth. *Act normal. Don't let him know how his proximity is making your heart race in the worst way and your lungs fight for every breath.* I tilt my head to the side, studying the psycho. "Not so weird, because one, I have classes here, and two, you have my schedule. I'm not an idiot, Milo. I know you've been following me around. Doing all of this crazy shit to scare me."

He slowly shakes his head. "Your fear is simply a byproduct. This is revenge. Payback for your interference."

I wet my lips. Wrong move. His gaze zeroes in on my mouth like a heat-seeking missile. I swallow hard. "What was I supposed to do? Let you burn the school down?"

"That's the first fucking time you've admitted it." He chuckles darkly. "But I've always known it was you who submitted the tip. That judge put me away in that hellhole to let them poke around my head. They said it'd help me. Well, guess what? I didn't need help. I don't need to change for the better. I like myself exactly the way I am." The air heaves from his lungs, and his eyes wander back to my lips. His head dips down, lips brushing mine as he finishes his thoughts. "After everything we've been through, you tried to have me put away. Why would you do that? My pretty Star. You do remember what I told you I'd do if you ever told anyone what I was up to."

Oh, I do. And this is what I've been afraid of ever since I realized he was stalking me.

Milo pushes me up against the wall at the bottom of the stairwell, the full length of his body pressing to mine. I shudder. As usual, his dick's hard, and he rubs it against my body, like he's done so many times in the past.

"HEY, *pretty Star. Are you awake? Brother's got something for you.*"

Roused out of a sound sleep, my throat immediately catches. There's a solid body behind mine and arms wrap around my torso like tentacles of an octopus. One leg is thrown over mine. I can't move. My heart rate ratchets up, the thudding in my chest almost unbearable. No. I told him no. That the two of us weren't a good idea. But he won't stop.

"I know you're awake. It's okay, you don't have to talk. No one has to know what we like to do. It's just you and me." The subtle shift of his hips forces his erection up against my backside. And then he starts to move in earnest, grunting and thrusting as he holds me locked against his body.

Tears stream down my face. Think about something else. Anything but this. I have a test in my French II class tomorrow. I begin to conjugate verbs in my head, like I know I'll have to do tomorrow. Madame Drury will be so proud.

Milo's ragged breathing clues me in that he's almost done. His hands squeeze my breasts roughly, kneading them like he's handling a pair of stress reliever balls. It hurts. I cry out in pain, but he doesn't stop because he's grinding into my ass like he can poke a hole through my pajama shorts with his dick. "Oh, fuck yes. Fuck. Yes, pretty Star. You're all mine. You'll always be mine." He jerks, then pumps a few more times as he groans and writhes with pleasure behind me.

I lie on the bed, shuddering, his cum seeping through his flannel pj bottoms all the way to mine. I can feel the sticky mess on my backside. I cry and try not to vomit.

"You won't tell anyone. Because you know me now. You know what I'm capable of. And you aren't going to say a damn thing to anyone. You know what I'll do. You

*tried to tell your mom about us. And look at what
happened to that poor cat of yours. Next time you try to
tell, it'll be worse. I'll take these little shorts off and stick
my dick inside you."*

I TAKE A DEEP BREATH, willing my nerves to calm
so I can get myself out of this mess. "Milo, this needs to
stop. I'm sorry you feel like I've betrayed you. But I
couldn't let you hurt people. Those gym bleachers were
full that night. Never mind the fire, people would have
been crushed in a stampede trying to get out of the building. And you had already blocked the doors. I did the
right thing. And I know you don't understand that
because it's all twisted up in your head." I look into his
crazed eyes. "Leave me and my friends alone."

"Pretty Star, we're just getting started. You want to
make sure I don't mess with your friends anymore?
Maybe you should stay the fuck away from them. Otherwise, I'm gonna rain terror down on them. Your little
friend who was in the car accident? I'll run her and her
boyfriend off the road. Make it a wreck that neither
survives. And the other? The pretty cellist? I met a lot of
unhinged individuals during my time locked up in that
loony bin." His lips twist. "It'd be a shame if she had to
relive what happened to her at the hands of her TA. And
I'll tie up her boyfriend and make him watch. Can you
imagine?" He snorts. "Yeah. I've been doing my research,
pretty one." He yanks me forward, then slams me against
the wall.

My head hits with a hard smack as he presses against me again, his raging boner between us about to throw me into a panic. I struggle hard, but I can't get free. I want to knee him in the junk but he's so close, I can't do anything.

"Why do you have to fight me when we'd be so perfect together? Maybe I should fuck you right now and get it over with." He leans in and licks my cheek, making me shudder. "But no. I'm not ready yet. I want to draw out the anticipation. Make it good for both of us." A wicked smile slides over his lips. "Maybe your guy would like to watch. See how it's really done. You know he's a fucking loser, right?" When I jerk my face away to dodge his tongue, he laughs, continuing. "I found his ex-girl-friend on social media. She filled me in on their breakup. Apparently, he has all sorts of daddy issues. And lemme tell ya, he f-f-fucking s-s-stutters like a motherfucker. She mentioned it." He chuckles, malice dripping from him. "But I'd already seen it firsthand in speech class." He tilts his head to the side. "What? Didn't know that about K-K-Kellan?" He smirks, grinding himself against me.

My chest tightens as I process this information. I've heard Kellan, once or twice, stumble over a word or two. I haven't seen true evidence of what Milo is referring to. But if he's saying it, it's probably the truth. *Kellan.* My heart twists and claws in my chest. Fury filling my veins, I look directly into Milo's darker-than-sin eyes and spit, "Keep his name out of your fucking awful mouth."

"Not a chance, baby. Not if you can't stay away from him." His mouth hovers over my sealed lips before his tongue darts out to lick a stripe over them.

The door behind us bangs open, and a harried-looking professor freezes when he sees us. "You can't be doing that here. Take it somewhere else," he huffs.

The man's appearance makes Milo back up just enough that I'm able to tear myself away, run back out into the hallway, and make my escape.

It's not until I sink into the seat behind my computer in the lab that I realize what'd been on the chain around Milo's neck.

My goddamn missing ring.

TWENTY-SIX
KELLAN

I'm in misery. All I want to do is find Star and talk this through with her. She has to know that I care for her—that I'd go to any length to keep her safe. So, for her to say she needs to be alone to deal with this hits me right where it hurts. I've trusted her with so much already, and we've come so far ... but now she's throwing up walls between us. Does she not see that I'm trying so fucking hard to be who she deserves, that I don't want her to deal with any of this stupid shit with her stepbrother on her own?

Fuck. My head is so messed up over it, I feel like I'm going in circles. I get that she doesn't want to lay anymore bullshit at our door. But at this point, we're already waist fuckin' deep in it. She has to realize that separating herself from us isn't going to work. The guy is a loose cannon. Who knows what he'll do next.

I slide into one of the last remaining seats in speech class. This is about the *last* place I fuckin' wanna be. *Jesus.* I do my best to listen to the lecture, knowing damn well I'm not going to retain any of the information. I exhale heavily and run my hand over my jaw as I doodle all over the top of the page where I'm supposed to be taking notes.

"This is so fucking stupid."

I glance to my left where some guy is mumbling to himself. But—he's actually looking right at me. He gestures at what everyone else is doing. *Oh, fuck.* "What did I miss?"

The guy gives me a lopsided grin. "I figured you weren't paying attention. I've been watching you draw for the last twenty minutes. You're good."

"Thanks, I guess." I sigh, then turn the page in my notebook, picking up my pencil again.

"We're supposed to be working on interpersonal communication." He snorts. "You know, like fucking small talk or something. I dunno. Seems pretty mundane to me."

I clench my teeth and nod. "Right. Well. Okay." This is the kind of shit that I hate.

"It's fine, I'll start. Are you an art major?"

"Yep. You?"

"Computer science."

I clear my throat. "I know a girl who's good with that stuff."

He grins. "See, now we're getting somewhere. My girlfriend is, too. Security mostly. She's like a cute little hacker."

I bob my head. "Cool." My eyes fix on the necklace he keeps messing with. And that's when I notice the chunky silver ring attached to it. I swallow, pieces clicking together in my head. "That's a nice necklace you've got there." I give him a tight smile, but frown inwardly. Maybe I'm reading too much into this. Maybe I'm wrong. This guy has been sitting next to me in this class for a while now.

"Thanks. I like to keep my girlfriend's ring on it. Makes me feel close to her. We've been together for years. Since we were young."

"That's a lot of personal information ..." My eyes flick to his. There's an almost mocking laughter in them. "Sorry. What did you say your name was?"

"I didn't say." He shrugs. "Neither did you." And then this crazy ass has the gall to wink at me.

The bell chimes signaling the end of the class period, and he's out of his seat in a flash and to the door before I can process what I think I know.

Fucking Milo has been in my speech class all goddamn semester. *Motherfucking fucker*.

"HEY!" I shout when I spot Raven and Lux up ahead of me on their way back to the dorm. I jog to catch up with them as they turn around. Their eyes light up when they see me.

"Hey yourself." Raven's head tilts to the side, assessing me. Gotta wonder what the hell that means. She gives me a tight smile. "Have you talked to Star?"

My brow furrows. "No. Why?"

Lux grits her teeth. "We didn't see her all morning,

then she got to our psych class just as it was starting, so we never got a chance to talk. She was closed off in class —like she wouldn't have wanted to try to make conversation even if we were able. Leave it to Professor Severn to go on and on with a crazy-long lecture. We never got a break where we could ask if she was okay."

"And she seemed jumpy. Upset." Raven crosses her arms over her chest. "She took off like a bat out of hell the minute the lecture was over." Spinning around, she scans the area. "She'd normally walk back with us, but she just left."

I nod, a defeated sigh leaving me. "I don't understand what's in her head." My jaw tenses, the muscle twitching.

Lux shakes her head. "I don't get it either, and I know we all have our issues, but damn, that phone call with her mom and stepdad. That was just stupid."

It *was* stupid. I hate hearing how they treat her. How they completely ignore her concerns.

Raven's brow furrows, and she reaches out to pat my arm. "You're torn up over it."

I draw in a breath, unwilling to agree, but knowing Raven is spot-on. I run one hand through my hair, tugging on it out of frustration. "Would you tell her I want to talk to her?"

"Sure. If we see her." Lux frowns as she notices my backward retreat. "Where are you going?"

"I need to think." I hold up my phone. "Tell her to text me."

AT THE GYM, I let my frustrations out on a punching bag. I fire hit after hit, jab after jab, and hook after hook into the bag swinging from the ceiling, all the while imagining it's that fucker Milo who's been watching me while I had no clue. I feel like an idiot. But how was I to know that the enemy had crossed lines and was hiding in my goddamn bunker with me?

A snort from off to the side of me makes me jerk my head up. Hawk stands there, eyeing me like I'm about to go off the deep end. "If that damn thing were a real person, you'd have beaten him to a bloody pulp by now." Hawk raises his brows. "I just got done in the weight room. Mad let me know you were here."

My forehead pinches into a line.

He bobs his head, catching his lip with his teeth before raking them over it. "The girls told him they thought this is where you'd have gone. That or the art department, so I figured I'd check here first." He heaves out a sigh, scrubbing his hands through his hair. "They're as worried about you as they are about Star, who, by the way, isn't talking to anyone. She's locked herself in her room and won't open up."

I wince. I've been distracted by the phone sitting on the bench ... the phone that hasn't made any noise at all. I keep hoping that she'll reach out. But she's stubborn when she wants to be. Hawk steps behind the bag, holding it steady for me. "Talk."

My teeth grind together. "That fucker Milo. He's been in my speech class. You know, the one I've had trouble with. He's been sitting right next to me, observing me, watching me struggle half the semester." I slam my fists hard into the bag, first one, then the other. I stop, heaving out a breath. "I can't fuckin' remember when I noticed him. But he was there today, doing a partner exercise with me, just chummy as all fuck." Hawk waits patiently while I hit the bag a few more times. "Then he started saying shit about how his girlfriend is big into computers." Hawk says nothing, simply continues to hold the bag for me. "And how he wears her ring on the chain around his neck. He kept fuckin' playing with it, sliding it back and forth on the chain."

This time, Hawk's brow arches. "Wait. Didn't you tell me to keep an eye out for a silver ring that Star thought she lost in our suite?"

"Yep. Sure. Fucking. Did." Each word is punctuated with a punch to the bag.

"So. Is all this about you thinking she's like ... cheating on you or something?"

"Fuck no." I give him an angry look. "This dude has been messing with her from day one—with anyone who is close to her. I'm surprised it's taken him this long to home in on me."

"Or maybe he knows that you matter most." Hawk's head cants to the side so he can see me. "Am I wrong?"

I shrug. "Fuck. I dunno."

One hand still on the bag, Hawk points at me. "Stop. You do so. You're fuckin' scared is what it boils down to. That girl thinks you're *it* for whatever reason. And she's good for you and might help you get past some of the awful shit that's happened to you. I know you haven't ever told us the specifics. But I know it was bad. And I'm begging you. If this girl is helping you, don't give up on her just because she has her own shit to deal with and she's pushing you away."

I look down at my hands, my jaw tense.

"Kellan, she needs you right now, man. Be there for her."

TWENTY-SEVEN
STAR

I wake up Friday morning alone in my bed, more frustrated with myself and this entire shit show than I was yesterday. It probably has to do with me being cranky as hell because I couldn't sleep. Worst night ever.

When I first realized Milo was here, it hit me that he'd likely be watching, looking into the lives of each of my friends. Poking around where he doesn't freaking belong because he knows threatening them would upset me. Milo's never let me have a normal life, a boyfriend, or even friends. I bite down on my lip. *Shit.* I don't know why I thought Kellan had been spared. Because he hasn't been. This asshole has been biding his time all along, saving the person who matters most for last. For his grand finale. But what's he planning?

Grumpy, I pull my phone in front of my face. Seven o'clock. I have to be in my freaking history class at eight. With a dramatic sigh, I throw the covers back and slip out of my bed.

Twenty minutes later, I've showered and dressed. I

pretty much look like crap today since I haven't done laundry in forever, but I don't care. A pair of old jeans and a graphic T-shirt that reads *Computer Nerd* across the chest will have to do. If I take off now, I can hit the Bean for a cup of coffee before class. Grabbing my bag, I sling it over my shoulder, step into a pair of Vans, and snatch up my hoodie off the back of my desk chair.

I unlock and pull my door open and almost kick Kellan. I blink a few times, thinking maybe I'm still asleep and dreaming or something, but no. Kellan Murphy is sprawled out in front of my door with a pillow and a blanket, guarding me.

My heart flutters wildly in my chest. *Oh man, is this ever sweet.*

His eyes open, and for several seconds, we stare at each other, our green eyes locked. He lets out a raspy, "Hey." Nothing more.

"What are you doing, Kellan?"

"I'm not abandoning you because you're scared."

I nod, sighing. "You're sweet but I don't know what else to say." My voice sounds rough, so I clear my throat. "I have to get to class."

"Fuck. You have an eight o'clock." He sits up, scrubbing his hands over his face. "I can walk with you."

"Don't you get it? He'll make it worse for us the more he sees us together."

He lets out a frustrated grumble, then wets his lips. "Can you come find me after our art classes are done today, then? I want to show you something."

I let out a shuddery breath that I swear is torn right out of my soul. "It's important?"

"There's something I need for you to understand. So, yes."

I HAVE no idea what Kellan meant earlier, what he needs me to understand. Once everyone clears out of my class, I venture across the hall to the huge room where Kellan's class is prepping their art pieces for the show Sunday afternoon. There are paintings everywhere, each of them having three that have to be ready to go by the end of today. There's a huge open area on the first floor of the building that's perfect for student displays, which is where they'll set up the art show this weekend.

Scanning the room, it looks like everyone else is gone for the day. Instead of calling out to him, I walk toward the same back corner he's been in for the last couple of weeks while he's been working on these paintings. He's kept them mostly to himself, setting up so that he's facing the rest of the room while he works and no one else can see what he's doing unless they come around the corner and peek.

When I step into his area, he's still working. He's got one paintbrush tucked behind his ear, a smudge of paint on his chin, and he's working shirtless. My gaze roams over him, the play of muscles in his torso as he wields the brush like a weapon is impressive. Once I've gotten an eyeful, my gaze shifts to the final painting he's working on. I take a few seconds examining it. He's taken the first two abstract paintings, which were different, yet somehow part of the same set, and has combined them on the third canvas. They come together at the very center in a vortex of sorts. It swirls together, the two images merging as one.

"Thoughts?"

I startle, as I'd been so involved in studying every nuance. I exhale slowly, my eyes flicking to his. "It's breathtaking."

He smiles, his lip caught between his teeth, then nods. "I thought so, but I'm kinda biased."

"Are you gonna tell me about them? I want to know—from your perspective."

"Yeah. I will. But something else has to come first. Why don't you sit down? I'm gonna grab another chair."

I suck in a breath. I feel like we're at a crossroads of sorts—either this is going to work ... or it isn't. And I don't want it to be my fault.

Kellan comes back into view, a chair over his head. Steadying my breathing as he sets it down, I blurt out, "I need to tell you something before you get started."

He's placed the chair facing me, so close that his jean-encased legs are spread around mine. He leans forward, bracing his forearms on his thighs. "Okay, then. Go ahead." I wonder if he has a clue what I'm about to say.

"I'm sure you see already that Milo has it in his head that I'm his girlfriend ... even though he's my stepbrother."

Kellan chews on the inside of his mouth. "Yeah. I picked up on that more than once. Especially when I realized he's been squatting in my speech class. He's got your ring, by the way. I wanted to tell you yesterday, but—"

"I know. Do you ever get to the point where everything is too much, but you're scared to make the wrong move and set off a chain reaction that makes everything worse?" I heave out a sigh. "That's where I was at." I stare at my hands in my lap for a few seconds. "I—" My hands tremble.

"You can tell me, Star. Anything. And I'm not going to think less of you or assume you're lying." His voice is raspy, but somehow soothes my nerves. "I'll believe you."

Tears prick the backs of my eyes and make my nose sting. "Milo has been threatening me since ... well, almost since we met." I stop again, feeling Kellan's eyes on me. "It all started when he first got there. I thought he was nice. And we were two teenagers living in the same house."

Kellan reaches for my hand, automatically understanding that this is going to be a struggle.

"One night, we were watching a movie. And ... I let him kiss me. It was my first." I wipe my fingers under my eye to catch a rogue tear. "I told him the next day that I thought it was a terrible idea for us to do that again."

"Shit."

"Yep. That's where it all started." I take a few calming breaths before I can continue. "It was almost immediately after that he showed his true colors, wreaking havoc in my life, whether it was setting things on fire—he likes fire, obviously—breaking things and blaming the housekeeper, stealing things ... the list goes on and on."

"If that was the worst of it you wouldn't be so scared."

Kellan's soft green eyes study my face. "You can tell me, Star."

I nod, trying to prepare myself. "He'd come into my bed while I was sleeping. Hold me down and touch me. His favorite thing was to dry hump me until he got off." I suck in a breath. "And he's been threatening to rape me for years. That's how he kept my silence for so long. Everything else he planned to do, he's followed through on. So, I knew. I knew he'd do it if I told."

"That's why it was an anonymous tip that you sent in."

"Yep. When he told me that he wanted to set a fire at the school? I thought I was going to have a heart attack. I had to do something. And true to his word, that asshole barricaded the gym doors. Thank goodness they caught him before he could set it. People would have died in there, I know it. I know I was right to say something."

"But it made him angry, I bet."

"Yeah. He guessed it was me. Anyway, turns out his daddy, Raymond, worked out a deal with the judge. And I guess it was a good thing he was put away in a mental ward for a year and a half. But ... it clearly didn't help."

He huffs out a breath. "Nope." His jaw is clenched, muscles twitching. "And now he wants you to pay for ratting him out."

I nod. "I wanted you to know the whole truth. I was scared to tell anyone. But I'm not anymore."

Kellan squeezes his eyes shut for a moment. In that small span of time that he says nothing, I worry so hard that I've somehow told him too much. When he finally opens them, they're blazing. "Sorry. Trying to control the urge to find him right now and snap his neck."

Oh. Well, that makes more sense.

He takes a few breaths, then meets my eyes. "I wanted to show you the paintings today for sure. But I also wanted to tell you—" His gaze slides down and to the side.

I wait.

He blinks a few times before meeting my eyes again. "My dad. I told you what an asshole he is. He's always been hard on me because I wasn't like him. I wasn't built like him or my younger brother. I think he hated me a little because I reminded him of my mom. And she was dead." He pauses, and I can tell he's gearing up to tell me something more. "The way he'd look at me. It was bad. And I developed a stutter, especially when I was around him. I sometimes still have issues with it. Like in that stupid fucking speech class." He stops again, hanging his head.

"Kellan." My heart goes out to him, he's trying so hard to get this out. It makes me want to cry for him, but I have an idea that's not what he needs from me right now. "You can tell me. Just like I told you."

He lifts his head slightly, peering at me, and nods. "From the age of ten until I was fourteen, anytime he felt like I didn't meet his expectations—whether I didn't do well in a class or on a test or if I fucked up at the one baseball game a season he'd show up to—he'd get so damn mad. And then he'd take his anger out on me. It was his way of making a man out of me. Toughening me up. He'd put out his cigarettes on my shoulders and chest. Places no one would see. And he'd always hold me still with a big, meaty hand on my shoulder or around the back of my neck."

I blink, my eyes scanning over the tattoos. "I thought they were hiding something but—" My voice catches before I can finish my thought. Breathing has become difficult. Every inhale feels like fire in my lungs. My head is intensely overwhelmed with the idea that a parent could do something like this to a child. *Ten.* He was ten the first time.

"I had one girlfriend in high school. Tammy. She broke up with me because I wouldn't take my shirt off, wouldn't let her touch me." He lets out a flustered noise. "Tammy liked the idea of being the elusive, hard-to-get Kellan's girlfriend. But she couldn't handle it. She didn't understand. And maybe that was my fault."

"You weren't ready for anyone to know."

"No. I wasn't." He stares at me steadily, our eyes connecting. "But you've helped me more than you know."

TWENTY-EIGHT
KELLAN

My breath hitches. I want to do this. I need this. I'm ready. "Come here."

Star's eyes search mine. "Tell me what you need from me."

My voice comes out a bit growly. "I want you straddling my lap."

Slowly, she rises from her chair to stand between my thighs.

"Take off your shoes and jeans." I spread my legs to give her room to maneuver.

Locking her gaze on me, she toes out of her shoes and unfastens her jeans, slipping them over her ass and down her legs. I offer her my hands as she steps out of them, kicking them to the side.

My eyes zone in on a pair of simple black cotton panties, and what I know lies beneath them. I take a deep breath to calm the lust raging through my veins and lift her by the waist, helping her get seated right where I want her. Her toes barely touch the floor like this, so she's got a hand on each of my forearms. I'm well aware that this would probably be easier if she could press closer and brace her hands on my shoulders—if I were any other guy, she'd do just that without a thought.

And I want that. But I'm nervous, and my heart has taken off, speeding out of control. All the blood in my body rushes to my dick as all the things I'd like to do with her race through my mind.

Star breathes steadily, waiting for me to make the next move, or to tell her what I want her to do. She gives me an encouraging smile, her eyes soft with some emotion that I can't quite put a label on.

"I want to be skin to skin with you. Can I take off your shirt?"

She nods, then lifts her arms, waiting for me to do it. I tug it off, then bring my hands to her waist. Before I realize what she's about to do, she reaches behind her back and flicks the clasp of her bra open, letting it fall from her chest and slide down her arms. Her eyes don't leave mine as she dangles it from her fingers and lets it drop. "What now?" And she waits for me again, one brow arching.

I glance down at her body, her lush tits on display for me. "I need you closer." I wrap my arms around her back and tug her to me, bringing her pussy into contact with my erection, which is straining behind the confines of my zipper. "Hands on my waist."

"Yeah." She grips me there, then lets out a surprised gasp when I bring her body fully against my chest. Her cheek lands at the side of my neck, on my shoulder, the soft skin of her breasts in direct contact with my pecs.

She's touching at least five of my scars. My body is a live wire, electricity snapping below the surface.

For several seconds, I simply breathe and hold her. When I think I can handle more, I drag my hands up and down her back. "Can you put your hands on my chest? Just past my nipples." My voice is gruff, and my body goes rigid as her palms slowly begin coasting upward, over my skin. Her fingertips graze the taut peaks, then they're right there, touching an area of my body I've never let anyone come near before, with the exception of the kind woman who'd covered my scars with the tattoos.

"Are you okay?" Star's chest rises and falls quickly against me. I think she might be as nervous for me as I am for myself.

"Y-yes," I manage to croak out. I tighten my hold on her and bury my lips in her hair. "Can you—" I swallow hard. "Can you slide them up to my shoulders? Near my neck, then down my arms?"

She does exactly as I ask. The sensation of being touched like this is nearly overwhelming. "You know ... I can hardly feel them, Kel. But I understand."

I drag in a shuddery breath as her palms skim over the caps of my shoulders and down my biceps to my elbows. "And back up again, please."

Her hands glide over my skin, coming to a stop when they rest on my shoulders. "Can I put my arms around your neck?"

My brow pinches. I breathe deeply and nod.

"I won't ever hurt you." Her arms encircle my neck, and she turns her face to rest it at the hollow of my throat. Her lips make contact with a soft kiss.

My hands drift down to her ass, pulling her closer. We both moan together at the feel of her moving over my dick.

"Are you okay?"

So many emotions are bubbling to the surface, and my body is hyperaware of every touch, so unused to any of this—because I never thought I'd get to this comfort level with anyone. I don't know if I can fully answer her question, but I'll try. "I'm not having a panic attack, if that's what you're asking."

She lifts her head from my chest, our faces almost level. "If we were to have sex, would you be okay if I held onto your shoulders?"

Lust jolts through my system again. I hadn't intended to fuck her here. But I see in her eyes she's game. And now that she's said it, I want to, won't stop thinking about it until we do. I release a pent-up breath. "We could see if I can handle it."

She nods. "What about a safe word?" Her gaze holds mine as she tilts her head to the side. "I'm pretty good at following directions."

I nod, my eyes flicking to the painting behind her. "Trust." I lift her off my lap, and stand up, yanking the condom—the one I'd grabbed on a whim this morning, never imagining it wouldn't still be there by the end of the day—out of my pocket before dropping my pants and boxer briefs. While she slips her panties off, I glance around the room that is usually full of other art students. This is insanity, but I want to do it. Need to push my boundaries. Because I want this girl. And it's not that I feel like I have to do anything I don't want to with her.

She'd be willing to do whatever I needed for as long as it took—maybe forever. I stare into her eyes as it hits me. I'm in real danger of losing my heart to her.

Star is maybe the calmest I've ever seen her even though she's standing completely nude in a place where anyone could interrupt us at any given moment. She's managing any nerves she might have because she knows this is big for me. She's so in tune with me, she knows I'm probably inwardly wigging out. She's not wrong. She gives a swift nod. "Trust. Okay. You say anything that sounds remotely like that, and I'll stop."

I sit back down, bare ass on the chair, and tear open the condom, only to have her stop me with one hand on mine.

"Wait. I want to." She kneels between my legs and wraps her hand around the base of my dick. My body riots. Her tongue flicks out, licking the drop of pre-cum from the head before running agonizing swipes along the underside, tracing over veins, and humming out her pleasure. When she takes me in her mouth, she moans, and the vibration goes straight to my balls.

Her free hand is clenched, resting on her thigh, and it strikes me why she's doing that. "Baby. Touch yourself. You don't have to hold back."

She slides her mouth off me long enough to say, "I want this to be about you."

I touch my hand to her cheek. "No. It's about us. Now show me how wet you are."

Dipping her fingers between her thighs, she slips them inside, alternately stroking herself and bringing them up to rub her clit as she bobs on my dick. After a few seconds, she brings up two fingers, glistening wet. I groan out, "Okay, keep doing that. Tell me if you're gonna come."

She takes me back into her mouth at the same time she begins to pleasure herself, which results in her moaning around me, which I really fuckin' love. The wet warmth and suction, the slide of her tongue—all of it has me gasping out loud. My hips thrust involuntarily, and I thread my fingers through the hair at the back of her head, guiding her as she takes my cock over and over again. Her hips buck as she rides her own hand. She's sexy as hell like this. And she's mine. My brain is full of the sight and scent of her. And now I need her taste.

I catch her by the chin, easing her off me. "Sorry. You're gonna make me come, and I don't want to yet."

Her lips twitch at the urgency in my voice. "Never be sorry for that."

I pull the condom out, quickly rolling it on. She straddles me again, seating herself on my lap. Before making any other move, I take her wrist in my hand. At first, she frowns, but then I take the fingers that had been inside her sweet pussy and suck them clean. The taste of her shoots through me, making my head foggy, and I groan, needing the physical connection between us more than ever.

She lifts off my lap, grasping my dick in her hand, and sweeps the head through her arousal. She's fucking wet, I can tell, and the scent of her is intoxicating. She's totally fuckin' teasing me, but it's so good I might die naked right here and now. Then I wonder if that would really be so bad after all, if this is how I'm going out. At least I'd die happy.

My lips graze over her shoulder as I murmur, "Arms around my neck." She immediately does what I ask. We pause a moment as I take in the feel of her holding onto me.

"You good?"

"Yes." With my dick in one hand, I put the tip right at her entrance. "Baby, sink down on this cock," I rasp. We both moan as she lowers onto me, sheathing my dick inside her body. We're such a tight fit, it makes my eyes cross. "Fuuuck." We're still for a moment, her arms around me, her breasts smashed to my chest, and her pussy taking every inch of my cock. And then she crushes her lips to mine, a desperate cry escaping her lips as our tongues stroke together.

It's intense. Sex is still new. Having a woman wrapped around me like this, even newer. And while my heart is thrumming hard and my head is spinning with it, I think I'm handling it pretty well. And it's all because of Star. I've got my hands on her hips, she's riding me, and her fingers are threaded in the back of my hair, holding onto my head as we kiss. I like this. It's intimate having her right here, arms around me, our bodies glued together. Her soft, bare skin is soothing. She's not here to hurt me. Never has been. And I don't think she ever will.

Our mouths tear apart as we both gasp for air. The feeling of her moving over me is incredible, and my head drops back. I stare at the ceiling for several seconds until I feel her lips traveling over my cheek and bring myself back to her. "Are you okay?" she whispers near my ear.

"Yes," I mumble half-incoherently, licking at the skin on the side of her neck. My hands slide up her back, then back down to grasp two handfuls of bare ass. *Fuck.* Naked Star is bouncing on my cock. I think my brain is about to explode inside my skull, liquify, and leak out my ears.

She nips my earlobe before she snickers. "Thank God because this is so fucking hot. You feel so good. But I didn't want to let myself enjoy it in case you were freaking out."

I grunt, "There's a hot naked girl riding my dick. I will think of you, of this moment, every time I walk into this room for the remainder of my college career."

"You'd better," she laughs softly, but then renews her efforts, sliding up and down my dick so good I don't know how I've lived without knowing what this was like all my life.

But even more than that, I don't know how I've lived without this girl in my life. She makes everything better—heart, soul, and body. She makes me feel whole, and that's something I'm unsure I've ever felt before.

I hold her tightly as we continue to move together. My hands slide all over her skin, touching her everywhere I can reach. With her mouth a scant distance from mine, I whisper, "I need to feel your lips on my skin." I swallow hard as we continue to move together as one. "Will you do that for me?"

She stares into my eyes, then brushes her lips across mine. "Remember your safe word."

"I'm okay." I suck in a shuddery breath. "I need this." I need to replace all the bad memories with something that makes me feel good, instead of associating touch with anger and hate. I grip her hips, taking charge from below, slowly fucking her while she skims her fingers over my skin, finding every single scar, and putting her gentle lips on each one.

My heart pounds so hard, it's as if it's attacking my rib cage from the inside, and every touch from Star sends desire shooting through me like lightning strikes. I know I'm going to come soon, but I'll be damned if I do before she does this time. I catch her mouth with mine again, worshiping her with my tongue while I plant one hand on her ass and shift her just slightly until my pubic bone is rubbing her clit with every stroke of my body. My other hand wedges between us to find her breast. I roll her nipple between my thumb and finger, watching her for cues. Sure enough, she gasps and rubs her clit against me harder, her beautiful body seeking out exactly what she needs.

Her lips skim over mine as she whispers, "Don't stop. God, don't stop. I'm gonna come."

Heat washes through me, my balls drawing up at her words. "Never," I groan. "Fuuuck. Keep going, baby."

She writhes on my lap, and my fingers splay over her ass, holding her body tightly to mine. I love the way she's right here, living out this moment with me. Capturing her mouth, I kiss her hard and deep, my tongue mimicking the stroking of my dick.

Tearing her mouth from mine, unsteady breaths fall from her lips as she looks deeply into my eyes, her hands moving to grip my shoulders tightly. "You make me feel so good, Kellan." Her body stills for a split second as her eyes glaze over and her pussy begins to clench my cock. "Coming." Her body trembles in my arms, and it's clear the spasms in her pussy are all she can concentrate on as she clings to me and rides them out.

Without further warning, I thrust deep as my dick throbs and cum spurts from me. Dear fucking God. I've never come so hard. That was an explosion—of lust and of need and of something else I haven't quite come to terms with yet. But it's there, hovering on the horizon, waiting for me to acknowledge it.

My chest still heaving from the intensity of our union, I catch her head between my hands and drag her mouth back to mine for a searing kiss. Against her lips, I mumble, "*Her Fear. My Shame. Our Trust.* I trust you, Star, with everything I am. That's what that third painting is about. Our trust."

A tear slides down her cheek, and she drops her head to my chest. "I trust you, too, Kellan. I trust you with all of me."

TWENTY-NINE

KELLAN

The weekend has flown by. It's already Sunday, and the art show opens in about ten minutes. I'm not exactly sure who received invitations to attend. Maybe other faculty members? We were allowed to invite people, of course, and once my friends found out, there was no way to keep them from showing up, both in support of me and of Ryleigh. The lot of them are waiting outside to be let in. To be honest, I'll be glad when this part is over. This is not my thing. Creating the art, sure, but talking with total strangers about it, not so much.

Ryleigh gives me a reassuring smile as she pushes her glasses back up onto the bridge of her nose. "You're fine. Your paintings are bomb ass. Everyone is going to love them."

I inhale deeply through my nose, my lips drawn into a tight line. Finally, I let the air out in a rush, shaking my head at how ridiculous I'm being. This is what I do. This is what I'm at Shadow River for. "Yeah, you're right. And yours are fuckin' gorgeous, too. It'll be fine." Funny how

I'm trying to convince myself of this as the words drop effortlessly from my mouth.

"Let's get your mind off it. What'd you do this weekend? Gage told Matty that shit was still weird with that Milo guy."

I roll my eyes. "That dick has balls, I tell ya."

"Most dicks come with balls." Ryleigh sputters with laughter. "Sorry, trying to lighten up the mood a little."

I can't help but snort a bit. "Ry, you slay me. I never expect the shit that comes out of your mouth." When we finally stop snickering, I continue, "Yeah, so the guy's been attending my speech class to ... stalk me? Spy on me? I dunno. And he had the nerve to talk to me about his"—I throw up finger quotes—"'girlfriend.'"

"Oh." Ryleigh's lips hold the O formation long after sound stops coming out. "What a crazy fucker."

"Yeah. You can say that again. Star and I laid low all weekend because of it."

"Well, that sucks." Ryleigh wrinkles her nose at me, then lets her eyes scan the room. I guess it's not just me who is a little on edge with all this talk.

"I mean, I'm not one who likes to go out a ton anyway, you know me, but I don't like feeling like we have to fucking hide, if that makes sense." But with the knowledge that both Star and I had Milo run-ins on Thursday, we thought it best not to poke the bear any more than we absolutely had to. We'd even gone as far as having food delivered so we never left the dorm until we had to for this event.

"Of course. And you can't stay in the dorm forever. You have classes, and a life."

I swing my arm out, gesturing to all the paintings. "Yeah, we knew it wouldn't last because of this today. But it was nice to have a couple days of quiet." I chuckle to myself. "I will say, though, the joke's on him because the two of us needed the time alone together to continue to work through a few things."

"Was I right?" Ryleigh arches a brow. "About being honest with her and taking things slow?"

I let a breath hiss from between my lips as I consider how to answer. Finally, I nod. "Yeah. We had quite the conversation on Friday. Really got shit out into the open." I glance around to see who's within earshot. "She, uh, she's helped me with some of those issues I hinted at having. I mean, they're still there ... but we kinda have a way of handling it that works for us."

"Aw. Well, I'm super happy for both of you, then." She grins, pointing toward the entrance. "Speaking of. Here she comes, along with everyone else." Ryleigh hurries over to Matty, who scoops her up and spins her around before they head over to her pieces so he can see the finished products. She hadn't let him see any of it throughout the entire process, so it'll be an eye-opener for him to see what Ryleigh's been working on.

I scan the crowd until I see Star coming toward me, flanked by Lux and Raven, with Maddox and Hawk trailing behind them. The guys each lift a hand to wave. They totally know this isn't my scene. Hell, it's not their scene either, but they're here to support me, because that's what we do. I nod back at them with a small smile, then I have to focus on the girl in front of me because she's standing there hesitantly. It dawns on me that she's waiting for my go-ahead. I can't stop the wide smile that stretches my cheeks as I hold out my arms for her.

Star practically melts into me, putting her arms around my torso to give me a squeeze, while looking up at me with beaming eyes. "This is amazing. I'm so fucking proud of you, Kellan." She points at the paintings then glances back at our friends who have gathered around us in a semicircle. "Look, aren't they beautiful?"

Everyone takes a few minutes to study each piece, while Star and I stand to the side. She looks up at me with a soft smile. "I really love them. What happens to them after the show?"

"I don't know the answer to that. I know we keep a portfolio of work. I'm sure I'll be able to get my hands on them someday. Probably when I graduate."

She gives me a bright smile. "Don't get rid of them. Please. I mean ... if you don't want them."

I catch her chin with my fingers. "Are you trying to tell me you'd like to have them?"

She chews on the side of her lip for a second, then nods. "I would. They mean a lot to me."

"We'll keep them, then." I don't know if she understands the subtle undertone of my words. But that's how much she means to me. She's my person. She's got my heart locked away inside her chest. It's hers.

She nuzzles against my side and sighs. "I'd like that. A lot."

"Kellan." The deep boom of my father's voice hits me square in the chest, and my body goes rigid.

Beside me, Star also stiffens. "Is that your dad?"

I huff out a breath as I watch the man who will never

be anything more than a sperm donor to me walk in my direction. "Fuck," I grit out under my breath.

My father stops in front of our group, his eyes flicking to the paintings behind us and back to me. He ignores everyone, his gaze locking on me, a grim set to his jaw. "Seems like we may need to have a discussion, son."

The way he says *son* like I'm his biggest disappointment hits hard. "How did you know to come today?"

"Imagine my surprise when I got an invitation to some art show for students majoring in *art.*" He rolls his eyes on the final word, demonstrating to me and everyone standing here exactly what he thinks of my choice of major.

Shit. I didn't know they'd do that. Choosing to ignore the bit about my major, I give him a tight smile before murmuring low, "I would have invited you personally, but I didn't think you'd want to come."

"You'd be right, you little punk. This is horseshit." He stalks closer and gets in my face, poking at my chest. "No son of mine is going to spend all this money to be a fucking artist. It's ridiculous."

I bristle, fully aware that my friends are hearing this— as are complete strangers who've come to the show. "If this is how you want to end our relationship, I have no problem with that." Star's hand on my back is reassuring, and she hasn't budged an inch, even though my dad is close enough to both of us that I can feel his hot breath on my face.

Before I can say anything else, he puts his big hand on my shoulder and squeezes hard. At my side, Star flinches, and her hand taps my back. I know what she's telling me without words. I breathe in slowly through my nose while I stare at the quickly reddening face of my father. My blood running cold, I bite out for everyone to hear, "Get your fuckin' hand off me. I won't let you hurt me anymore." I jerk out of his hold without waiting for him to agree.

My old man backs away, his eyes squinting at me as he shakes his head. "You're cut off, son."

"I haven't wanted to be your son for a very long time. My inheritance from Mom means you don't get to torture me ever again." My chest is tight, squeezing my lungs so hard I can barely take a breath, but I don't care that we have an audience anymore. I only want to be done with him. "Leave."

When he turns around and storms out, I sag with relief, rubbing my hand over my jaw. No one says anything for what seems like interminable seconds. Star presses closer to me. I clear my throat. "I'm fine. That needed to happen."

She nods. "Yeah, it did. And I so wanted to tear his hand off you, but I knew it had to be you."

I let out a sigh, then turn us to face our friends, who I'm surprised to find are standing immediately behind us. I grit my teeth. "Sorry you had to see that." At their murmurs of concern, my lips form a tight line.

Ryleigh gives me a sad smile. "Are you okay?"

I tug Star closer and kiss the top of her head. "Yeah. I'm gonna be fine." I let my gaze slide over each of my friends, old and new. "Thanks for being here today. I know Ryleigh and I both appreciate having your support." I suck in a breath, feeling the need to be alone. "I'm going to take a minute, if you don't mind."

Star shoots me a worried look.

I stoop down, pressing my lips to hers. "I'm okay. I just need a sec to splash some water on my face or something." I swallow hard. "Be right back."

Ten minutes go by, and I'm getting antsier by the second. We've taken the time Kellan's been gone to walk around the room looking at all the other artwork. Hands down, Ryleigh's and Kellan's projects are the strongest.

I'm no dummy, I know everyone is wondering exactly what Kellan meant when he said his dad had hurt and tortured him. Their whispers back and forth are a clear indication, but it's not my place to tell them, that'll be up to Kellan if he wants to fill them in on the abuse he suffered for years at that asshole's hands. He may never tell them. And that's okay. I will keep his secrets forever. He trusts me, and that's something I don't take lightly. *Our Trust.* I smile again, my eyes drifting to his paintings.

Once Kellan returns, I'm sure we'll bug out of here and go get something to eat and hang out. The art show was ruined for everyone the moment Mr. Murphy walked through that door and opened his condescending mouth.

Matty and Ryleigh stand next to me, and I think she must see the worry on my face because she leans close and whispers, "He'll be fine, you know. I don't claim to understand everything about Kellan, but he tells me enough that I know he's got you, and you're everything to him."

I give her a surprised smile and tilt my head to the side, studying her. "Wow. Thank you for telling me that." I'm suddenly glad he's got this girl for a friend. I have no doubt she's been his sounding board this semester, definitely for art stuff but it would also appear he's comfortable sharing more personal things with her, too. And I get why because she has a way about her that makes her easy to talk to. I lean a little closer, lowering my voice. "I hated every second of what went down today. His dad—" Anger washes through me again just thinking about it. "Never have I wanted to knock someone out so much in my entire life."

She nods, smirking at my outburst. "Yeah. No shit. I'd have been right behind you. But it sounds like maybe he doesn't have to worry too much about mending that relationship if he has an inheritance from his mom. They aren't close."

"No, not at all. I didn't know about the money from his mom, but I hope it means Kellan's free of that bastard for good." I glance at my phone. Eleven minutes. "He's been gone a long time." I want to go to him. If he's struggling with this alone …

But my gut says he wouldn't lie about being okay. He probably just needed a moment to himself.

"Has he texted you?" Ryleigh gives me an encouraging smile.

"I can check." I open up our text message thread. But there are no new texts from him. Drawing in a breath, I decide it can't hurt to shoot him a message.

Me: Kellan, I think we're getting food after this.

I wait a few beats, then send another.

Me: Are you okay? Should I come find you?

After another minute goes by with no response, I frown. *Nothing. Maybe I should go find—*

My gaze snaps to the back hallway that leads down to all the classrooms. A flash of someone in black has a chill rolling down my spine. Whoever it is moves quickly down the hall and slams out the back exit. The floor drops out from beneath me. *Milo.* "Oh, fuck." *No.* He wouldn't be here. But oh my God, of course he is. "Fuckfuckfuck!" I whisper-shout, lifting onto my tiptoes, trying to catch sight of Kellan. But he's nowhere.

Lux and Raven join me, Ryleigh, and Matty in time to hear my outburst.

"Are Hawk and Maddox with Kellan?" The question rushes from me as my chest tightens unbearably.

"No, I don't think so. They went looking for a vending machine. Maddox is starving." Raven lays a hand on my shoulder. "What's going on?"

"Kellan hasn't come back and"—I point down the

hallway with a shaky hand—"I swear that was Milo." My head scrambles. "He's going to try again." Matty and the girls stare at me, stunned.

"Please believe me." My lip trembles. "Don't wait. Call for help. Get outside. He's going to burn this place down."

Horror clear in her eyes, Lux quickly asks, "What're you gonna do?"

"This is my fault." I lock eyes with Matty and shake my head. "Don't you dare let them follow me." And I take off running. I hope I'm dead wrong, but if I'm not, I can't afford to waste time. I stop to flip the plastic barrier up on the fire alarm and pull down on the lever, setting it off. The alarm sounds over and over, the sound of it making my breath catch in my throat. From behind me, there's a huge commotion as people realize what's happening. I can only hope that the 911 call is being placed and help is on the way.

With my heart in my throat, I continue at a fast pace down the hallway. I bet Kellan went where he feels most comfortable. His art studio.

Back in the foyer, shrieks of terror sound. The doors won't open. Milo's done it again. They've been barricaded from the outside. My pulse skyrockets. Sirens scream in the distance. *Please, please, please hurry.*

I heave out a breath, skidding to a stop outside the art studio. What I see makes my heart thunder. There's a chain looped tightly around the two door handles, with not one, but two padlocks securing it, and there's smoke coming out from under the door. *Oh, shit.* This is real.

He's started a fire in the studio. I cautiously put my palm up to the wood. It's still cool.

I slap my hands to the doors. "KELLAN!" I don't know what else to do, so I try fiddling with the padlocks on the off chance that they were improperly secured. No. There's no way in. I beat my fists on the doors. "KELLAN!"

Strong hands grasp my biceps, pulling me out of the way. At first I struggle, trying to get back to the door, but then Maddox's deep voice is in my ear. "Star, let us try."

A shuddery breath falls from my lips, my eyes wild as I stare first at Maddox, then Hawk. "He's in there. I know it. Milo did this."

Hawk's steady gaze meets with mine. "Okay. We'll get to him. But you should get out of the building."

"No." My jaw clenches hard, and I hold my ground, pointing. "I'm not leaving without Kellan."

Maddox's expression is grim, but he nods and pulls what looks like a lock-picking kit out of his pocket. "Fuck, I knew this little set would come in handy someday." He looks carefully at the two padlocks, then pulls a few instruments out. I don't claim to know what they're for, but I need them to work.

Hawk holds out his hand for some of the tools, then roughly says, "Together?"

Maddox nods, a look of determination crossing his face as they both squat down to get a better look at the locks. "Yeah," he says gruffly, "We don't have time to wait."

Working intently, they move the metal tools this way and that. Maddox springs his open, and two seconds later, so does Hawk. They pull the locks from the chains, and the chains from the door handles, then, each grasping a handle, yank the doors open at the same time. Dark black smoke billows out. The smell is acrid, and it burns my eyes. The sprinkler system has already activated, and water sprays everywhere.

The guys immediately surge forward into the room, but very quickly, Maddox grits, "Oh, hell. Down," and they drop to hands and knees. I have to imagine there are all sorts of things in an art classroom that are flammable—oil-based paints, cleaning solutions, and there would be a literal ton of paper and canvases on hand in the storage closet. This is a fucking huge place, but I know where he'll be. I scramble to my knees and follow behind Maddox and Hawk, shouting, "The back corner. His station is that way," then cough hard as I inhale smoke.

"Dammit, Star, go back," Hawk growls from between clenched teeth when he glances to see me behind them.

I shake my head, pointing to the corner. "No. He'll be all the way back there." I pull my sweater up over my nose and mouth, but it doesn't help much.

Resigned to the fact that I'm coming with them, Maddox shouts, "Which way?"

"Left back corner," I shout back as loudly as I can. My heart thuds hard. There's a pile of who knows what burning at the far side of the room near the windows. "Faster!"

"Oh, fuck." Hawk's voice barely reaches me over the noise of the cracking fire.

I blink, my eyes tearing and my nose running. And that's when I see Kellan on his back near the wall.

Unmoving. I spring to my feet, hurtling past the guys, and come down next to Kellan. My shaking fingers go to his throat, feeling for a pulse. "H-he's alive." I pat his face, hoping to rouse him. "Kellan. Kellan!"

"Let us get him out of here, Star." Maddox grips my shoulder. "You'll need to lead us out." He and Hawk get Kellan in a two-man hold just as one of the curtains catches fire. The blaze races up to the ceiling. "Fuck," he grits, "We need to go *now*."

Hawk readjusts Kellan in his arms, meeting my terrified gaze. "It's okay. We're getting out of here. Crouch and run, sweetheart. We're behind you. Stay as low as you can."

We make a mad dash for the exit, darting around various pieces of furniture and easels. My heart pounds loudly in my ears. When we finally burst from the room, I almost don't hear the commotion coming at us from both the front and rear of the building. I blink, realizing help is here.

One of the firefighters puts an arm around me, and we hurry to the back exit. I glance over my shoulder, watching as my whole heart is being carried out, still unconscious.

Outside, I think every ambulance and fire truck within a twenty-mile radius has been called to the parking lot. I'm ushered over to one of the emergency vehicles and am immediately seated on a stretcher.

A man I recognize as the older EMT from the night Raven was taken to the hospital starts going through his procedures checking me over. "Where'd this blood come from?"

Startled, I look down at where he's got my hands in his gloved ones, cautiously turning them this way and that, then lets his eyes roam my body for evidence of injury. I shake my head. "It's not mine." My face crumples. "It must be Kellan's."

"Okay. Well, your friends are getting medical attention, too." His voice is meant to be calm and soothing, but I'm inwardly panicking. "Let me see what I can find out." He pats my hand as another EMT comes over. I pay no attention to what she's doing, but my eyes follow the gray-haired guy over to the other ambulance, and then he disappears from sight.

"Star!" Lux gasps my name as she jogs over to us with Raven right behind her. "Are you okay?" Worry etches both of their faces, and they scramble to get close, each grabbing at my hand. Instead of a group hug, we've got a group handhold going on.

"She's gonna be okay, ladies, but please give her some space." The EMT quickly assesses me. "I'm going to put an oxygen mask on you, and then we'll head for the hospital to have you looked over."

I nod. "Okay." My throat is sore, and my chest burns a little, but I think I'm okay. "Have you seen the guys?" I look first at Raven, then at Lux. They exchange a glance. "Tell me."

Raven swallows hard. "Maddox and Hawk are okay. They're bitching about going to the ER." Her lips twist a bit. If I wasn't so worried, I'd laugh.

"They must be okay if they're complaining, right?" Lux gives me an unsure smile before biting her lip and looking away.

"And Kellan?" My voice is rough. Raspy.

Another disturbed, fearful look passes between them.

"They already took him in the ambulance. He was still unconscious."

Lux looks down at my free hand. "Oh God, that's from his head, isn't it?"

THIRTY-ONE

STAR

From what we're hearing, the fire in the art department building is out. Everyone was safely evacuated once the pieces of wood that Milo had used to keep the doors from opening had been removed.

I've already seen the police officers, and I've given them more than I'm sure they were ready for. Milo's description so they can track him down, where he lives, works, his dad's name, and every single sick thing I can remember him doing, including what he's been doing to me all these years. They'd been most interested in his botched attempt at setting the fire at our high school, as he'd followed through with exactly the same plan this time. And when I told them this was all about revenge because I'd gotten him caught the last time, they assured me that I likely won't have to deal with him in the future. He's eighteen now, so he's in deep, deep shit—especially since he's added attempted murder to his repertoire.

I also informed the officers about his stay in the psych ward, as well as the fact that I know he signed himself out because he was eighteen—but it was against his doctor's wishes. I may have told them that he told me that, just like he tells me all the other sordid details of his dirty deeds.

It was a little white lie. I'd hacked into the computer system at the psych facility and saw that he'd left against medical advice. I was going to give the information to my mother, but I'd wanted plenty of proof to back it up before I presented my case. Unfortunately, I'd never gotten the chance to do more research.

I watch as Raven and Lux whip back the curtains separating me, Maddox, and Hawk. They've given us three ER beds right in a row, and we've all been checked over, so I'm okay with it. Kellan would have died in that building if Hawk and Maddox hadn't come, and I would have died right there with him, on the other side of the door. There's no manual for how to navigate a situation like this. And I don't know how I can ever thank them enough.

Maddox is on my left, with Hawk on his other side. He winks at me, then gruffly says, "Good job showing us where to go and getting us out."

"Thanks." I give him a pained look that I hope reads that I wish I could have done more. I wish I'd been able to get to him faster. I wish I hadn't brought Milo down on all our heads. The guilt is very real. It's suffocating. My chest is tight with it. "Thank you for helping me."

Hawk shakes his head. "Not necessary. He's our brother. But ... you. You surprised us."

I frown, not quite following.

"You're feisty, Star. That's what he's saying." Maddox

shakes his head. "And smart as fuck. Pulling the alarm before you knew there was an actual fire."

"I appreciate that. I went with my gut." I let out a ragged sigh. "I knew Kellan had been gone for too long. And then I thought I saw Milo leave out the back. I knew I'd never forgive myself if I didn't act."

Lux sits down next to me, grabbing for my hand, and gives me a soft smile. "You did great."

"And they're going to catch Milo. You'll never have to worry about him again." Raven sits gingerly at the foot of my bed. "Everything's going to be okay."

That's what everyone keeps saying, but we haven't heard anything about Kellan's condition yet. I'm trying valiantly not to freak the fuck out.

Maddox bristles, his expression going stormy as he shifts to a more comfortable position on the bed that's barely big enough to hold him. "It's fuckin' bullshit that his dad's not here." We overheard some nurses talking earlier about how Mr. Murphy had been contacted but wasn't coming. *Asshole.*

I screw up my courage and boldly state, "That's okay. Kellan doesn't need him anyway. He has us."

"Damn right," Hawk grunts.

"Is there someone here for Kellan Murphy?" A woman's voice travels to us from the ER waiting area, and I sit straight up on the cot.

There's some low talking from beyond the curtain, then Ryleigh's firm voice. "Yes, we're his friends, but you need to let Star St. James back see him."

"But *she's* a patient. We don't usually do that."

"She's his *girlfriend* and saved him from a mother-fucking fire. Let. Her. See. Him!"

I *knew* I was right about her. My brows shoot up, and I cover my mouth with a few fingers as Raven gets up and pulls the curtain back before anyone else can do it. "She's right here. And yes, she'd like to see Kellan."

At the height of the commotion, a nurse appears from the double doors where we've seen them take other patients. The newcomer rapidly assesses the situation, glancing from us to the woman who doesn't want to let me see Kellan.

"They want to send one of the ER patients to see another patient."

The nurse frowns, nodding toward me. "This one? Don't be silly. Put her in a wheelchair for transport, and I'll take her myself."

I guess Ryleigh's earlier outburst already had people in motion, because a patient transporter is right there with a wheelchair. As he helps me get settled, I scan the faces of our friends and almost start crying.

"Tell him we said to behave, okay?" Lux blows me a kiss.

Maddox rolls his eyes and huffs out a laugh. "Yeah, tell him the staff would probably like it best if he wore his hospital gown at all times."

And despite not knowing how Kellan is doing yet, I grin at him while everyone laughs. "You got it."

We take off down the hallway, and once we've pushed through the double doors, the nurse murmurs from behind me, "It's nice that he's got good, loyal friends."

I nod. "They're kinda the best." And I guess I'm not hiding my emotions very well, what with my voice cracking the way it is, because she lays a hand on my shoulder and squeezes.

"His doctor can tell you more, but he's going to be okay. He took a hit to the head, maybe a piece of wood? We're not one hundred percent sure, and he couldn't tell us."

"He's awake?" I look hopefully back at her as we zip down the hall and around a corner.

"Yes, he woke up for a little bit, but he might be napping again. He doesn't remember much except he'd gone off alone to calm down after an altercation with his father. The rest is foggy for him. He has a concussion and needed a couple of stitches. They didn't intubate him for the smoke inhalation, so that's a great sign. We'll keep him for a few days to be sure, but he should be okay."

I want to say that's a relief, but I'm going to worry until I see him myself. We stop in front of a door, and she turns me around so she can back me in.

Once inside, all the air whooshes out of my lungs at the sight of Kellan lying in the bed, an oxygen mask covering his nose and mouth, his eyes shut. A tiny whimper escapes my lips as the nurse pushes me right up to the side so I can take his hand in mine.

"I'll be back to check on you in a little bit," she says softly, patting my shoulder. But I'm too busy feeling the warmth of Kellan's skin and the pulse in his wrist to answer.

I don't know how long it is that I sit and watch him breathe, skimming the pad of my thumb over the back of his strong artist's hand. Finally, I can't stand it any longer. I rise onto wobbly legs and lean over the bed, thankful that his IV is on the other side. I press a soft kiss to his smooth-shaven cheek, then drag in a shaky breath. "Kellan, you're going to be okay. You hear me? You have to be because I need you in my life."

Kellan shifts on the bed, "Hey, baby." His words are muffled from behind the oxygen mask, but his pretty green eyes are glued on me. "I need you, too."

My heart lurches. "You're awake."

"I am." I can tell speaking isn't going to be easy for him right now, his voice is all raspy—not that he's ever huge on words.

I carefully lift my hand to his face, brushing his messy hair from his forehead. "How are you feeling?"

He grimaces, but it slips into a smile as his eyes roam over me. "Better now that you're here. Can you climb onto the bed with me?"

My lip catches between my teeth as I consider. "I won't hurt you?"

He shakes his head. "No. But you wanna tell me why you're in one of these fancy hospital gowns?"

Like a deer in headlights, I pause, staring at him. "Do you really not know?"

He coughs a bit, then gestures for me to join him and helps me get settled. "The police officer might have mentioned it."

"Oh."

"You shouldn't have put yourself at risk like that."

"I was the only one who knew what was happening. There was no way I was leaving you."

He tries to swallow, and it's visibly difficult. "Mad and Hawk helped you?"

"Yeah. The doors were locked together with a chain and padlocks. I tried but I couldn't get it open, and I was in a panic. They showed up, and Mad whipped out this lock-picking kit, and they went to town on it. And you can't get mad at them for not making me leave, because they told me to. But they wouldn't have found you as quickly—I knew where you'd be." I draw in a breath and stop to cough before continuing. "They picked you up, and I led the way as they hauled you out." I shift, touching his chest as I do.

And he winces.

I grit my teeth. *Scars. Shit.* "I'm sorry. I wasn't thinking."

He shakes his head. "No. It's not that." Plucking at the snaps that run from the collar of his gown down to the sleeve, he pops them open. "I want to show you something."

"I don't understand. Did you get burned in the fire?" I purse my lips, staring at his hand that's clutching the edge of the hospital gown, my heart rate picking up.

Kellan pulls the oxygen mask down and wets his lips. "Do you remember how I took off at ten this morning? Told you I needed to help set up for the show?"

I nod, my brow furrowing.

He removes his hand from the gown. "Look under there."

"Are you sure?"

"Yep."

Cringing for a second, I suck up my courage and

cautiously pull the gown down. What I see floors me. I'm speechless. I cover him back up for a moment, only to pull the fabric down again to stare.

After a solid thirty seconds, Kellan murmurs, "Do you like them? Because there are more."

My teeth scrape over the skin of my lower lip as I release it, and my gaze flicks between the stars outlined on his shoulder and the questioning expression on his face. "Are you telling me that you got— How many are there ...?"

"Stars. Sixteen."

"The same number as—" I bite back my words. I can't say it.

Kellan nods. "Yes." His eyes scan my face, worry lines marring his forehead. "You didn't answer my question."

"Do I like the stars that you marked your body with? I mean, I hope I'm not making too big of an assumption. They're for me?"

Kellan nods solemnly.

"Why?" My heart flits around my chest like a hummingbird.

He tilts his head to the side. "Because you're my person, Star. You understand me. And I want to have you with me always, the same way I have the roses for my mom. They were her favorite."

I'm all choked up. I know it took a lot for Kellan to say all that to me. And in my head, the words I want to say are clear. *I love you.* But all I can manage to do is to bury my face against his chest and hold onto him tightly. *How did I fall so hard so fast?*

It seems like it's been forever since the art show, but it was only a week ago that Star's fucker of a stepbrother bashed me in the head and left me for dead. The good news is, I feel a lot better now, but the best news is that Star doesn't ever have to deal with that asshole ever again. He's totally ending up in prison for everything he's done. Her mother was so upset at the turn of events, she actually showed up to apologize to her daughter. Star had been so surprised, she kept questioning after her mother had departed whether it'd actually happened.

"Kellan, can I help you?"

I glance over my shoulder as my girl approaches. I've just washed and blotted dry my new ink. My lips curve with a smile as I hold out the little tub of aftercare ointment they'd given me at the tattoo shop. This has become our little ritual every morning and evening. I think she likes taking care of the ink I got for her.

She unscrews the lid and sets it on the counter, then

washes and dries her hands carefully, peeking at me in our reflection. "Ready?"

I blow out a breath. I don't think having someone touch me will ever be easy for me. It'll always come with that swift feeling of apprehension, but with Star, I know everything will be okay. "Yep, go ahead." I never would have let anyone help me with this in the past.

She gives me a flirty wink before carefully beginning to dab the ointment over each star across my shoulders. She's become a fixture in my life in such a short amount of time. A rock. Someone I can depend on, no matter what. Everything I'd want in a partner. "I can't wait until these are healed and I can put my lips on them." She comes to stand in front of me to work on the ink on my torso and biceps, her fingers gently gliding over my healing skin.

"Fuck, I like it when you talk like that."

She grins up at me. "Oh, yeah? What else do you like?"

"You know what I like."

"Do I?"

"Yep. You're obviously able to read my mind. You always know what I need." My voice has gone unexpectedly husky.

Her brows draw together. "Kellan Murphy, are we having a moment?" Her tongue darts out, sliding over her lip. I can't help but watch it and wonder where else she could use it on me.

I grasp her by the nape of her neck, lowering my lips until they brush hers. "I want all my moments to be with you."

That wicked tongue of hers flicks out, tracing my lips. My heart responds, pumping blood to my dick. I don't know if it'll always be this way between us, but shit. Right now, everything about our relationship is good, especially this part. She grips my waist, tugging my pelvis to her at the same time she slips her tongue into my mouth. I can't help it. I groan aloud at the rush of desire moving swiftly through my body.

We kiss, only parting to pull Star's shirt over her head. Otherwise, we remain in a lip-lock, shoving the rest of our clothing away from us until we stand naked and breathless together.

She presses up onto her tiptoes, kissing the corner of my mouth. "I have a surprise for you."

My brows slowly arch at her playful tone.

"I went on the pill."

I peer carefully at her. "You what now?"

"When we first started messing around. I went to the clinic on campus to get on birth control." She waits a beat. Bites her lip.

It's like a cattle prod to my dick when I realize what she's hinting at. "Um. Are you saying what I think you are?"

With a devilish gleam in her eye, she pivots, placing her hands on the counter, then arches her back, bringing her pussy into contact with my cock. She glances over her shoulder. "What are you waiting for?"

There's barely enough blood in my brain to respond. "Not a damn thing." I take myself in hand, slowly stroking as she angles herself back toward me. I drag the head of my cock through her wetness, let it enter her the smallest bit, then pull back.

She gasps at the loss. "Kellan, please."

"You're sure?" I know she thought she had the upper hand here. "Maybe we shouldn't." I slip my dick in maybe an inch, but immediately pull back out. *Fuck, she feels good like this.* Reaching around her body, I cup her breasts and groan, "You have the best tits." I tease them until the nipples are stiff peaks, and she's moaning and thrusting her ass back into my groin.

Star lets out a choked cry. "Please."

I curl my body around hers, nuzzle her neck, then nip her earlobe. Summoning all my willpower, I slide my hand over her sweet ass, then reach between her legs, stroking my fingers through her arousal. "Mm. I like to play with your little pussy, baby,"

She lets out a shuddery laugh. "I like it, too."

Grasping my erection, I slide it between her legs again. A wave of heat slams into me, making me dizzy with want. I'm going to put my dick in this girl, no barriers between us. My breath heaves from me at the thought of it. "You trust me?" I grit out.

"Yes. Always."

This here, with her, is the only kind of fire I ever want to feel again. I fucking burn for her. "You want my dick?"

"Inside me. Now."

I notch myself at her entrance, grasp her by her hips, and watch her reflection in the mirror as I enter her inch by ridiculously mind-blowing inch. Her mouth has dropped open, her eyes dilated with desire. Our gaze locks in the mirror as I begin to thrust inside her wet warmth.

"This is so good," Star mumbles between pants.

Trying to maintain control, I slide my hands around to touch her, to claim as much of her body as I can. I want my hands to have been everywhere—the valley between her breasts, her belly button, her soft thighs. My blood roars in my head as I find her clit and begin to rub her swollen bud in tight, fast circles. Her back bows at the sensation, and she meets my every thrust with her own.

My brain is on overload. Hot girl bent over in front of me. Hot girl looking at me in the reflection of the mirror. My dick inside her pussy. Nothing between us. *Holy fuck, I'm gonna come.* Heat flashes through me. "Fuck. Fuuuck," I groan. "Baby—" The pads of my fingers work furiously over her clit until she's writhing against my hand, and her eyes connect with mine in the mirror. "Star, you're so beautiful when you lose control." My breaths are ragged as I pound into her tight body. "Show me how you're mine."

"I love how good you fuck me," she chokes out right before her pussy clamps down on my dick, and her hips roll as wave after wave of intense pleasure hits her. I see every moment of it play out in her reflection.

The euphoric expression on Star's face as she comes sends me right over the goddamn edge. My hips jerk against her ass, and my cum shoots from my dick into her pussy.

We're both loose as noodles, standing there in the middle of the bathroom, still intimately connected. It blows my mind that I have this girl who understands me so well that she can anticipate my needs. If I'd never found her, I don't know how much good stuff I'd continued to have missed out on. And I'm not referring to sex, but that's definitely a part of it. I've expressed that I want a reminder of her with me always. I had those stars inked all over my body for a reason. I think she gets it. But it's time I said the words.

THIRTY-THREE
STAR

I'm glad Kellan is behind me, holding me up, because my legs are trembling like they're going to give way any second. He slowly eases out of me, then picks me up in a cradle hold and whisks me out of the bathroom, laying me down on the edge of the bed.

Kellan kneels before me and pushes my legs open, my swollen flesh like a feast for his eyes. A rumbling, growling sound works its way up from his chest. His fingers dig into my thighs, almost reflexively, as he studies me. "This might be the hottest thing I've ever seen in my whole fucking life," he mumbles, his voice rough.

A wave of heat knocks me sideways. I can feel his cum dripping from me, and I know he's watching it, and that's exactly what he's referring to.

He takes two fingers, swipes at the moisture coming out, and ever so slowly pushes it back inside me. "Fuu-uck," he groans, bringing his face in close to inhale deeply right before he uses his fingers to expose my clit. With the flat of his tongue, he licks over the sensitive bundle of nerves before he sucks on it, making animalistic, hungry noises. It's never been more obvious how much he wants me.

My back arches as pulses of desire shoot through me. Every touch of his hands on my skin makes me ache with need. Every pass of his tongue makes me shiver and shake. And I wonder what I did to deserve him. Or maybe it was nothing I did or anything he did either. Maybe we're simply two life-roughened souls destined to find each other—to care for each other.

That's about as poetic as this computer science major gets.

Tension coils quickly, already on the verge of shattering into a million pieces. I moan, clutching fistfuls of Kellan's hair without realizing I'm doing it. The orgasm begins as a barely there shimmer, then quickly develops into more, the rippling pleasure spreading outward. I can't help but rock my pussy against Kellan's face, I'm so lost to the all-consuming feelings flowing through me.

While my body continues to pulse, and I'm still off in some other world, Kellan slides his dick inside me again. Moans erupt simultaneously from our mouths, and I grab his ass with both hands, urging him to move faster. I don't know if it's that he already came inside me and I'm wetter than hell because of it or what, but my body is rocked almost immediately by another orgasm that makes me cry out and leaves me breathless.

Kellan gathers me close, bringing my mouth to his and kisses me deep. Like he means it. Like this is the beginning of everything. At that thought, my heart threatens to erupt from my chest. He makes several more languid strokes, then locks eyes with me as his orgasm overtakes him. Groaning against my lips, he breathes out, "Fuuuck. Star. So fucking good."

He collapses on top of me for a few moments, completely out of it. Catching my lip between my teeth, I gingerly allow myself to trace outside the ink of a few of the stars on his shoulders as I wait for him to get some blood back into his brain. I'm not so much worried about touching him anymore—not because of his scars, anyway —but I am a little concerned for his new tattoos.

After about a minute, his head lifts, and he stares into my eyes. "Hey. I have something I need to say to you."

I skim the arch of my foot over the back of his calf muscle. "Oh yeah? Must be pretty important." I lean in, softly brushing my lips over his.

"It might be. Let's get cleaned up first."

———

TURNS OUT, cleaning up consisted of a shower— together, of course—which led to round three. I'm not complaining.

Once we're finally settled in bed, we're quiet for a little while, so I startle when Kellan speaks into the silence. "I wasn't sure if you understood what I was saying to you with the new ink. You know—when we were talking in the hospital. Words aren't so much my thing." As if he's sorting through what to say in his head, it all comes out in a deluge.

My brows draw together as I prop myself up on my elbow so I can see him better. "I mean, I think I understand?" It comes out a tiny bit like a question. I want so bad for him to say the words to me. I know in my heart that we're feeling the same thing because I can't be feeling this alone. *I can't.*

He takes a deep breath. "I will never forget the way you've helped me. That's why I wanted the stars. As a reminder that it was you." He smiles down at me, tracing his finger over my face. "You've set me free. And—" He pauses, cupping my cheek. "I'm so in love with you, Star."

A great wave of relief crashes over me and tears threaten. I blink several times, my eyelashes fluttering hard as I try to hold them back.

"Are you okay?" he whispers, searching my expression for an answer. I swear, he can see straight inside my mind with those inquisitive green eyes.

My lip trembles. "I feel so connected to you, and we've been through so much. But I wasn't sure if I'd ever hear you say the words."

He pulls me close and kisses my forehead. "I know. For a long time I believed I was completely damaged by my family. But you're in my head and in my heart, and I don't ever want to let you go. That's why I couldn't keep the words from you any longer. I've loved you for a while now. You're fuckin' stuck with me."

"Stuck with my sweet punk is right where I want to be." Lying here with our bodies wrapped together, hearing that Kellan loves me—I've never felt more secure in who I am and what I want. "I love you, Kel. Nothing in our past matters anymore. Because we have each other now."

"Exactly. This? Us? It's everything we'll ever need."

EPILOGUE

KELLAN

The new year is a time for new beginnings. I've never paid a whole lot of attention to it before, but with all the shit that's happened lately, it's safe to say our entire crew is looking forward to the new year, the spring semester at Shadow River, and getting a fresh start. *Together.* We've discovered through a variety of crappy situations that we're stronger that way. We've got each other's backs, support each other in a way most of our families never have. And now that we've come through it—walked through the fire, as it were—we're ready to move on with our lives.

We're due back at the university on January 3 to begin classes, but Ryleigh invited all of us to her home for New Year's Eve. Her parents are out of town, and we plan to crash here in River Rock for a couple of days before heading back to school.

It didn't take long before we pulled out the booze and got the party started. I'll be perfectly honest—we're getting a little rowdy, blowing off a whole lot of steam. I look around our circle of friends, smiling as they begin another boisterous round of toasting—totally an excuse for consuming as much alcohol as we can.

"How about, here's to finding love right across the hall?" Lux grins, pressing a kiss to Hawk's waiting lips.

Ryleigh shakes her head. "Considering Matty and I grew up next door to each other, you wouldn't think I'd think anything of it, but it's funny that all of you have ended up together. Three couples in two suites. You're all so perfect for each other, though."

Lux laughs. "I never would have dreamed it would turn out this way, but I'm so glad it did." There's a murmur of agreement throughout the group as we clink glasses and drink.

"I'm just pissed I wasted time hating you when the opposite is so much nicer." Hawk nuzzles Lux's nose, making her laugh. It makes my heart happy to see them like this. Gage lost his twin, and Lux almost lost her life. They deserve all the best after what they went through with Landon.

Ryleigh sips at her drink. "Well, I'm glad you've let Matty and me barge in on your little group."

I roll my eyes at her. "You and I have been art buddies a long time. And your man and Hawk are magic together on the football field. You aren't barging in anywhere. If anything, we've dragged you two along with us, kicking and screaming."

Matty chuckles with a playful wink. "You can say that again." He pokes Ryleigh in the side. "Where's your sister tonight?"

"Nope. Not talking about Farrah. She's a pain in my ass."

Hawk laughs. "I only met her one time, but I think I speak for all of us when I say cheers to fuckin' Farrah not being here to join us tonight!"

I've never met the girl, but by all accounts, she sounds like a piece of work. And I've got a jerk of a brother myself, who I'm no longer on speaking terms with, so I lift my glass and clink it to the others. Jamie and I will never see eye to eye. It's time I accepted that and moved on.

"Speaking of family members, I bet there are a bunch of us happy to be heading back to school and not surrounded by the crazy." Maddox nods and holds up his glass.

Maddox and his dad are on very precarious footing. While it's nice that his father has gotten his head out of his ass where his soon-to-be ex-wife is concerned, that doesn't necessarily make up for the fact that he and Lindsey were indirectly responsible for his mother's death. That's never going away. And I respect Madman for holding his ground. I'm glad for his sake that Raven came along when she did. It took some work, but her love has helped him through the worst of his anger, and now they're well on their way to happiness.

My girl is among the first to tap her glass to Mad's. We don't know exactly what's happening with Milo, but the police caught up with him not long after he tried to kill me and burn down the art department six weeks ago. He's currently in prison awaiting trial and undergoing a battery of psychological examinations. He won't ever hurt my girl again.

I also raise my glass because, true to his word, my father cut me off. But the good news is that my mother had the foresight to set up trusts for both me and Jamie. Dad can't touch them, and I've had access to it since I turned twenty. It'll cover my college costs, and I should be able to set myself up nicely after graduation. I don't know what the future holds for me with my art, but all I want to do is be able to create and, hopefully, make people feel something through it.

Raven holds up the hard seltzer she's been nursing all night. I've noticed she's still nervous to drink very much after her overdose, and I commend her for watching out for herself. "Here's to being done dealing with skeevy, asshole faculty members."

Spencer's on his way to prison, too. That stupid fucker didn't take the plea deal his lawyer tried to arrange for him. With the video evidence, there was no way he wasn't going to be put away for a very long time. I'm just glad for Raven's sake that there's not a chance she'll have to deal with him ever again.

Maddox snorts, "And no more foot fetish freaks, either. Even if Riddick did redeem himself with the scholarship." He catches Raven at the nape of her neck and drags her into a kiss steamy enough to make the rest of us groan aloud. That's Mad for you, though, he's always full throttle with everything he does, whether it's hate or love or even one of his stupid stunts. The man goes after what he wants.

I glance to my side where Star sips on a fruity cocktail. I think she's my biggest fan. Thank goodness the paintings I'd done for the art show had come out of the fire unscathed because Star may have taken Milo's head off if he'd ruined them for her. She swears she has plans to hang the paintings in our apartment someday. Because, yeah. This is the real deal. Someday I'm going to marry this girl. She's healed me in a way I didn't know was possible, and I've done the same for her. I'll be forever grateful and intend to show her how much I appreciate the love she shows me every day of our lives. *Fuck. Getting sappy. Or drunk. Probably drunk. Drunk and sappy.*

I hold up my glass as my gaze travels over these fucking amazing people who I consider to be more family than friends. Funny how shitty family situations can be the catalyst for closer-than-close friendships. "Here's to letting go of the past."

"And here's to our very bright futures." Star grins and brushes her lips over mine.

The entire crew raises their glasses, smiling. *Yep.* We're in this together. Every shared class, every art show, every party, every study session, every cello concert, every late night, every football game, every accomplishment. Everything.

Together.

ALSO BY LEILA JAMES

DEAR READER

Did you love Kellan and Star?! Honestly, I was so damn excited to write my first male virgin, I didn't know what to do with myself. He whispered that secret in my ear one day, and my eyes got really big. *Kellan. That makes a lot of sense. Thank you for telling me.* Haha. But really, how swoony was he? And I think my favorite scene was in the art room when he let her touch him. Gah. *My heart.*

And Star—we all knew she had a big secret, too, but no one seemed to have any idea what it was. Including me. She didn't tell me for a little while either. But dang, something was obviously going on because she had me slip a few clues into the first two books. Did you notice in *Beautiful Nightmare* when she said she thought someone had been in her room? Yep, Milo was there, as early as Book 1, lurking in the dorm, then in *Perfect Chaos,* started pulling the fire alarm. He was there the entire damn time. Sneaky little bastard.

So, as you can imagine, I'm having some serious problems over here. I never want to leave Shadow River University. Did you love the cast of characters from Shadow River? I know I did. It all started with the guys' images for the covers ... and their story took on a life of its own from there. Every time I start a new book or series I have a moment of what-the-hell-am-I-doing? That's where I am now. What am I doing and what's next?

All I can tell you for now is that I have options ... and I'm waiting for my muse to whisper in my ear again. Will it be something set in an academy? A college? Is it bully romance? MM? RH? A little bit of everything? Who knows! But if you want to be among the first to find out all the details, consider following me!

Follow me on Amazon: author.to/LeilaJames
Follow me on TikTok: https://vm.
tiktok.com/TTPdhy1aNd/
Follow me on IG: instagram.com/author_LeilaJames
Join my Facebook Reader page:
Leila's Loves & Bully Bad Boys
And join my NEWSLETTER through my website:
https://www.leilajames.biz/newsletter-signup

Until next time,
   XO *Leila* XO

ACKNOWLEDGMENTS

To Krista Dapkey, your emoji comment was the most professional thing I've seen in my entire life. It also might be my favorite ever. I've saved it. I'll remind you of it every once in a while because I'm fun like that.

To Diana TC, you slayed with Kellan's cover. Everyone loves him so much.

To SM, how am I already done? WTH just happened? Can we go back and start over? I remember when this series was just a couple of images and some fragmented ideas.

To Shauna Mairèad, girl, let's sprint! Thanks for helping me get my ass in gear. It's so good to work with someone who has similar goals.

To my ARC and Street Teams, thanks so much for all your support! It's appreciated.

To my family, XOXO Love you!

ABOUT THE AUTHOR

Leila James has one goal: keeping you up past your bedtime turning the pages of her books. She writes emotional, angsty, and swoon-worthy new adult romances with lots of unique characters and plot twists.

Leila's family will tell you she's as big a reader as she is a writer. And ... she's completely obsessed with both. She resides in Virginia with her husband and two children.

Connect with Leila on FaceBook & Instagram:

Printed in Great Britain
by Amazon

37447361R00179